RAIDEN: GUARDIAN OF LIGHTNING

The irregular universe

BOOK 1 OF RAIDEN'S TALE

DARRYL BARNES

Cover art by Terrence Gray

Contents

Prelude: Guardian 2
Raiden 16
The man who hunts 25
The hunt begins 29
Somebody's watching me 33
The Hunt's end 41
A hot date 46
Guardian vs Guardian 57
Be the hero, Raiden 64
Lords of Lightning 70
Kagutsuchi 82
Happy Birthday 88
Guardian of Nature 98
The one who can see the fate of the world 114
The challenge 126
Three Way struggle 137
Father and son 144
What lies at the end of a rainbow? 154
To catch a firebird 173
The hardest choice 183
Raiden Vs Zeus 191
Even if your heart should break 200
Aftermath 206
Crime & Punishment 217
Saying goodbye 223
Tales of what's to come 232

Prelude: Guardian

It was always easy to see the stars at night in Albuquerque, New Mexico. It was one of the things that attracted people to the city the most. The warm weather was perfect for people who hated the cold but weren't quite ready to move on to blazing levels of heat. The city was the perfect size; not being too large that it made you feel insignificant in it, yet not feeling so small that you couldn't go anywhere without bumping into someone. There was plenty to do and see, if you knew where to look. It was a near perfect city, even factoring in the giant bird soaring through the sky; clutching a young man in its claws.

"Let me go!" The young man bellowed, wildly swinging his arms. The young, dark skinned boy had known exactly what this creature was, considering he had more than a few run-ins with the deity. "Thunderbird! Drop me!" He continued to bellow; his ear length dreads flowing in the wind as they ascended higher and higher.

"Hania Hawke, stop moving. Now." Thunderbird spoke in a surprisingly calm voice, even though the young teen had begun punching the massive leg that Thunderbird had been carrying him in. It wasn't like it hurt or anything though, it just served to annoy the majestic creature. Thunderbird looked very similar to an overgrown eagle, except being completely brown, yet it had this sort of...regal appearance that set it apart from other creatures. Perhaps it could have something to do with its golden eyes that were focused straight ahead on its destination and the streaks of lightning that appeared after every flap of its enormous wings.

Hania's brown eyes widened as he finally was able to see where he was being taken to; a large hole in the sky that he was positive wasn't there at first. The two flew through the hole and came out the other side to see an entire new world. Tall buildings lined the ground below Hania and Thunderbird, with designs reminiscent of cultures once passed. Aztec structures taller than they ever had been during their prime sat directly next to a cluster of Japanese shrines to make for the most confusing layout of a city ever. What was most bizarre about this place, however, was the bright, shining blue sun that sat in the sky. “Where are we…?” Hania asked in a state of pure wonder. The air felt heavy to him; forcing him to be painfully aware of each breath that he took. He felt dizzy and even slightly nauseous. It felt as though he were going through several G’s of gravity and he was terribly underprepared to do so. Yet Thunderbird seemed perfectly fine soaring through the sky, as if it were no more trivial than taking a stroll. *“Stupid deity...”* Hania couldn’t help but think.

“We are in the realm of gods. The fact that you haven’t passed out yet is a feat within itself. You should be proud. I know I am.” Thunderbird spoke to Hania as though he were meticulously picking his words. His speech was slow and deliberate, likely attributed to the fact that he walked on eggshells with Hania. Deity or not, Hania was always ready to dish out a verbal lashing.

“Keep your pride to yourself; I don’t want it.” Hania retorted, rolling his eyes so hard that he could probably see his own brain matter. The rest of the flight was filled with an awkward silence; Thunderbird flying forward while stealing glances at Hania every so often, and Hania making sure to put his full concentration on the environment around him. Every time he looked at the bright blue sun, he felt an intense wave of vertigo overcome him.

“Don’t fret, we’re almost there.” Thunderbird motioned ahead to a large, spiral shaped tower. Although it was the tallest building he had seen thus far, it seemed relatively plain. Its gray brick design seemed rather dull compared to the rest of the world. Yet it seemed...fierce and intimidating; an ever-present storm cloud floating over top, with bolts of lightning striking down in every which direction. It screamed power; something that attracted Hania.

The two landed beside the front door of the large tower; narrowly avoiding a bolt of lightning as they entered. They walked through a dimly lit hallway, with Hania struggling to follow his guide. It was dimly lit and smelled of storm water, with the occasional lightning strike illuminating the hallway fully. They were approaching a metal door that opened on its own as soon as Thunderbird approached it. Hania breathed a sigh of relief when it did so, considering the door had to weigh at least a ton. The room they entered was covered with stark white tiles; the type of white that it seemed every famous person's teeth were. It was a little eerie to Hania. To his left was a large pool filled with some type of golden liquid, which Hania wasn't quite sure what it was. It seemed deep though, and considering Hania was unable to swim, he decided to stay away from it all together. Hania cleared his throat and it echoed in the near empty room. Whatever this room was, Hania was not a fan. "This room needs a window or something." Hania spoke softly to try and avoid the echo. He failed.

"Hm. I've never considered that." Thunderbird seemed to genuinely consider it. Hania had stopped paying attention though, and instead shifted his gaze to the large, vibrant red door that stood before them. Hania absolutely hated the color red.

"While you're at it, repaint this door." Hania scoffed.

"I'm rather fond of the color red." Thunderbird added. It was a little bizarre to watch his beak move as though it were a human mouth.

"I know. That's why I hate it." Hania cut his eyes and pushed open the door; albeit with some trouble. It wasn't quite as solid as the other door looked, but it wasn't any ordinary door.

The room he entered was rather dark, besides for a large hole in the ceiling that allowed cerulean rays of light to beam down in the center of the room. Every time the thirteen-year-old Hania looked at this light, he felt a little woozier. He wondered why, but mostly grew irritated at his inability to look at the light. He saw it as a challenge, and he hated to lose.

"Hania." The voice was deep and powerful; making Hania jump a bit. The voice came from above him; belonging to a man sitting atop a storm cloud. Hania finally took the time to examine his surroundings a little more carefully. Several storm clouds floated above him, all of which were occupied by some strange figure. He assumed that they all were deities, like Thunderbird. He couldn't be sure though, considering Thunderbird was the only deity he had ever met, much to Hania's disgust. Of course, a Native American god was the only one who bothered to reveal themselves to him. Probably because he was half native American and they didn't want to cross streams or something.

“How do you know my name?” Hania questioned, squinting to see who the person talking was. He was answered with a bolt of lightning crashing down in front of him, shooting off arcs of electricity every which way. To Hania, it felt more so warm than causing him harm; with a slight tingly sensation traveling down his bones.

“I know everything there is to know about you, boy.” The lightning slowly changed shape to become an actual, if not pale, man. He stood over Hania with relative ease, appearing to be about eight feet tall. He wore a simple toga that left most of the left side of his torso exposed, and his veins were prominent throughout his muscular physique. The man had a long beard that was as white as freshly fallen snow, with long, straight hair that reached his shoulders in a matching color. One look and the word power came to mind; so much so that Hania tried to avoid the gaze of his electric blue eyes. Somehow, Hania knew who this was. He was looking into the face of Zeus, one of the most famous deities.

“I know about you too, Santa Claus.” Hania retorted in his usual snarky self. He wasn’t about to be intimidated by anyone, even a deity. “Is that a tiara?” Hania added, pointing to a small golden crown that appeared to be tattooed onto the center of the lightning god’s forehead. It was a joke that Hania would instantly regret, as bolts of lightning began wildly flowing from the deity’s body. Unconsciously, Hania took a step back. That single step, was a sign of weakness in both Hania’s own eyes and Zeus’.

“Are you finished yet?” Zeus was completely serious. He had no concept of humor; the opposite of Hania. He clearly was proud however, that the mortal before him had feared him. Hania automatically decided he hated him.

“Alright Zeus, since you want to keep things super serious, mind telling me why I’m here?” Hania figured now wasn’t the time for games. Besides, he genuinely didn't know why he was here and to say he wanted an answer would be a bit of an understatement. His eyes looked around at the figures above him; all of which their names flew into his head just the same as Zeus'. All the deities above him were ones that were known to control lightning; the muscular, dirty blond standing off to the side was the deity that Hania recognized as Thor. He smiled at Hania while making a rather obscene gesture at Zeus from behind his back. Thor just became Hania's new favorite god. Plus, it put him at ease to know that Zeus wasn't omnipotent, just a pompous ass.

"You've been selected to become the new guardian of lightning. You should feel honored to have this privilege. "Zeus didn't exactly give off a very welcoming look; he looked at Hania as though he were no more than a spec of dirt. Maybe that's how he viewed mortals in general.

"Did I enter a sweepstakes or something? Or is this more like a timeshare?" Hania's response earned a snicker from Thor in the background. Why couldn't every deity be more like him? Zeus responded with another display over his control of lightning, having it bounce around him. "C'mon Zeus, you and I both know that lightning won't hurt me." The thirteen-year-old mused, pointing out the previous attempt. *Crack!* A bolt of lightning found its way down to hit Hania, causing him to reel back in pain.

"You weren't hurt last time because I made it so. Don't get full of yourself. To me, you are no more significant than a grain of sand." Zeus barely moved a muscle when he sent down that bolt of lightning. Hania however, had been hurled over trying to compose himself. Hania was gifted; blessed with the power to control lightning. He had never known what it felt like to truly be struck by lightning or harmed by electricity. He wasn't used to his entire body burning, or the numbness that set in afterwards. His insides felt like they were on fire, his bones were still shuddering from the blow, and his pride had been shattered into pieces. Hania's eyes gazed up at the rest of the deities floating above them. Thunderbird looked like he wanted to strike Zeus for the attack, while Thor looked impressed. Not with Zeus, but rather his gaze was directed towards Hania.

“*You’re less fragile than I expected. Glorious! Let’s ride into battle together!*” Thor’s look practically spelled it out for him. Hania’s eyes met another deity whom had been sitting atop a cloud on Thor’s left. His skin was an annoyingly vibrant shade of red, while multiple golden jewels adorned his body. Immediately, Hania understood that this was Indra without having to fully know who he was. Such was the power of the gods, Hania figured. He looked rather indifferent to the entire thing. No, he looked bored in all actuality.

“Can we be serious now?” Zeus mused. He took slight pleasure in Hania’s pain; something he took no care to hide.

“Seriously serious. Dare I say, deadly serious?” Hania quipped back. His body may have been in agonizing pain, but his mouth wasn’t. “What exactly does a guardian of lightning do?”

“Guardians. There are multiple guardians, each designated to a different grouping of lords.” Thunderbird chimed in from atop his cloudy perch.

“Lords? You mean gods, right?” Hania looked on puzzled.

“All lords are gods, but not all gods are lords. The specifically powerful ones whom are in control of the human world are referred to as lords.” Thor blurted out. He seemed to be yelling, although it wasn’t easy to see if this was on purpose or not.

“Seems snooty.” Hania shrugged his shoulders.

“Very much so.” Thor chuckled, pointing at Zeus while his back was turned. Zeus cleared his throat; signaling for everyone to be quiet.

“A guardian is picked to represent the lords back on earth. We cannot freely roam about on earth without tearing it apart, and so we nominate a... lesser being, usually a human, to do so for us. They fight on our behalf, as well as disposing the monsters that escape down to earth that we cannot be bothered with. In trade for the privilege of representing us, and the power that it presents of course." Zeus' explained in a rather blunt, cold fashion.

"It also lets us see through our guardian's eyes, so that we may view the human realm without having to enter it ourselves." Thunderbird chimed in.

"So, y'all are definitely not omniscient. Well, I think I'll decline. My ancestors would be mighty upset if I willingly became a slave." Hania always had a hard time hiding his irritation, but with Zeus it overflowed. The way Zeus spat out the word "human" lingered in Hania's ears. It lingered on his lips, like the stench of alcohol after a night of drinking. It reminded him of the thousands of other occasions he had been referred to with a racial slur. No wonder why bigotry existed in the world; the gods themselves invented it. "Pick someone else." Hania added.

"Do you think we actually picked you for this? To me, you are no more significant than a blade of grass." Zeus began to say something else, but Thor interjected.

"Do not fret, young warrior! You are a blade of grass in a sea of dead flowers!" Thor always seemed to yell whenever he talked. "You were chosen by our oracle!" Thor talked as if Hania should know what that was. He didn't even seem phased by his troubled look.

"The who?" Hania tilted his head. "You know what, it doesn't matter. I really don't want to be involved with this."

"But you already are involved in our matters! You killed a chimera!" Thor pointed out. It was true; last year a chimera attacked Hania's middle school and he took it down. Not that it was remotely an easy feat, of course. But no one had told him to do it; he did it to protect the people around him.

"Not the same thing, and we both know it. I don't want to be a guardian and taking orders from any gods or lords or whoever y'all decide to call yourselves. I want to be a hero. Heroes go where they're needed, not where they're sent." Hania explained. A few murmurs were exchanged between the lords above him; Zeus looking particularly annoyed and Thunderbird looking particularly pleased with Hania's response.

"So, what's stopping you?" Thunderbird interjected; silencing the murmurs. "Be our guardian but be the world's hero. These matters that we send you on aren't for our personal gain. We cannot freely fret around your world, using our might to vanquish foes. But we cannot let the world suffer from our creatures, our mistakes, and our creations. Does this sound more your speed now?" Thunderbird seemed to genuinely care about the human world, which was a refreshing change of pace. But Hania couldn't help but focus on how the bird-like deity closed his eyes whenever he spoke. It seemed like every one of these gods had some type of habit that came out whenever they spoke. Zeus always let lightning bounce around him as if it were a show of might, as well as interjecting with frequent insults, and Thor did the equivalent of talking in all caps.

"Fine, as long as I don't have to deal with prophecies or something." Hania said, after a few moments had passed.

"Why would we deal with prophecies? We aren't creative enough to think of a prophecy every time we want you to do something." Zeus said, with a straight face.

"It would be pretty cool though." Thor added. Before Zeus raised his hand to silence him.

"Are you ready to start this process?" Zeus moved so that he was behind Hania, faster than his eyes could track. And Hania had some pretty good eyes. He nodded his head in response. Zeus led him over to the area where the azure light had been hitting the center of the room. Hania hated that he had to avert his eyes to avoid passing out, where as everyone else in the room could look at the light so casually. Without looking directly at it though, Hania could tell that the light had grown brighter. No, brighter wasn't the right word to describe this. The light had grown aggressive; he felt it seeking out substance like a starving plant seeking sunlight. Little tendrils of light plucked at the hairs on his skin as he got closer. His body screamed run away, his heart raced, and his bones began to chill. Luckily for Hania, he wouldn't have a chance to run away, since Zeus spartan-kicked him directly into the center of light.

The noise Hania made could hardly be considered human. It was the personification of pain; a blood freezing cry that would have you think every single organ was shutting down in his body. Every cell in his body felt as though it were on fire; each individual molecule roaring out to stop. His blood felt like they were replaced with daggers; cutting him on the inside. Hania felt like throwing up, but nothing would come out but his own, pitiful voice. He was sure that this was what it felt like to die. No, this had to be worse than dying. For the second time in his young life, Hania had truly wished to die. His name might have meant spirit warrior, but he felt more like a cowering infant longing for his mother to kiss his boo-boos better. Just when Hania couldn't take it anymore; when he had nearly made the decision to beg for someone to kill him, the pain stopped. The pain was replaced by a surge of power; a strength so large that it coursed through his veins. His body felt lighter, faster, and more durable than before. Lightning danced wildly around him; emitting from his body in a brilliant display. As though he were being branded; he felt a searing sensation on his right shoulder. Hania could feel a small thunderbolt shaped symbol being engraved onto his right shoulder.

"It is complete." Zeus nonchalantly stated, before returning to his perch upon the clouds.

"That's it? No explosion of power? I expected my hair to turn gold or something. It's a little underwhelming." Hania was bluffing, of course. He felt like he could take on the entire room of deities and survive for at least thirty seconds; about twenty-nine seconds worth of added confidence in his own abilities.

"That's it?! You haven't tested your might yet! All your abilities have been amplified and imbued with magic properties! Better strength and speed, more lightning and more healing! You haven't even donned your battle garb!" Thor nearly fell off his cloud in his own excitement. Hania could tell by that crazed look in his eyes that Thor wanted to fight Hania. But the way Hania's life was set up, he enjoyed living it, and decided to decline if he was challenged.

“Battle garb? Are we talking suit of armor or spandex and underwear on the outside?” Hania questioned. Thunderbird looked at him and Hania instantly became annoyed. He knew that Thunderbird was about to open his beak to spout a few words.

“It’s whatever you may desire. The symbol on your back is the source of the magic flowing within you. It will create your new clothing based on whatever image you shape in your mind, and it will serve as minor protection against attacks. You simply have to will it into existence, and it will appear at any time.”

Hania thought about this for a few moments. He had thought about designing a costume for at least a year now, while he sat in his room toying with the idea of being an actual superhero or not. To be honest, he still wasn’t completely sure if he wanted to be a superhero. Just in case though, he had to think carefully. He needed something that would make it harder to identify his face, but something practical as well. Superheroes were still a rather new thing in the world; currently there were only two confirmed superheroes, and maybe a dozen or so unconfirmed reports of others. He didn’t exactly have a lot of options to model his look after.

“Could you hurry?” Zeus rolled his eyes as he watched Hania deep in thought.

“Shut up, gramps! I think I’ve got it…” Hania furrowed his brow and began to envision the costume he had picked out. The magic that Thor mentioned he was now embedded with reacted to his thoughts, and the small lightning bolt tattoo that was on his shoulder began to shine bright. His clothes were gone; replaced with a cape-length, gray cloak that ended at the back of his knees, adorned with golden lightning bolts engraved along the trim. His cloak was complete with a hood that draped over his head in such a way that it formed a beak down to his nose. Magical shadows left his mocha hued chin and mouth revealed while completely obscuring the rest of his image. His brown eyes also peered out through the shadows that were created by his magical outfit. Beneath his sleeveless cloak, he now had on a rather snug, blue shirt and matching pants; both trimmed with the same lightning bolts that adorned his cloak. A golden belt was around his waist, with the buckle forming a lightning bolt, with flat shoes that had the same golden tone.

"The bottom half of your face, and your hands are completely exposed, as well as the front of your neck. Horrible design choice. You know you don't get a second chance at this, correct?" Zeus pointed out, in typical hypocritical fashion considering half of Zeus' body was out.

"Pot calling the kettle black, much? I'm well aware about that fact, but well...it's important to me...to a lot of people, that some of my features are shown. That the world knows that I'm black. Well, half black at least. That I'm a minority; yeah that sounds better. Anyway, there aren't too many people for minorities to be able to see themselves in or to aspire to be. So, I want to add to that very tiny list. I don't know why I'm explaining this to you lot, I guess it's something that's lost on gods, right?" Hania had a slight smile as he spoke.

"Don't understand that at all." Seemingly every deity in the room proclaimed in unison, like the start of the world's most mythical Christmas carol. Hania had figured that his explanation was going to be lost among deities with hardly any concept of race in general. Still, saying it out loud felt good.

"So, here stands Hania the hero…" Thunderbird began, before he noticed Hania shake his head.

"No, not anymore. Don't call me Hania when I'm wearing this." Hania had thought long and hard about this. Not only was Hania such a rare name that he was certain people would put two and two together, but this was a chance for Hania to make a new name for himself. To be something more than Hania, the boy with abandonment issues. To be more than Hania, the boy who got kicked out of his first two elementary schools. This was a chance to be someone who meant something.

"Very well. What shall you be known as?" Thunderbird questioned.

"Call me…"

Raiden

"Come out with your hands up!" Chief Valo of the Albuquerque police department blared over his megaphone; facing the New Mexico Credit Union. Like the rest of his men behind him, he was clad in swat gear with only his dull brown eyes showing. The response he received came in the form of bullets, as five men wielding assault rifles came flying out the front door. The police and the robbers entered a vicious shootout, but it was apparent that these criminals were no amateurs. Two officers went down with well-placed shots to their thighs, while the rest couldn't get a good shot in.

"We just have to get to the car. Form up." The leader of the criminals, the largest of the five men spoke in a deep, menacing voice. His words were slow and calm, but the rest of the men fell in line on instinct; either from fear or respect. More likely, it was a mixture of both. Like migrating birds, the men formed a V pattern with their leader at the center.

"Don't let them get to that car!" Chief Valo directed. He had been referring to a windowless white van that was parked to the right of them. "Eyes up, damn it!" Chief Valo screamed. Two of his men were hiding behind their squad cars despite the spray of bullets soaring in the opposite direction. "Rookies." The Chief couldn't help but mutter, before he popped his head up and fired a burst of rounds from his assault rifle, only for the bullets to harmlessly collide with the leader's ballistic shield. "Where the hell did they get their hands on that…" Chief Valo figured they had to have some type of military training. He ripped off his face covering and hat in frustration, revealing his brown stubble and completely bald head. Their formation was perfect, lacking in blind spots completely. They didn't fire all at once, making it so there was always a constant rain of bullets flying down at their targets, and their leader was making it easier to get to their van by shielding their movements.

"Think they're irregulars?" An officer to the chief's left questioned. An irregular was what the public had referred to those with superhuman abilities. It was mostly derogatory, as that implied that those who had extraordinary gifts were barely human, but it was only to be expected. Super powers were incredibly rare and no one had really understood how they even sprouted up in society. Or perhaps they had been in society for longer than anyone even knew about and have just recently been brought into the limelight.

“I don’t think so. Or at least...I hope not.” Chief Valo muttered. Chief Valo had been on the opposite end of an irregular’s fury only once, back before he was promoted to Chief. The experience left him comatose for a month.

“Chief, at this rate…” One of the younger sounding officers began, crawling his way over to Chief Valo.

“I know! New plan; shoot out the van’s tires!” Chief Valo couldn’t contain his frustration at the situation.

“We can’t sir. We can’t get a good angle on the tires because that short wall is blocking them.” Chief Valo sucked his teeth at the news delivered by his officer. If they got in that van, they would be forced into a high-speed pursuit and even more innocents could be harmed. But if they simply cut their losses and let them escape, the group could always come back and do this all over again.

Crack! A bolt of lightning struck down directly on the van, rendering it inoperable. All gunfire immediately ceased. Everyone was left in awe at what they were seeing. “Oops. You didn’t need that did you?” The lightning formed into a hooded figure as it spoke.

“Of course, you had to show up, Raiden. Friggin’ freak of nature.” The leader of the robbers spat after regained his focus and commanded all his men to aim their assault rifles at Raiden. Nearly eight years had passed since that fateful meeting with the deities of lightning, and Hania, currently going by his superhero persona known as Raiden, had matured since then. He was a few inches taller, and lean, with even longer dreads that were just past his jaw, although they were currently hidden away thanks to his costume. Luckily, his costume had grown and evolved with him. His cloak fit closer to a cape; leaving his rather toned arms exposed. His previously golden shoes were now black, and significantly less gaudy. His pants also lost the golden trim, and since he got tired of bruising his knuckles, he began wearing fingerless gloves that matched his shirt.

"Don't be rude! I was in the neighborhood and figured I'd stop and say hello." Raiden enjoyed poking fun at criminals. Normally, it threw them off and made things easier for him.

Raiden had officially been New Mexico's native superhero for about a year now, although he had been helping the city as Raiden for a little longer than that. Just long enough for him to be recognized by criminals and policemen alike, although they didn't know much about who he actually was. The public referred to him as the lightning irregular, which was only half true. Plus, he was currently New Mexico's only known irregular after Chief Valo killed the last one, so he had a huge advantage over the local crime. His approval rating was pretty high though, so that was enough for him. He grinned; his white teeth offsetting the shadow formed on his face by his beak like hood and his own natural burnt sienna toned skin. The robbers let loose their guns simultaneously, but Raiden was ready. He became a bolt of lightning and zipped between the bullets easily. "Last chance guys. You can't win, and you know you can't win. So how about you make this easy for me and give up. Or don't. It's really your choice. I like beating people up too." Raiden watched as the men reloaded their guns. "Oh good, option B it is!" The hero quipped. His personality was still nearly identical to how he was several years prior.

A blast of lightning flew from Raiden's hand and smashed into one of the criminals' guns; launching it straight from his hands and into pieces. Using his two index fingers, Raiden knocked the rest of the guns out of the thugs' hands with lightning and began floating an inch or two off the ground. The dark-skinned hero flew towards his opponents and easily knocked four of them out with a single punch each. "My men…" The leader looked almost like a lost puppy as he watched them all be knocked unconscious.

"Yeah, you might want to fire them for napping on the job." Raiden spoke after landing a foot away from the leader. "Just you now, big guy. Wanna give this up?" Raiden offered. The leader looked like he was seriously contemplating it for a minute. But he was taller than Raiden, and definitely more muscular than him. It was like watching a track star face down a linebacker. Maybe with a well-placed punch…

The leader charged Raiden with his ballistic shield in front of him. At the last second, he moved it out of his way and threw a haymaker so beautiful that Mike Tyson himself would swoon. He missed, but that didn't diminish the beauty of it. "That's a nice shield ya got there." Raiden teased while dodging the two follow up strikes that the leader attempted. Raiden was way too fast for the man to hit, plus his left hand was occupied by the shield. Still, the shield at least was making Raiden hesitant to use his lightning. "It would be a real shame…" When the leader charged at Raiden again, the superhero drew his fist back. "...if someone were to break it!" Raiden cried while he punched directly through the ballistic shield in the middle of the man's charge and used his momentum to carry his punch directly into the man's chest. No matter how tough the shield may have been, it couldn't stand up to Raiden's super strength. The man slumped onto the ground with all the finesse of a sack of potatoes. Idaho potatoes, specifically. The officers stared in awe for a moment, before rushing out with handcuffs to arrest the bank robbers.

"Thank you, Raiden." Chief Valo never knew how to talk to the hero. In truth, he thought Raiden was annoying, but he couldn't deny that Raiden got results. Even if he was an irregular.

"No problem Chief!" Raiden flashed a grin as he spoke, before raising his hand up and waiting, until the now confused Chief Valo slowly raised his up to match Raiden's. Raiden swiftly high-fived the chief, before flying off into the air.

"Sometimes, I really hate that kid…" Chief Valo murmured as the hero flew out of sight.

Raiden loved flying through the city; his city. Seeing the people below carrying on through their daily lives, the aroma of all the fresh food being cooked, the spectacular view. Of course, Raiden wanted to protect this place. After all, he grew up there. His focus shifted though. He was flying away from the city, not deeper in it. His destination was a much quieter place.

Raiden landed at a small, beige house in the outskirts of Albuquerque, before his costume removed itself in little bolts of lightning, leaving him standing in a simple black t-shirt and a pair of faded blue jeans. His mid-length, brown locks framed his face and extending to the nape of his neck, with a short strand or two hanging above his brown eyes. The sides of his head were shaven, although this wasn't immediately apparent due to his untamed dreads falling to obscure his sides from view. He was what would be referred to as "baby-face;" something that he hated to be pointed out. So much so, he got a stud piercing in his nose to take attention away from his chin. "Mom, your favorite son came to visit!" He walked into the house after announcing his presence and stuck his hands inside his pockets. His mother's house was a little bigger than the outside portrayed, but not by much. It was a simple ranch-style house with two bedrooms and one bathroom. The tradeoff was that it was cheap to live in and filled with fond memories.

"You're my only son, Hania." Hania's mother retorted, putting down a book that she had apparently just started. She was relatively young at only a month into her forties, but she already had developed crow's feet, though he called them smile lines whenever speaking to her. She still was rather beautiful, to the point where even Hania couldn't understand why she remained single. The two looked rather similar in all honesty; same skin complexion, same 'classic' Native American high cheekbones, same slightly heart shaped face, even the same almond shaped eyes. The only real difference was that his mother's hair resembled her Native American side more, whereas Hania's resembled his African-American side. That, and Hania's nose was more beak-like compared to his mother's slender nose.

"Good, I don't like competition." Hania walked over and hugged his mom tightly. For the majority of his life, it's just been the two of them against the world. Their bond was unbelievably tight. "Did you see me on TV? If not, don't worry about it. You can always catch it when they run the story again this evening." Hania's mother laughed softly at her son's excitement.

“Yes, Hania. Or should I be calling you Raiden now?” Hania’s mother smiled warmly at her son. He was her pride and joy, even if the rest of the world didn’t know about his superhero antics, she certainly did. She was actually the one who pushed him to become a hero in the first place.

“If you call me Raiden, then I get to call you Naira. Call me by the name you gave me, and I’ll call you by the name I gave you. Well okay, I didn’t exactly name you mom, but you get the point.” Hania said.

“Fair enough, *Hania.* By whatever name you go by, I am so very proud of you. I just hope I’m not holding you back.” Hania was taken aback by his mom’s words.

“Holding me back? Mom, if it wasn’t for you, I wouldn’t even be doing this. I’d still be hiding my powers away from the world and pretending I’m normal!” Hania countered. He hated being called an irregular, since it felt like just another racial slur, but at least he had the chance to be who he truly was.

“Perhaps. But I feel like you only stay in New Mexico because I’m here. You could be helping the entire world out, not just this state.” Naira rubbed her son on the head, before walking past him into the kitchen.

“That’s not true! New Mexico has the best tacos!” Hania called after his mother, before walking around her living room. The wall was plastered with pictures of the two of them together. He saw pictures from the day he graduated high school, his prom picture with the cute exchange student from Ghana, even pictures from him in elementary school. But his trip down memory lane was interrupted when he came across a particular picture. The same picture he found himself looking at every day since he was younger. In the picture was his mom, on her nineteenth birthday judging from the fact that she was four months pregnant with Hania, standing in front of a taller male. It was easy to see that he wasn’t mixed like Naira, but rather fully Native American. He almost looked like a stock photograph found by googling his race; with his silky black hair tied into two braids towards the end, and a single large feather sticking out at the top of his head. He had the same beak-like nose that Hania had, which was perhaps one of his more distinctive features. He looked older than Naira by a few years, but just as happy to be with her as she appeared to be with him.

"Pasta's your favorite food, go to Italy!" Naira walked out of the kitchen only to freeze when she caught Hania staring at the picture.

"Why do you still keep this phantom's picture up?" Hania didn't remove his eyes off the picture. He only remembered seeing his father three times in his entire life: right after they were kicked off the reservation, on his tenth birthday, and right after he came to terms with his desire to be a hero around two years ago. The last time, it took all Hania's willpower not to just blast him with lightning right then and there.

"Don't call him that, you know that isn't fair. Your father cares deeply about both of us, especially you. He's just too important to stay here." Naira tried to comfort her son, but he took a step away from her as soon as she got close.

"Mom, I'm twenty years old. When are you going to stop making excuses for that man? He just doesn't want to be here with us." Hania's eyes flashed gold for a brief moment as a spark escaped his body. Whenever he had a particular powerful surge of emotions, or he was using a large amount of his lightning abilities, his eyes shifted from dark brown to brilliant gold. Naira opened her mouth to speak, but Hania quickly cut his mom off. "I don't want to talk about this anymore, mom. Let's go make dinner." His eyes shifted back to normal, and he left the photo as though it were some diseased roadkill.

"Sure, darling, anything you want." Naira followed behind Hania as he walked into the kitchen.

Night had fallen, as a man sat inside his home watching the evening news. "Thanks to the efforts of local hero, Raiden, the men were stopped…" The newscaster on the man's TV spoke. He chuckled a bit before standing up from his recliner and walking over to his wall, which was covered with mounted heads. He looked at his most recent additions: a wolf, a bear, a lion, a tiger, and a human. More specifically, the wolf was a werewolf, stuck in wolf form. The mounted bear head belonged to a hyper intelligent bear that was wielding a sword. He took down the lion and the tiger together after hearing how the two creatures were working together to terrorize Singapore. The human kill was the latest one, and still fresh in his mind. It belonged a man claiming to be some type of super soldier, apparently able to wield any weapon at optimal efficiency. It was a glorious fight, but ultimately the super soldier was killed during the very same sword duel that he suggested.

"Now that's what I call big game." The pale, muscular man chuckled before reaching for a crossbow that was resting on the wall, below the mounted heads. "That'll be my next hunt..."

The man who hunts

Three nights had passed since Raiden's face was shown blasted on the small screen. It was all that the man could think about. The big game hunter, as he liked to refer to himself as, was meticulous. Once he found something that he had an interest in hunting, he sank his fangs into it like a ravenous beast. The past two days, the hunter had his crimson eyes glued to the television and his computer, visually digesting all manner of information relating to Raiden. He was studying how he fought, the powers that he had, even how he talked and his non-verbal mannerisms. The plan was to know Raiden so well, that the two could breathe in sync. The big game hunter had relocated to New Mexico at this point, although considering when he saw the news article he was in Arizona from a previous hunt, it wasn't a far trip.

"It's almost time to start hunting...." The man muttered to himself. This time though, he wasn't referring to Raiden. Raiden's hunt would come later in the week after he did his usual prep work. He had been tracking another were-animal in the area that was running from a few states over, and for the big game hunter, it was perfect. All were-animals acted similar, he had notice. They never stayed in one place, and they operated mostly at night. All of them were skittish, and avoided spot lights. Factoring in that the creature would be headed towards Texas, all the man had to do was wait. He even had a rough idea of the pathway he would take, based on his predictions and estimates.

The big game hunter was dressed in all black, with a claymore resting on his back and two handguns on his belt. Night had fallen, so this was the perfect camouflage. His breathing became shallow and scarce, and his heart beat had slowed significantly. His hunting mode had been in full-effect at this point. If he wanted to, the big game hunter could have stayed prone for forty hours without moving when he entered his zone. After that, he would need to drink some water and stretch his limbs, before returning right back to the same position. A handful of people had walked past his view without noticing him thus far. None of which were his target. It would be a lone man, which meant that he was being hasty and not using his wits. The smarter option would have been to blend in with a group when trying to hide. Sure enough, after only three hours of waiting, a pale and slender man walked into the big game hunter's view. The man's scraggly beard and uneven buzzcut suggested someone who hadn't been in a steady home for weeks. Combined with his tattered pants and shirt, with his overall demeanor that screamed "please, don't push me," were all dead giveaways that this was the prey that the big game hunter was looking for.

"Stop right there." The big game hunter had left his hiding spot so silently, the were-animal hadn't even noticed until it was too late. This was on purpose, of course. Were-animals tended to be resistant to long range attacks, and most times, they were practically unkillable whenever they hadn't fully morphed. Strange, considering they were so much more powerful in their were state. It was almost as if the animal within them rejected the death of their human form.

"Can I help you?" The were-person spoke with a gruff voice. He looked at the big game hunter and scanned the weapons holstered on his body. "You don't want to do this." He had come across all manner of people who wanted him dead before, albeit none with crimson eyes. The big game hunter said nothing, but simply drew his claymore. The way he held the weapon in his hand showed off his expertise; his stance perfect for both attacking and guarding.

"I do." The hunter muttered from behind the mask that covered the bottom half of his face. He watched as his prey rapidly morphed to reveal his actual form; a were-scorpion. The bones of the man cracked and shifted in a disgusting display, before he became a human sized scorpion; his black shell gleaming in the moonlight. His hands had become rather large pincers, while a long tail had grown from his back. The only part of the were-scorpion's body that wasn't covered in a black shell, was his face. The hunter sighed at the sight. A were-scorpion would be too easy of a target. As long as he didn't get himself stung, there would really be nothing the were-scorpion could do. Plus, he had fought creatures significantly faster and stronger than what he imagined a were-scorpion was. "Cut off the tail, cut off the head." The hunter spoke, mostly to himself, as he dodged two swipes from the were-scorpion's tail. Not only was the were-scorpion unimpressive as a species in general, but this one was sloppy. The hunter guessed that he was recently changed. If this were a hunt for fun, the hunter would have simply left and went to do something else. Hunting things that didn't interest him generally wasn't his style. However, he was getting paid for this one, so his hands were metaphorically tied.

"Got you!" The were-scorpion lunged at the hunter when it seemed like he was losing his footing. A ploy, no matter how clever it was. With a quick adjustment of his footing, the big game hunter sliced off the were-scorpion's tail. A blood like substance the hue of dull copper spewed from the newly severed appendage, but to the hunter's surprise, the were-scorpion stifled his screams of pain. "Damn yo-" The were-scorpion found himself looking up at his own body. In one swift motion, the hunter had severed his head right as the creature started to lunge.

"Cut off the tail, cut off the head." The big game hunter repeated, as the were-scorpion's body made an audible thud against the floor. He walked over and picked up the now taciturn head and placed it on the back of its body. The hunter crouched down next to the torso and pulled out his camera phone. "Selfie!" He mused, before sending the photo evidence to his client. The hunt may have been boring, but for sixty-five thousand, being bored had its rewards. Plus, now he could focus on his actual target.

Back in his hotel room, the big game hunter had documents spread out all over his bed, and a large white board posted up on the wall. "I know for sure that he's African American and since he isn't hiding this means that he is proud. His actions show that he's cocky, and judging from the smoothness of his skin, I'd put him in his early twenties." The big game hunter had been talking out his thought pattern while writing his notes on the whiteboard. "Any footage of him shows that he is normally coming or going from one of three different directions when he flies, and he is active during all types of hours. One of the directions he comes from coincides with the University of New Mexico and that matches with the age I'd place him at. Not to mention the fact that he speaks like someone who has some type of education whenever he's on television. With his age, personality, and how active in heroism he is...he's probably poor, or lower middle-class. Mapping out the city, this area that he occasionally flies to and from is one of the cheaper areas for rent. I'd wager he lives around that area. This third area though...it's towards the outskirts of town. I can't quite place this one...maybe a parent or sibling lives in this direction. Or a friend." The way the hunter's mind worked was frightening. He pulled out his laptop and as though he were a former employee, effortlessly accessed the student files for the University of New Mexico. "Based on all the information I have, there are only three students who may fit that profile. I'll study a little further...but I'm positive it's this kid." His finger tapped on a student ID in which the student was both cheesing from ear to ear and winking. "Hania Hawke, eh?" The hunter closed his laptop and grinned. He had found his target.

The hunt begins

"Lakota tribe Chief found burned to death outside of Cheyenne River Indian Reservation." Hania read aloud from his laptop. He felt conflicted hearing the news. On one hand, it was an innocent life lost by unknown means. The superhero in him thought about flying over and doing his own personal investigation. On the other hand, the tribal chief was kind of an ass. He was the same tribal chief who made Hania and his mother's life a living hell. The tribal chief didn't agree with the relationship Hania's mother had with his father, just because of who he was. He already didn't like her to begin with because she was mixed, and he was a self-proclaimed "blood purist." Still didn't give him reason to boot out a single mother and a three-year-old. Hania's mom didn't even try to refute the eviction, nearly eighteen years ago. She just found an affordable home and spent all the money she had on the move to New Mexico, hoping for the best. No thanks to his phantom of a father, but they managed to make it.

"Whatever." Hania closed the laptop before he got any more irritated than he already was. It was time to go on patrol and blow off some steam. A small lightning bolt shaped symbol on the center of Hania's right shoulder lit up as his costume enveloped him. "Let's go catch some baddies!" He exclaimed as he flew out of his apartment window into the sky.

Raiden kept looking from side to side as he flew. Particularly because he really wanted to see some crime so he could save the day, but mostly because something about the night seemed off. It was a feeling he couldn't shake but lacked a proper basis. At least it did, until an arrow flew directly into his right shin. "Sonova b-" Another arrow flew towards him, but Raiden was prepared. In one fluid motion he caught the arrow directly in the middle and flung it back towards the ground, adding an aura of lightning on its return trip. Whoever fired it had moved, unfortunately. Raiden landed and ripped the arrow out of his leg, tossing it hard against the floor so that it split in two. Raiden had a high pain tolerance acquired from his year of being a public superhero, and his endeavors prior to his superhero career, but that still made him tense up. The sensation of the exit wound widening as he pulled it out made him make a note to himself not to try that again. "Who are you?!" Raiden took a step and felt his foot catch what he could only guess was fishing line. A grenade rolled next to him and gently tapped his foot. "Crap and a half!" The grenade went off milliseconds after Raiden noticed it.

Thankfully, that was enough time. Raiden became a bolt of lightning and planted himself atop a nearby building. The young hero winced a bit from the pain in his leg. Sure, he could heal, and the open wound would shut in a few moments or so, but he wasn't impervious. It hurt like hell, honestly. He had no idea who was attacking him, and the pain was dulling his thoughts. Plus, his brain was moving a million miles a second as a side-effect of transforming into lightning. All he knew was that this attacker was good. A bullet whizzed by and slit his right cheek; the bullet only missed whatever its intended target was because Raiden had been rapidly shifting side to side at the speed of lightning to keep himself safe. His attacker was far, judging from the fact that they were using a sniper rifle. Within this singular battle, he had been hit more times than he ever was since exiting the guardian basic training program. "If I paid more attention in Physics class, I probably could have figured out where that shot came from. I just had to be a psychology major." Raiden murmured as a second shot hit him in his shoulder. No amount of training should have helped whoever this sniper was, correctly hit him when he was moving as fast as he was. Some type of magic, powers, or science had to be involved. Whatever the case, Raiden needed time to heal. At the very least, he needed to get out of the sniper's line of sight. He was woozy though and was strongly fighting the urge to run. Raiden had fought many people who shot at him, more than he would ever admit to his mother, but he was never actually hit. Sure, bullets had grazed him before, but this was his first time being actually shot. The entire experience was a zero out of ten for Raiden. Would not recommend to a friend.

Raiden regained his composure and dove off the side of the building, just as he heard another bullet whizz by his ears. He scanned around, searching the environment he was in. Only now did Raiden realize he was around older, decaying buildings with boarded windows. Graffiti and trash littered every street in sight. The area he was in was abandoned, which made sense. His attacker could hide without people getting in their way and would have had enough time to set up his traps. Which meant…

"*Do they know who I am?*" Raiden froze; his eyes widening and heartbeat quickening. Raiden typically flew past this area when leaving his apartment to throw his trail off, although he admittedly forgot this area was abandoned. Did someone tail him or was this a coincidence? Did they know of his true identity as Hania? Another arrow flying towards his face snapped him out of his thoughts in time to disintegrate it with a well-placed bolt. "Enough!" Raiden slammed his hand onto the ground, covering about a city block radius in lightning. He couldn't risk anything more than that or he might creep into a populated area. Even still, he took care to weaken the force of the attack in case any homeless were in the area.

"Ugh!" A voice cried out in pain; echoing from the empty buildings. It was a male's voice, judging from how gruff it was. Raiden rushed over to the area he heard the scream from, taking the most direct path he could think of… through the walls of the buildings. He arrived at where he had heard the cry of pain, just in time to come face to face with a flashbang. Raiden's body was extremely durable, and his pain tolerance was off the charts, due to his powers. The tradeoff was that he was weakened to internal damage. Drugs, sound, even light-based attacks damaged him much more than they would the average human. He winced and covered his eyes, barely keying in on the sound of slow footsteps shuffling away. Lifting a hand, he shot a bolt of lightning towards the footsteps and hoped for the best.

"Bloody hell!"

The man cried out in a forced British accent, the bolt obviously hitting its target. He tried to follow up with a second attack but could tell that his attack missed. Raiden heard the dull roar of a starting engine, followed by the squealing, spinning tires. "Get back here!" Raiden cried, attempting to fly towards the speeding car. Not that he was able to get very far however, as he felt himself being propelled into the wall by something that could only be described as a miniature rhino. Raiden grunted, while wondering if his chest had caved in. Several moments passed and his vision returned. Looking down to his hands, he found himself clutching a literal ball of heated iron. It was shot out of something, Raiden had to guess, because it was still hot to the touch. “Is this guy a pirate or something?” He couldn’t help to ask himself; picturing an old school pirate complete with eyepatch. A few words were engraved on the ball, Raiden noticed, as he thumbed the small cannonball over.

“The hunt begins…” Raiden read to himself. He stood up, his eyes glowing an Olympic gold color and a bolt of lightning struck the iron ball so intensely that Raiden was left holding a pile of ashes. “You’ve got that right.” Raiden murmured in response. He flew up, searching for any trace of the criminal. The problem was that Raiden was blinded for a lot longer than he thought. Sure, he heard the general direction that the car went, but it was long gone when he came to. Plus, he didn’t seem to be the type to be caught by driving away. More than likely, he would have switched cars by now. Not to mention that the flashbang was so perfectly timed that he didn’t even get a good look at the guy. It would be a gross waste of time to search him out, Raiden determined. Instead, he flew home as his eyes were still sensitive; taking care to move faster than before just in case someone was tailing him.

Somebody's watching me

"Hania!" Hania's head snapped up after hearing his friend shout at him. He had visible bags under his eyes and a general disheveled look to him. For the past three days, he had been both paranoid, that his little stalker knew who he was, and so thirsty for revenge that he had been flying around every night searching for him, despite not knowing what he looked like. It had begun to take its toll.

"Sorry, I must have dozed. What did you say?" Hania was regaining his awareness, as he panned the room. He was in the college library, helping his favorite little redhead study for their psychology exam.

"You need to get some sleep soon. I asked if you could help me with a report on Greek mythology, since you're so good at that too." His friend, Kylie, smiled sweetly as she spoke. At one time, the two used to be a couple but decided they worked better as friends. There was still a strong connection between the two, and an obvious mutual physical attraction. Hania kind of had a thing for redheads. Ironic, considering red was his least favorite color.

"Yeah, sure. How about I go take a nap and we can meet up a little later." Hania stood up and pulled Kylie into his chest. If he wasn't so tired, he probably could have counted the freckles on her face.

"I'll text you later then. Get some sleep, dreadhead. The nightmares aren't coming back, are they?" She pushed herself away from Hania and started gathering her belongings off the table. She lingered a bit, waiting for the answer. A few years ago, Hania went through a bout of night terrors. Granted, the two were dating at that point and thus his well-being was a larger concern than it should be currently, but they were still friends. She still cared, even if she was currently keeping a healthy emotional distance.

"I'm okay, don't worry about it, fire crotch." Hania whispered his nickname for Kylie and quickly dodged the book she tossed at his head. Deflection was just one of Hania's many talents. Of course, the night terrors weren't back. They never left to begin with.

Hania stepped outside the library and had nearly made it off the campus, when he felt something smack into his left shoulder. It was a small beanbag, but it stung too much to have been thrown. Another one smacked him directly on the forehead. Definitely not thrown considering how much force was behind the impact. It had to have been shot. Someone was stalking him. He stepped to the left and another bean bag shot at his foot. The same thing happened when he took a step back, but he was left alone when he walked forward. Someone was guiding him; someone who was an excellent shot. His eyes widened as he came to the realization that it must have been the guy who hunted him three nights ago. He knew who Hania really was, and that was a huge problem.

The area he was in was way too populated to try and attack his stalker. One person knowing his identity was bad enough. He'd have to play along for now.

Hania had walked half a mile as per his silent instructions; with his stalker taking care to tag a few nearby pedestrians with bean bags every few feet. He was showing Hania that the entire city was his hostage. He ended up having to walk all the way back to the site of their first battle, giving Hania an hour and a half to stew in his anger. For the first time, he was face to face with his attacker. The male dressed rather plain; wearing an all-black bodysuit that showed off his rather muscular physique, and a pair of metal gauntlets. What little skin that showed was sun kissed, and he had shaggy, dirty blonde hair. The bottom of his face was covered with a gas mask, while his eyes peered out. His eyes were the one, extraordinary thing about him. They were a bright, almost glowing, red with his pupils giving off the appearance of a cross. "Nice to finally meet you Raiden. Or should I call you, Han?" The man's voice was a mixture of a terrible British accent and an equally terrible Australian one.

"First off, you sound like a dying narwhal. Take some acting lessons. At this point, I'd even pay for them myself. Secondly, only my friends call me Han, and I hate you more than that Narwhal song." Hania couldn't take his gaze away from his assailant's peculiar eyes any better than he could mask his hatred of the horned sea-cow. The fact that his pupils resembled a crucifixion was off putting. Plus, they were a deep shade of red which Raiden hated even more than his stupid accents.

"Really? Then what does Kylie call you?" The man grinned under his mask, causing it to move slightly from the action.

"You even think about touching her and I swear I-" Hania's rage was quelled instantly when he felt a needle fly into his neck. His thoughts became hazy and his words slurred. Suddenly he felt so...and then he plopped down onto the floor.

"Where...am I?" Hania's consciousness returned, but he still felt groggy and his thoughts were hazy at best. Hania was restrained down in a chair, in what looked like a log cabin. Normally, the metal cuffs should have been digging into his wrist, but they weren't. The chair felt unnaturally soft as well. "Rubber." Hania whispered. The insides of the metal cuffs, as well as the chair itself, were made of rubber. He wouldn't be able to shock his way out of this situation in his current state. About a half dozen human heads were stuffed and mounted on the wall to his right. On his left were a dozen different weapons; a few swords, a staff, a group of guns, and at least two that he had never seen before. The big game hunter wanted a more...homely touch, so he decided to buy a small lodging for his stay. "I've gotta get out of here." Hania spoke slowly, methodically. He was having trouble getting his words to form. He definitely was still drugged. An open window indicated that it was sunset, meaning that around six hours had passed. Hania couldn't help but wonder what type of drug he used to knock him out for so long.

"Oh good, you're awake." The man's accent was French this time, much to Hania's dismay.

"Listen up, you stupid hunter or whatever your name i-"

"Oh, it's Hunter. Charmed." Hunter quickly cut him off. Hania paused for a moment, completely blank face.

“Seriously? Hunter is your actual name?” Hania’s delivery was completely deadpan. He made a noise that fused annoyance and disgust perfectly. “I want you to know, I hate you more than life itself.”

“Yes, I’m sure. So, tell me, what makes you tick? How did you get your powers? What are you?” Hunter moved a little closer and poured himself a glass of whiskey.

“*As if I’d tell you.*” Hania thought to himself. “I’m the Guardian of Lightning. I was handpicked to be the champion for the Lords that rule over lightning, like Zeus. I’m connected to all of the lightning on earth.” Hania quickly shut his mouth. He just started spewing words out with no control over it. Thankfully, he hadn’t told Hunter everything. Still, it was strange that he couldn’t lie, like he wanted to. “Did you use sodium thiopental on me?” Hania asked his captor, whom seemed taken aback.

“I’m impressed you figured it out. You truly are a worthy hunt. Certainly not your run of the mill irregular.” Hunter clapped as he spoke to his prey. Truthfully, Hania had studied various drugs and the side effects they had, back when he was trying to determine what weaknesses he had a few years back. It was more surprising that Hunter figured out what his weakness was, after only one encounter. Was Hania that sloppy, or was Hunter that good?

“I guess there’s nothing I can do then.” Hania managed to slur out. As powerful as he was, sedatives always seemed to work a little too well on him. In fact, maybe it was because of his powers that they worked well. Sedatives seemed to confuse his healing ability, causing it to either halt completely or increase the potency of the drug. That was the case with all medicines. Even Nyquil could knock him out near instantly if he took it.

“Zeus is real, huh? You don't say. Maybe I’ll have to start hunting Gods next. Are Lords the same as gods?” Hunter inquired.

"No." Hania admitted. He hated that he couldn't control his words. Sodium thiopental normally wasn't an actual truth serum, although it did make it more difficult to compose a lie. For Hania, however, it absolutely was functioning as a truth serum.

"How about you explain to me the difference between guardians, lords, and gods then." Hunter sipped his whiskey and awaited the answer.

Hania managed to sigh rather loudly, which surprised him considering he was practically under Hunter's control. "Gods are more like a species or race. They all have powers and exist in a separate realm from us. Lords are normally, but not always, Gods. They are the only ones who are ever capable of entering the human realm, even if briefly. They're normally elemental based and are responsible for bringing those elements to the human world. Guardians serve the lords directly and represent them in their stead, as well as do missions for them occasionally." He managed to leave out a few minor details somehow, but that was still a lot more than he had intended to tell.

"That was very informative. Good job. So, you aren't an irregular, but someone handpicked by the Gods?" Hunter questioned. Hania remained silent as long as he possibly could.

"No, I'm not an irregular." Hania answered. It was essentially the truth. To this day, the public believed that all irregulars just woke up one day and suddenly had powers. No one knew what caused it, or if there were differences in their origin at all. Hania however, was born with his power. Becoming a guardian simply amplified them.

"Interesting. Anyway, here's how this is going to work. I'm going to put you back to sleep and have you dropped off somewhere on this island. Then I'm going to hunt you down and either you will stop me, or I'll add your head to my collection."

“And what's to stop me from flying off this island?” Hania tugged at his restraint. Whatever he was drugged with was still flooding his system, draining his strength.

“Because if you do, I’ll put a bullet directly into Kylie Schaefer's forehead. But I won’t stop there. I’ll get your mother, and everyone you’ve ever bothered to even breathe on, Hania Hawke.” Hania narrowed his eyes after Hunter’s threat. This was a problem that he wouldn’t be able to smart talk his way out of. “I’m not completely unfair though. If you kill me, before I kill you, there is nothing in place that will reveal your sec-”

“I don’t kill. I won’t kill you.” Hania answered.

“Oh, you’re serious about the whole hero thing? So, you won’t kill me?” Hunter asked, to which Hania responded by shaking his head. “Even if I’m trying to kill you?”

“Even if you’re trying to kill me.” Hania had a fierce look in his eyes.

“I wonder how long those convictions will last. Your power incites challenge, I hope you know. People are going to continue to want to test their strength against you.”

“So, I’ll stop them. Without killing them.” Hania reiterated.

“I get it. Don’t want to be judge, jury, and executioner. You’re naive, but it’s admirable. I hope you can hold on to that innocence. Even as you realize taking a life would be easier than protecting people from the same villain who keeps slaughtering innocents. Because once you take a life, it changes you forever.” Hunter seemed to be genuinely giving Hania advice, which would have meant a lot more if he weren’t doing it in one of his ridiculous accents. “Well, if you survive, it’ll be interesting to see how you handle that. So, let’s revise those rules. If you stop me, I won’t tell your identity, nor would I go after any of your friends. I’ll even give you warning next time if I decide to hunt you again.”

“Fine.” It wasn’t as if Hania had much choice. “First though, I want to know who you are and why you decided to attack me.”

“Fair enough, since you’ve been so forthcoming with information.” Hunter had an annoying Irish accent now. Normally whenever Hunter hunted prey, he spoke in his normal voice. That was because he was positive that his foe would never see him again. The fake accent and the attempts to hide his features was more of a compliment to Hania’s skills. For the first time ever, Hunter wasn’t confident that he’d win this battle. “I’m a descendent of Judas, cursed to be a living weapon. A betrayer of my own humanity. I’m also a big game hunter, and what could be bigger game than a superhero irregular? You see, I had been watching you while you spent this year in the spotlight; gathering clues as to who you really were.”

Hania was taken aback. Did he just indirectly create a supervillain by being himself? Hunter implied that he was the first superhero he had ever hunted, and it was all because Hania had made himself such an easy target. He felt himself getting drowsy again and when he looked over there was another syringe sticking out of his arm. *“I really need to pay more attention.”* Hania had his last thought, before his eyes shut.

The Hunt's end

Hania woke up and immediately hopped onto his feet. He was outdoors, covered in dirt and surrounded by trees. He sniffed the air with two quick breaths. "Water?" Hania flew into the night sky just enough to see the landscape. "This is Rattlesnake Island…" A shot whizzed by Hania's ear, forcing him to land immediately. "A warning shot eh. Alright then…" Hania's costumed enveloped him with a bolt of lightning. "...Raiden is here to play."

A shot flew in Raiden's direction, but he darted behind a tree to dodge the blow. He returned fire with a blast of lightning but could only assume he missed. If only Raiden could find out where he was exactly.

"Hey Hunter, can you come out and play?" Raiden's shout was answered in the form of an arrow firing at him. Raiden flicked his fingers and a bolt of lightning struck the arrow from the sky. "I just want to thank you for the lovely nap. I feel refreshed!" Raiden was hoping to draw him out. If he could just find out where Hunter was, Raiden could put him down. Another arrow flew at Raiden's face, but he managed to smack the arrow with a small blast of lightning. What he didn't see, was the second arrow flying in the direct shadow of the first one. It was so close to him, too close to dodge. A small barrier of wind appeared around Raiden, slowing the arrow just enough for Raiden to snatch the arrow up.

"That was weird...what the hell…" Raiden didn't have wind powers, as far as he knew. Maybe it was related to his power of flight. A bullet digging into his side snapped him out of his thoughts and back into reality. "Mother of Zeus, that hurts." Raiden turned into lightning and zipped away. Once he returned to human form, he felt the ground underneath his feet give way. What he thought was a solid piece of ground, was actually a pitfall. Luckily, he caught himself before falling onto the spikes located at the bottom.

"A pitfall? Seriously? What type of mystery team, monster of the week strategy was that?" Raiden shouted as he floated out of the pitfall and back onto the ground...which promptly gave way again. "I can friggin' fly, what was the point in this?" Raiden shouted again, obviously more annoyed than before. He figured it was time to stop touching the ground. He needed a way to see the entire island without having to fly around. Essentially, he had to be in multiple places at once. A glint caught Raiden's eye just in time for Raiden to see a sentry gun pointed at him from in between two trees. "Craptastic." He took off as fast as he could with a spray of bullets trailing close behind. Raiden dipped out of the way, just barely dodging the shots. Once he was far enough away, he whipped around, turned into lightning, and charged full speed into the sentry gun. Needless to say, it did not survive. Raiden's normally brown eyes shifted gold from the usage of his powers.

"Now there's an idea…" Raiden slowly flew into the sky and raised both of his hands above his head. Lightning bounced around his arms, expanding outwards to deflect the few arrows that Hunter shot at him. Then, six large lightning bolts began consistently striking the island in different locations. Raiden was the champion for the gods of lightning, no matter how much he disliked them. Except Thor. Thor was pretty awesome. Like the gods of lightning though, Raiden was connected to every piece of lightning on earth. He closed his eyes and was able to see the area that the lightning was striking. He just had to find Hunter and get to him before he could evade him or set a trap. Luckily, Raiden hadn't revealed this power to him.

"Found you." Raiden transmuted into lightning and dashed halfway across the island, towards Hunter's perch in a tree. He tore through a piece of thick rope placed five hundred feet in front of Hunter, which caused the branch Hunter was sitting on to fall away. Hunter hit the ground just as Raiden turned back into his human form and punched a hole into the rather large tree that Hunter fell from. Hunter was right in front of Raiden now and even the plethora of weapons he had collected on his person wasn't going to save him. That didn't stop Hunter from trying, however.

Hunter whipped out his sniper and attempted a beautiful rendition of a first-person shooter fan's greatest achievement: the no scope. Raiden easily dodged the haphazardly fired shot and moved close enough to grab the barrel of the gun and fling it out of Hunter's hands, sending it far away from his grasp. Without missing a beat, Hunter pulled out his bow and jumped back while notching an arrow and firing. "Nope!" Raiden teased while catching the arrow right at the end. Raiden used the arrow tip and shred through the string of the bow, but Hunter hit him in the eye with its remains. The momentary shock gave Hunter an opportunity to drop a live grenade at Raiden's foot and leap away. Raiden sent lightning down around the grenade; drilling a hole into the ground that the grenade harmlessly fell into.

Three throwing stars lunged into the superhero's arm but failed to slow his charge back towards Hunter. "Back off!" Hunter dropped the accent game while drawing a hunting knife from the right holster of his chest, and a pistol from the left. Raiden slid to the left and dodged three shots fired at him, and wedged Hunter's shooting hand into the air. Hunter stabbed at the hero, but his wrist was caught by Raiden. "Got ourselves a bit of a standoff huh?" Much to Raiden's annoyance, the accents were back. He went with a Japanese accent this time, which just sounded horribly racist.

Instead of responding with words however, Raiden opened his mouth and projected a ball of lightning out of it. It smacked Hunter hard enough to knock him back several feet, but not enough to seriously wound him. "Ow." Raiden's voice was raspy, and he spit out a bit of blood. Before he could complain about his now burnt throat however, he was forced to duck and allow the claymore that Hunter swung to pass harmlessly over him. He then stole the swiss longsword that was resting on Hunter's back. The two began a furious sword battle. Thankfully, he had some brief training under his belt by Oya, the warrior goddess. Every guardian underwent training with some sort of war deity in order to prepare for the rigorous demands that the role required. Raiden wasn't exactly the best swordsman, but he was extremely fast. It didn't do much against Hunter's supernatural swordsmanship abilities, however. In a short amount of time, Hunter managed to launch Raiden's stolen sword directly from his hands and into the base of a nearby tree. Keeping up the pace, Hunter slashed down towards Raiden's head. The guardian of lightning however, caught the blade between his two palms and charged the sword with lightning.

"Christ on a cracker!" Hunter's hands were singed as he dropped the blade. Just as the crimson eyed villain reached back to draw another weapon out, Raiden delivered a rib cracking kick that sent hunter skidding along the island floor.

“Hope I didn’t overdo it.” Raiden muttered as he approached Hunter’s stagnant body. Over the years, Raiden had gotten pretty good at throttling his strength. “Please, don’t be dead. Come on, not dead, not dead.” Raiden turned over Hunter’s body so that he was on his back. “Yay! Not dead!” Hunter coughed out a bit of blood. “You need a hospital. Alright, let’s go.” Hunter raised his hand to stop Raiden.

“I’ll be fine. Leave me.” Raiden burst into laughter, much to the wounded Hunter’s annoyance.

“Leave you? You’re going to jail, man!”

“I didn’t commit any crimes. You can’t do that.” Hunter’s retort made Raiden laugh again.

“You literally hunt people. That’s pretty illegal, without counting the kidnapping and drugging me.”

“Semantics.” Hunter sat up and clutched his broken ribs.

“I hate you. I really friggin’ hate you. I hate you more than the sun hates the moon.” Raiden facepalmed and closed his eyes just long enough for Hunter to dig a flashbang out of his pocket and throw it directly in Raiden’s face. It went off and blinded him just as he heard a helicopter overhead. “No! No! No!” Raiden shouted while flailing his arms. It must have been on autopilot. Either that or he had paid off some random person to actually be his pilot.

“You win this round. I’m impressed Raiden, I must admit. Don’t worry, we’ll meet again. I can see that hunting you will require...strategy.”

“I really need to invest in sunglasses.” Raiden’s vision returned after the helicopter, and Hunter, were both long gone. He sighed a bit but couldn't be too upset. Sure, Hunter got away, but Raiden felt like he would keep his secret. Raiden flew off and went back towards his apartment, with unaided sleep being the biggest thing on his mind. That was, until he checked his phone and saw the fifteen missed text from Kylie. "Yeah, she's going to kill me." Raiden muttered, typing an eight hour too late response as he flew into the night sky.

A hot date

Hania sat inside of his psychology class, staring out the window. About a week had passed since he fought Hunter, and he disappeared without a trace. All he could do was replay the battle over again in his mind, and mentally point out each mistake he made. If only he had shot lightning at the helicopter instead of panicking and flailing his arms about. No, if he did that then he might have killed whoever was flying the helicopter. Unless it was an unmanned drone…

"Mr. Hawke!" The voice of his college professor snapped Hania out of his daze. The room was devoid of students now, with Hania being the sole exception. "As much as I know you enjoy my class, it ended several minutes ago. You're free to leave." If Hania wasn't so dark, he'd be as red as a tomato.

"Sorry, Professor Greene." Hania excused himself and darted out the room without another word. Once he stepped out of the classroom, he saw Kylie darting towards him. She lunged into his arms and squeezed him as tight as she possibly could; a large grin on her face.

"I aced my exam!" She finally let go of her best friend and backed away a few small steps.

"Congrats! I knew you could do it!" Hania joined in on her celebration, now that he finally knew what they were celebrating.

"Yeah, thanks to you, dude! Let me treat you to lunch. And I'm not taking no for an answer, so you might as well shut up and come get in my car." Kylie grabbed Hania by the wrist and began dragging him towards the direction of the parking lot.

"Hania walks willingly. Hania is a good boy." Hania teased, shuffling behind Kylie.

Kylie took Hania to a little cafe just outside their campus; a place they visited rather frequently since they started at the University of New Mexico. "I don't understand how you can eat so much, and never gain any weight." Kylie muttered as their server brought their food to them. Whereas Kylie had picked a rather modest sized salad, Hania had ordered five tacos, smothered in sour cream and salsa.

"I stay pretty active." Hania retorted, only after swallowing a rather large bite from one of his tacos. "Fast metabolism too. All that jazz." The pair had decided to eat outside and enjoy the nice weather. It was the start of Hania's favorite month, April, so it was much more comfortable to be outdoors in the seventy-degree weather versus inside, where it would be either too hot or too cold.

"Yeah, I've noticed." Kylie eyed Hania up and down rather quickly, while he wasn't looking. "Oh, did you hear about the fire just outside of Albuquerque this morning? It took like five hours to put out." That peeped Hania's interest quite a bit.

"No, I didn't. That's like the fifth unexplained fire in the past two weeks, isn't it?" Hania was a little concerned that the fires seemed to be moving closer to them. He decided to keep an eye out for any fire related activities when he went on patrol as Raiden this evening. Something about this didn't sit right with him, and after the incident with Hunter, he was definitely going to trust his gut feeling. His train of thought was interrupted, when he felt someone tap his shoulder.

"Excuse me. Are you Hania?" The voice belonged to an admittedly attractive female, with long and wavy hair the color of sunrise. Hania smiled at her; trying not to let her catch his eyes resting on a small, jagged scar on her right cheek.

"Well, that's what my birth certificate says. Can I ask what your name is? And how you know me?" Hania was trying his best not to be rude, but he had been on edge and extra paranoid over the past few days. Every time his eyes gazed upon her; his shoulder tingled like miniature bolts of lightning were hopping around.

"Sorry, I'm being rude." The woman's pale face turned brighter than her hair for a split second. "My name is Laura Belle, and I guess you could say I'm a friend, of a friend, of a friend." Laura smiled sweetly, running her hand through the fringe of her hair. Hania had placed her age around twenty-seven or so, which only made Hania question why she was approaching him even more.

"Nice to meet you, Laura. How can I help you?" Normally Hania wouldn't have entertained the conversation much, but in all honesty, she was pretty much a redhead, and his weakness was rearing its ugly head.

"I was wondering if you were free this evening. Maybe for dinner?" Laura was about as red as the filling in a cherry pop tart at this point. Hania hesitated for a second, his eyes fixated on her body for a second, which only caused Laura to blush even further.

"Sure, dinner sounds good. I'll pick you up at eight." Hania took out his phone and allowed Laura to type her number in and watched as she happily skipped off. He kept staring at her back as she left the area, before realizing that he had forgot to introduce Kylie. "Sorry Kylie, that was rude of me."

"Whatever, it doesn't matter." Kylie stood up rather abruptly and placed the money for their meal on the table. "I've got something to do, so I'm going home." Hania might have been the one with the lightning powers, but Kylie had a storm cloud brewing above her head.

"Don't be jealous." Hania was joking, but now was clearly not the time nor the place. Kylie turned her head around so quick; she may have gotten whiplash.

"I am not jealous of whatever bimbo you decide to date. Whatever we had in the past, or whatever I felt for you is irrelevant! Same thing with if I do still have feelings for you or not! I only care because over the last year you've become incredibly distant and we've been growing apart, even though we're supposed to be best friends! You're hiding things from me and every time I see you, you're exhausted! So, when I finally get you to step out and talk to me, you can't even give me a few hours of your time! That's why I'm pissed off! That's why I'm going home!" Kylie stomped off.

“But you’re my ride…” Hania’s words were ignored, as Kylie left him standing at the table. Hania felt like a jerk. Correction, Hania was a jerk. She needed the time to cool down though, before she’d accept his apology. “Guess I’ll just fly straight to my mom’s house…” Hania left to find a place secluded enough to take off from. The one problem with Hania going on a date was that he didn’t own a car. He knew how to drive, although admittedly not very well, but he never bothered to save up for his own car since he could fly. It was too late in the evening to try and rent a car, and plus he was under twenty-five so it would have been an extra three hundred dollars. He couldn’t ask Kylie to borrow hers, considering her reaction just now either. That only left him with a single option.

“What happened to that nice Kenyan girl you were dating? I liked her.” Hania’s mom felt the need to point out people that she did like, whenever she didn’t agree with Hania’s choice in women. She preferred someone more like Hania culturally, and in truth Hania normally preferred that as well. However, redheads would always be an exception to that rule.

“It didn’t work out.” Hania answered matter-of-factly. These conversations annoyed him, but this was the price he had to pay in order to borrow her car. Plus, this was the second lecture that he had gotten today. Hania walked towards the bathroom, to change out of his jeans and pullover hoodie.

“A shame too! She was cute!” Naira called after Hania. “Besides, you know I get nervous whenever you date a white girl.”

“Yes, I know mom. You’d rather see me with someone my color. This is only the third white girl I’ve ever went on a date with, it’s not like an every time thing.” Hania rolled his eyes, only because he knew his mother didn’t have X-ray vision.

“Hania, I want you to date someone because they make you happy. Period. I don’t care if it ends up being with a white girl.” Naira’s voice had a little bit of annoyance laced within it that wasn’t missed by her son.

“Then why…”

"Because this world is cruel, and I fear for you. For every white person with good intentions who loves people of color for the person within their skin, there's another who are only interested in you because of your skin tone. There's those who keep the company of others who see us as lesser. There are white people who will stand besides us when it's time to fight for our rights, and there are those who are part of the problem by remaining silent. They don't wear name tags, so unless you get to know their character beforehand, you'll never know." Naira now sounded more panicked and worked up than before.

"Mom, I know, and I get that." Hania did know this. His mother had given Hania "the talk," that people of color must give their children about being safe and aware in this world. He knew that his mom never worried when she started dating Kyrie, because they had known each other for long enough that her character was never in question.

"As your mother, I don't ever want to see your heart broken. Or any harm come to you." Hania couldn't help but chuckle at his mother's words, which he immediately regretted when he realized she had moved right outside the bathroom door.

"I get the heartbreak thing, but what makes you think harm would come to me? I'm kinda a superhero and all that jazz." Hania hoped his mom didn't hear him chuckling.

"Yes, but you are not invincible. You've seen the news. You don't have to be armed to be taken as a threat, and I'm not talking about the fact that you're secretly the most powerful person in the state." Naira pointed out. Hania touched his side as Naira talked. Thanks to his powers, the parts of his body that had been shot were perfectly healed. There wasn't a physical scar either. But Hania knew it was there, somehow. He'd trace over the marks and his fingers could feel the tears in his flesh. If he stared hard enough, his eyes would start to trace the scars on his body as though they were fresh.

"I promise, I'll be careful. I know the rules for borrowing the car. Be safe, be compliant, and no sudden moves. Now, how do I look?" Hania finally stepped out of the bathroom and pushed the thoughts of being shot again out of his mind. Hania was now wearing a black blazer with a white shirt underneath, and black slacks. Dressy, but not overly dressy in Hania's opinion.

"Oh, my wičháȟpi! You look so nice!" Naira often called Hania by his Lakota nickname, star, whenever she was excited by something he did. That was often these days. At least the tone of their conversation was shifting into a more comfortable tone.

"Thanks mom! I'm going to head out now. "He grabbed the keys to her ford focus and walked out the door. He had an hour to drive before he reached the hotel that Laura texted, she was staying at, and he didn't want to be late.

It was a little odd that Laura insisted that they ate the restaurant inside of her hotel, but the food at least smelled good. She was wearing a black cocktail dress that showed off the curves that Hania noticed from earlier in the day, and she looked even more shy than earlier. They made small talk, but it mostly consisted of Hania asking questions about Laura, whom sheepishly answered them. Her answers lacked a lot of important information sadly. He learned that she had graduated from the same college that Hania currently attended and was in town for a business conference. Laura also said that the common link that Hania had with Laura was one of his professors, but that just raised more questions than it answered.

"What does your mom do?" Laura asked.

"She's an accountant now. Took her a long time to get to that point but seeing her graduate college for her degree was definitely my proudest moment." Hania answered, with a big grin on his face. Sometimes it was hard to tell who the parent was and who was the child whenever Hania talked about his mother, but he couldn't help it. They were all each other had for most of their lives.

“And your father?” Laura regretted asking as soon as she saw Hania’s face. The atmosphere completely changed.

“He currently has a doctorate at being a piece of crap, but he’s also a CEO.” Hania sputtered out.

“Oh, which company?” Laura didn’t realize she was being set up.

“Phantom fathers. They’re that company that specializes in leaving their families to fend for themselves. He really climbed his way up the corporate ladder, but when you’ve been there for so many years that's to be expected.” Hania didn’t mean to let his anger get the best of him, but he couldn’t help it.

“I’ve never heard of that company.” Laura looked as though she wanted to look it up online.

“Probably because I made it up.” Hania was kind of upset that he had to point that out. He apologized for his outburst. “What about your parents?”

“My parents left me at a store when I was twelve. I don’t know their jobs. I think my dad might be a bus driver.” Laura stated, without hesitation.

“Okay, family talk is over.” Hania quickly spat, praying for the return of awkward silence.

“You look nice.” Laura randomly mentioned, right as their food came. The two had exchanged compliments when they first met up, so even if it wasn’t exactly unwanted, the statement was oddly placed in the evening.

“Thank you. So, do you.” Hania raised an eyebrow at Laura, but it went unnoticed. Instead she just consumed herself in her spaghetti; only looking up from her plate to flash smiles at her date. Hania sat for a moment, as though he were waiting for something to happen, before allowing himself to enjoy his seafood alfredo.

“I have access to the roof, and I’ve heard it has a lovely view of the city. Do you want to go?” Laura asked after several uncomfortable moments passed. They both had finished their food about ten minutes ago, and evidently had run out of things to talk about. Hania still looked like he was waiting for something, and Laura still was too shy to meet Hania’s eyes. Whenever they did lock eyes, she seemed to sweat a bit and turn away. It kept the tingles in Hania’s back to a minimum at least.

“Sure, let's go.” Hania paid the waitress, making sure to tip her well. Hania was a waiter for a short period of time and he still had nightmares about it. The two went onto the roof from an elevator just outside the restaurant and walked over to a small wicker bench that was set out. The two were completely alone, and if the entire date wasn’t so awkward it might have been romantic. “Are you cold?” Hania asked once they sat down, fully prepared to give her his blazer. The temperature had dropped a bit with the setting of the sun.

“Oh, I’m never cold.” Laura spoke with an eerily unfamiliar amount of confidence as she slid closer to Hania. “I wouldn’t mind a kiss though.” She puckered her lips and moved slowly towards Hania’s. He went along with the kiss, puckering his own lips and slowly approaching his dates. They were centimeters away from locking lips, when Laura opened her mouth to go for an open mouth kiss...and spat out a stream of fire directly at Hania. Once the flames subsided, Hania revealed himself on the other side of the roof.

“I bet you were waiting all night to do that.” Hania, unharmed, teased.

“Oh, I missed. How did you know?” Laura covered her mouth, as though the fire was nothing more than an unexpected burp.

“How did I know you were the guardian of fire? At first, I didn’t. See, whenever we locked eyes, my body would start to tingle, just like how you started to sweat. When guardians lock eyes, their body reacts in some type of way, but I couldn’t really figure out what was happening at first since you’re the first guardian I’ve met. But your symbol glowed just enough for me to see, without others noticing. It's probably something only other guardians can see honestly." Hania explained, oddly level-headed compared to his usual, cocky behavior.

"Oh, I see!" Laura rubbed her hand over a flame shaped symbol on her shoulder, and then pointed at where the lightning shaped symbol was on Hania's shoulder. "You're right! Yours is glowing too!" Her excitement was unsettling for Hania.

"So, were you the one setting all those fires? I'm guessing it's not a coincidence that most of them were located somewhere that I've been." Hania's questioning caused a wide smile to etch itself across her nearly vampiric toned face.

"I wonder." Her response was short, nonsensical, and delivered in a crazed tone of voice. She reached to the back of her black dress and unzipped it; stepping out of the dress and revealing to Hania her completely naked form. Hania couldn't help but let his eyes trace her figure.

"Oh, hardwood floors." Hania muttered, as though his curiosity was satisfied. "I'm confused. Are you here to fight or fu-" Hania was cut off when a ball of fire slammed into him, burning most of his clothes off. A wall of fire had appeared in between Laura and Hania, which the former walked through rather slowly. Her now crimson eyes were wide, and the way she stood with her head slightly tilted made her look...off. Laura, naked and partially enflamed, with that wide smile on her face made Hania realize that she was perhaps the most deranged individual he had ever faced. Her costume; a form-fitting, black bodysuit with a flame pattern on the right side materialized onto her body in very much the same way that Hania's came whenever he willed it to.

"Call me Phoenix. Tell me, what do you want carved on your tombstone?" She swayed in place, as though it were a tremendous task to stay still. Hania said nothing at first, but simply summoned his costume onto him. This would be the first time he'd be fighting someone who was on the same power scale as him, and that both excited and scared him. What if he really did lose? No, now wasn't the time to lose confidence in himself. Raiden let lightning bounce around his body, matching Phoenix's flames that were rising from her feet.

"Right. Definitely here to fight then." Raiden charged at Phoenix, hoping for the first strike.

Guardian vs Guardian

Raiden flew at Phoenix and threw a quick right hook at her. His attack missed when she ducked down, and he was hit square in the stomach with her kick. Thinking quickly, Raiden slammed his hand onto the ground and let off a few sparks of lightning just powerful enough to knock his opponent off her feet. "Got you!" Raiden cried out, delivering a chop at Phoenix as she dropped onto the ground.

"Don't underestimate me." Phoenix had caught Raiden's hand between her own and kicking flames out of her feet. Raiden was forced to retreat in order to avoid being burnt by them.

"*Super strength, check. Fire, check.*" Raiden thought to himself, taking a moment to regain his composure. The two guardians were about even in strength, but Raiden was faster. It was time to use that to his advantage. The guardian of lightning began darting around the roof, trying to throw Phoenix off his trail. Suddenly Raiden charged directly towards Phoenix, who responded with a large fireball in his direction.

"Where…" Phoenix realized that right before the fireball hit its target, Raiden was gone. Seconds later, she was hit with a lightning-infused punch to the back of the head.

"Are you unconscious yet? Please be unconscious, I really don't like fighting girls." Raiden walked over to the still floored guardian.

"Good thing I'm a woman then." Phoenix shot up, keeping her feet firmly planted on the ground in such a way that she relied solely on her knees to get up. She started giggling, switching to a hearty cackle a moment after.

"Really doesn't make this any easier…" Raiden muttered. He couldn't let this fight drag on. Eventually he wouldn't be able to keep her flames from catching the entire rooftop on fire, and there were still people inside of the hotel. Or even worse, they would eventually hear all the commotion going on and come up to investigate. There was definitely no way he could fight her and defend other people from her attacks. It was a little annoying, and not his style, but he'd have to fight a little harder against her. Raiden cocked his hand back and let loose a stream of lightning from his entire palm. Phoenix countered with a stream of her own chosen element; the two attacks colliding in the middle and canceling each other out. "*I'll have to try harder...*" Raiden thought to himself.

Raiden charged at Phoenix straight out; no tricks, no feints, nothing of the sort. He intended to deliver a hard punch to her side, hard enough that it would make her hurt like hell once it connected. Raiden wanted to force her to give up, instead of making it into a drawn-out fight. Once he was within striking range, he used his momentum as added power, and flung his fist directly at her right side. Phoenix quickly moved her hand to guard, but Raiden kept pushing through until he heard the sickening snap of a bone breaking. Raiden jumped back, watching as Phoenix's arm went limp at her side. "You only have one arm now. How about you back off, so I don't have to break anymore limbs." Raiden was hoping that Phoenix would be too hurt to continue, but she just smiled again. That wide smile showing all her teeth and most of her gums. That smile that caused her head to cock to the side, as though the sheer weight of her insanity was too much for her to bare. Flames consumed her arm and within seconds, she was swinging it around as if nothing happened.

"You're sweet to worry about me, but I'm just fine. "Phoenix teased, taking care to work out any stiffness in her newly healed arm. Raiden stood in awe, frozen in place. A wound like that would have taken him at least two or three days to heal from, and yet it barely took her thirty seconds. It didn't matter how strong Raiden was, if he couldn't hurt her enough to make her back off, then there was no point. But even if her healing factor was faster than his, it had to have a limit. Raiden was unique among the guardians, or so he was told, and even his healing factor would fail if he kept taking damage. It had to be the same for her.

"Good to know. You heal pretty fast." Raiden tapped his foot against the ground as he spoke. "Let's see what gives up first: my fists or your healing." Raiden blitzed Phoenix faster than she could comprehend, let alone prepare herself for. He had switched his body to lightning to quickly close the gap between the two, turning into human form directly in front of her. Raiden didn't have enough training to fight with any distinct style. He was barely better than a typical brawler in all honesty. But he was fast and strong, and that was the basis of his technique. He delivered a quick and powerful punch to Phoenix's right arm, breaking it again instantly. Without losing pace, he delivered a punch to her left arm. Broken. Phoenix tried to move back, but Raiden slammed his hands into her ribs. Broken; at least three of them. Phoenix kept trying to get some distance, but Raiden wasn't allowing it. He delivered a kick to her ankle, breaking it. But Phoenix was almost...enjoying the beating. Her cheeks were flushed, and between grimaces, she managed to smile. She pivoted on her good foot and revealed that her arms were healed. It was time to counterattack.

Phoenix shot flames at Raiden, using them as a distraction. Once Raiden had successfully dodged them, Phoenix lunged forward and connected a hard punch to his jaw. Phoenix could outlast him in a straight-out fight. Using his distraction to her advantage, she kneed him in the groin and caused him to hunch over. "That was rude of me. Are you alright?" Phoenix asked, pausing her attack to rub his back. It was frustrating, at the very least.

"Get away from me." Raiden flung his fist out, but she was already gone. "I friggin' hate you." Raiden recovered from the low blow and stood up straight, eyeing her down. He made a mental note to make a doctor's appointment to check that his little swimmers were still swimming properly.

"I'm guessing you aren't going to call for a second date?" Phoenix sounded almost innocent. If Raiden wasn't fighting her right now, he might have believed her. Raiden stared at her, as if he had to take a few minutes to process what she asked.

"No!" Raiden finally responded, once he figured that she might have actually been serious. She pouted her lips, looking visibly disappointed.

"Something I said?" Phoenix, now fully healed, kicked a few balls of fire at Raiden as she spoke. The flames flew in a fan pattern, with one catching Raiden on the leg as he fled.

“You’re just not my type.” Raiden retorted, rolling past another jet of fire onto his feet, and flicking an arrow shaped bolt at his foe. “I might never date again after this. Definitely no more redheads.” Raiden went on, calling a bolt of lightning from the sky to strike Phoenix. He had to throttle the power to avoid letting the bolt go through the hotel roof. It managed to stun her however and give Raiden the chance to dash at her and kick her so hard, she flew off the roof and towards the street; seventeen stories below. “Crap, crap, crap!” Raiden ran, prepared to jump down and catch her, until he saw her floating slowly back up.

“You almost killed me, hero boy.” Phoenix teased, once she had both feet planted firmly back on the roof.

“You can fly? Of course, you can fly.” Raiden was rather annoyed that he showed even a minuscule amount of compassion. He floated a few inches off the ground; Phoenix following his example. The two flew at each other, going blow for blow once they were in range. Neither of them fought with any identifiable style. No fancy throws, stances, or chops. They relied solely on instinct. Phoenix barely bothered to dodge Raiden’s attacks, while Raiden was focused on making sure he wasn’t getting hit. Seeing an opening, Raiden let loose an arc of lightning and followed through with a barrage of punches to her arms.

“Hurt me more!” Phoenix excitedly cried, slowing Raiden up just enough for her to spew fire her open mouth. She was too close, and the fire was coming too fast, for Raiden to transmute into lightning and escape. He barely had time to put his arms up and was sent sliding along the rooftop like a ragdoll. He flipped up on his feet just in time to see his worst fears being realized: two hotel staff members had flung the door open.

“Get back!” Raiden yelled, zipping over to them just in time to block a ball of fire with his body. The two staff members were frozen with fright and weren’t going anywhere. And he really, really needed them go to anywhere but here. “No choice…” He slammed the door shut, and used a close range burst of lightning to weld the door permanently shut. Raiden turned to Phoenix right after he heard a thud. The older of the two staff members must have passed out from fear. Raiden had to get Phoenix away from the roof, and as far away from civilization as possible. Raiden transmuted into lightning and flung himself at Phoenix; turning to normal in time to grab her and throw her high into the air. He pursued, firing bolts of lightning at her as she was in the air.

Phoenix stopped herself, about twenty-five feet above the rooftop. Raiden wanted her higher, but he'd have to settle with this for now. Phoenix used flames from the bottom of her feet as thrusters to fire herself at Raiden and latched on tight. Flames enveloped her and began to burn Raiden, leaving him forced to respond by shocking Phoenix with as much lightning as he could muster around his body. It was a contest on who could take the most punishment without giving up. At least it was, until Phoenix leaned up and kissed Raiden. Both elements fizzled out, with Raiden being forced to focus on pushing her off him. Raiden was probably more confused over the duration of this fight than upset.

"What? Our first attempt at a kiss was interrupted." Phoenix said, in a matter of fact tone.

"By you! You attacked me, remember?" Raiden made sure to point out, putting extra emphasis on the word remember.

"...Semantics." Phoenix's answer infuriated Raiden. He officially hated the word after his dealing with Hunter. Now another supervillain was using the word. Semantics evolved to quite possibly the evilest word Raiden had ever heard. Prior to these two encounters, he had thought destiny was the preferred word for the evil inclined. "In any case, I'm glad. Now I won't have any regrets when I boil your blood." Phoenix went on, smiling as she touched her lips.

"You haven't been able to do it so far, so I'm not exactly afraid of you saying that now." Raiden was lying. He was burnt badly, and only half of his wounds had healed. He had turned into lightning so much that he could barely focus his thoughts anymore. They were erratic, shifting from the current battle, to tacos, to his unfinished homework, to Kylie's anger, to the meaning of his existence and a few dozen things in between. He made another mental note to donate to ADHD research, because he couldn't imagine feeling like this all the time. Plus, he was running low on energy reserves after using so much lightning. Still, he was determined to win this fight.

Raiden charged at Phoenix, a little sloppier than before, but still relatively fast. He imagined even Phoenix had to be getting tired at this point. She was using less of her fire now, and it didn't burn nearly as bad whenever he was hit by it compared to the first few times he was caught. He punched Phoenix in the shoulder, attempting to dislocate her arm. He failed but managed to leave her stunned in place long enough for him to knock her towards the ground below. "Why did I do that." Raiden muttered, realizing the mistake his erratic mind made a fraction too late. Phoenix was now low enough to attract a crowd on the streets, and have people pressed against the windows of the hotel and nearby buildings. It was about ten at night on a Saturday, so of course barely anyone was sleep. Raiden dropped down a bit to Phoenix's level.

Raiden deflected the blast of fire that Phoenix had shot upwards and attempted to close the distance between the two. If he could get close enough to throw her back up, he shouldn't have too much to worry about. The same trick wouldn't work twice though, unfortunately for him. Once he grabbed her, Phoenix engulfed her entire body in flames strong enough to burn the palm of his hand. He withdrew his palm and settled on a close-range blast of lightning. She went flying back, and then was hit with a bolt of lightning from the sky. Again, Raiden flew at Phoenix in an attempt to throw her away from the growing crowds on the ground, but once he latched onto her ankle, she kicked him directly in the throat. Raiden released his grip, but not before crushing the bones in her ankle.

Phoenix and Raiden both took a few moments to recover, before charging at each other again. They locked themselves in another close ranged fist battle, this time with their strikes being embedded with their respective elements. Phoenix's strikes were growing weaker, whereas Raiden's remained the same strength, if only sluggish compared to when the fight began. Raiden knew in his head, if it kept going at this pace, he could win. Her healing was slowing down too, and she was leaving a lot of openings for Raiden to strike. All Raiden needed was a well-placed strike to the back of her head, or to generate a large amount of lightning to knock her out. Victory was practically in his grasp. At least, it was. That all went out the window, once she turned her fireballs onto the crowd below them.

Be the hero, Raiden

The flame zipped passed Raiden and approached the crowd with rather quick speed. “No!” Raiden screamed as he turned. His overwhelming desire to protect the innocents around the two overrode his exhaustion; allowing him to transmute into lightning and zip in front of the blast. He turned back to human form just in time for the fire to slam into him. “Run! Go find shelter!” Raiden shouted while fanning his arms away from him. He then set his attention back on Phoenix, who had her preferred twisted smile etched onto her face. Raiden had to stop her, no matter what.

Raiden took off at full speed for Phoenix, engaging in a close combat fight. The difference between the two at this point was practically night and day. Phoenix was tired; her body giving out on her during the assault several times. Raiden was tired too, but his willpower was forcing his body to cooperate with him. He dodged two of her sluggish punches, and then assaulted her with a barrage of fist that connected with the entirety of her torso. He ended this assault with a roundhouse kick that sent her flying. He raised his right arm and summoned a bolt of lightning from the sky. Raiden’s eyes closed, allowing his vision to connect to the lightning as though it were a manned drone. The aerial view gave him a better look at which citizens were endangered during this fight, as well as a sweet sense of satisfaction as he watched Phoenix be struck with the bolt. It made it seem a lot more personal. “That wasn’t a good idea.” Raiden muttered, breathing hard. He could emit lightning from his body relatively easy, but summoning lightning from the sky required a lot more work. It was taking its toll on him.

“I’m going to kill you! That'll make Kagutsuchi proud of me!” Phoenix rose from the ground and screamed at Raiden. Raiden had never met Kagutsuchi, but he knew that Kagutsuchi was the emperor of fire, just like how Zeus was the emperor of lightning. But why would the leader of the fire gods be proud of Phoenix for killing Raiden? He was distracted from his thoughts when he saw Phoenix shooting another few balls of fire toward the crowd. Raiden zipped over to the crowd and swatted one of the fireballs so hard it dispersed into embers.

“Crap, that burns!” Raiden waved his hand to put the flames out, while using his free hand to shoot lightning at another fireball right before it smacked into a fleeing citizen. Phoenix had fired two more during the struggle that Raiden noticed at the last second. He charged both of his hands with lightning and caught the flames, being pushed back by the pure power that the blast had. “Go up, go up, go up!” With all his might, Raiden forced the blast to go upwards and explode into the sky. It almost looked like fireworks. Deadly, murderous fireworks that wanted to wreak havoc on all of humanity. Still pretty though, Raiden couldn’t help but admit.

“Burn! Burn! Burn!” Phoenix cried, shooting multiple blast of fire at Raiden. But she had lost her tactical advantage. The streets were now essentially empty, and Raiden was free to move about without protecting anyone. He had to finish this soon, before he passed out from exhaustion. He couldn’t risk shooting lightning from the sky or turning into lightning with his low energy reserves. Using his normal flying speed, Raiden started dodging the fireballs until he got close and charged his hand up with lightning. Phoenix expected a punch, but what she got was an open palm lunge that connected with her head. Raiden used his momentum and tossed Phoenix hard, making her hit a nearby Hummer and slump down onto the ground. However, Raiden made a mistake of his own volition by taking a moment to catch his breath. Raiden figured that Phoenix had been defeated but was proven wrong when she transmuted herself into fire and flung herself into a nearby apartment building through an open window.

“Crap! River of crap! Seven layers of fu-” Raiden used the last bit of his energy reserves and transmuted into lightning; following behind his opponent. The window had led to the second story hallway, which was now on fire. Raiden had to push himself, he had to beat her before she created anymore damage to the building. She had to be on the brink of exhaustion as well. He just had to outlast her. Raiden ran at her, jumping onto the wall of the hallway and using it to leap at her head. He connected with his knee, just as she grabbed his ankle. Despite reeling back from the blow, she still managed to throw Raiden into the inflamed wall and hold him there. She laughed maniacally as she held him in place; his back becoming charred.

“Enough!” Raiden bellowed, putting up a weak aura of lightning around his body to shock Phoenix. She released him, and he sprung off the wall and began barraging her with body blows. He could hear the screams of the residents of the building as they realized their hallway was on fire, but for now the flames were contained to the floor they were on. They would be able to escape from the window at this height. It sucked, but Raiden had to tell himself to focus on Phoenix. His opponent swung her fist at Raiden, who ducked and delivered an uppercut to her chin. She stumbled back, spit out a bit of blood, and took a few steps back. She needed to get some distance, or else she’d lose this battle. Phoenix’s eyes darted around the environment, looking for something to give her an advantage.

A second too late, Raiden realized what Phoenix’s plan was. Phoenix opened her mouth and pointed it directly at the ceiling, unleashing a huge wave of fire that engulfed the entire ceiling. The worst part out of the entire thing, was that the flames were spreading at an alarming rate. The building was going to come down, and there was no way everyone would be able to get out from all five floors. “It’s time to be the hero, Raiden. Or do you just want to keep beating me like the savage you are?” Phoenix grinned as she delivered her ultimatum. She was completely spent at this point. Raiden could stop her, but he probably would have to sacrifice everyone on the fifth floor. Possibly even the fourth floor. But if he left her to her own devices, he could save everyone. Raiden didn’t say a word; taking off towards the stairs. He pushed himself to move as fast as he could, flying straight to the top floor. He figured that he could save everyone from the top and work his way down.

He had severely overestimated himself, however. Flying to the top floor, combined with the large amount of thick smoke that had surrounded him, was much more than he could handle. Once he stepped onto the top floor, Raiden hit the ground and collapsed. “I can’t…” His energy reserves were practically zero. His costume flickered on and off, like a child was playing with a light switch. His brown eyes grew dull and nearly lifeless. “Move, damn it! Move!” Raiden pleaded with his body. It didn’t work, however. He just needed to rest. He was so tired…

“Help us! Somebody help us!” A cry from one of the apartments was what kicked it off. Others who were stuck as well joined in, until there was a chorus of voices sounding off. A concert of torture and anguish that hit Raiden's ears and danced around like an unwanted guest.

"It doesn't matter if I can't...what matters is, I will!" Raiden's eyes shifted to gold, as he put all his power into standing back up. "C'mon...C'mon!" The flickering from his costume ceased; showing his renewed resolve and surge of energy. It was time to rescue everyone.

The fifth floor went by relatively fast, with only three out of the eight apartments having residents. Raiden grabbed the older couple who resided in the first apartment he stopped at and flew them to the ground safely via their window. "Call 911 and tell them we need the fire department, just in case they haven't already sent them." Raiden made sure to instruct them before heading back up. The fourth floor was significantly more challenging than the fifth floor to clear, mostly because each of the five families had several young children. After a second to think, Raiden decided to get all the younger children out first before getting the adults. None of the families complained. He informed everyone to gather in the furthest back apartment for convenience, and because the smoke was significantly less intense back there. By the time he got the children of the fourth floor out, he noticed that everyone on the first and second floor had made it out of the building by climbing out of their windows. One man from the second story had broken his ankle, but he was at least safe from the immediate danger.

"I'm going to get your parents now, okay?" Raiden announced to the children; most of whom were crying and calling to their families. He flew back into the window and began grabbing the adults two by two. Unfortunately, one of the adults had passed out due to all the smoke. She was still breathing, but her kids shrieked once he had gotten her safely onto the ground. The sounds of sirens wailed in the distance; barely audible over the sound of the kids. "When the ambulance arrives, you direct them to her first okay?" Raiden told a younger looking male, before heading back into the building. His costume was magical, but it didn't give him much protection against the heat, smoke, or flames. The only thing it really did was magically patch itself whenever the flames wore a hole in it. Immediately, Raiden realized that he should have started with the third floor first.

If he hadn't transmuted into lightning, he probably would have reached that conclusion a lot earlier.

Black smoke consumed the hallway, oozing into the apartments with ease. A few people had already jumped out of the window, suffering broken ankles or legs. Others however, had passed out in their homes. Only two people were still conscious when Raiden reached them. Instead of his usual two at a time, he forced himself to carry at least four people down at a time. It wasn't a far trip down so Raiden figured he could take it. The firefighters arrived after his first trip down, and they immediately entered the building to help Raiden. Due to their help, Raiden only had to make three trips, even though there were nearly twenty people on the floor by the time he had reached them. The fire was put out relatively fast once they arrived, but the building was still in ruins. Everyone was safe, minus a few that needed to go to the hospital due to smoke inhalation or broken bones though and that was all that mattered. "Thank you, Raiden. Thank you." A middle age woman ran over and hugged Raiden. This set off a chain reaction, with everyone left in front of the previously burning building joining in on the hug. This was why Raiden became a hero.

"I'm just glad you're all safe." Raiden smiled, before removing himself from the group. He was pretty much out of energy, his body hurt all over, and he really needed to sleep so that his healing factor would have time to recover. First though, he had to try and locate Phoenix. He flew into the air, and headed out of town where he assumed, she would be heading. Raiden only got just out of the city limits, before he had to land. There was no way he would find her, he had to accept. Plus, if he traveled any further then he wouldn't have enough energy to fly home. Raiden sighed loudly, before catching something out of the corner of his eye. "Great. That's the last thing I needed." Raiden muttered to himself while looking towards the sky. A large, brown bird was making its way towards Raiden. The bird had to be around three times the size of Raiden, with white streaks going through its coffee toned wings and body. It was the Thunderbird, the lord of lightning that Raiden hated the most. Its giant wingspan kicked up dust as it landed in front of a visibly annoyed Raiden.

“We need to talk.” The voice that emitted from the Thunderbird’s open beak was rather deep. It then started to shrink down; taking on a more humanoid form. Before it had fully transformed however, Raiden cocked back and punched it dead in the face. The Thunderbird hit the ground hard but made no sound of pain. Instead it just continued to complete its transformation; turning into its human form that was almost alien to Raiden, despite how often he had seen it in photographs. “Was that necessary?” The Thunderbird asked, brushing the dirt out of his silky, black hair. His golden eyes looked Raiden up and down, giving off an odd sense of pride. Raiden hated that look.

“What? You wanted to talk right?” Raiden was overcome with fury when he looked at the Thunderbird’s face. “Let’s talk, dad!” Raiden cried, charging his father. He didn’t care about his exhaustion anymore. He didn’t even care about Phoenix. All he cared about was punching his father in his stupid face until his own knuckles bled.

Lords of Lightning

Raiden charged and punched his father directly in the face. This time however, the deity barely flinched. Raiden sucked his teeth as he jumped back, panting hard. His body was being fueled by the sheer level of annoyance that Raiden had for his father. Thunderbird simply looked on at his son, as though he were no more than a child throwing a tantrum. In some aspect, this fact was true. "Is this really necessary?" Thunderbird reiterated as he looked on at Raiden; brushing off his deer-skinned, war shirt.

"I have a strong hatred for phantoms, so yes, it is." Raiden responded, visibly irritated. He hated how much he resembled his father. While Raiden had the same heart shaped face as his mother, the shape of his eyes and his slightly beak shaped nose were traits received from his father. Thunderbird's human form was smooth shaven just like Raiden's, and his eyes were a permanent shade of gold. Raiden didn't have enough energy to fly, but he was determined to at least knock that feather out of Thunderbird's jet-black hair. That stark white feather, with the red tip that Raiden often saw in his dreams.

Raiden unleashed a flurry of blows on his father's face, whom simply sat there and took them. Raiden was so exhausted that his blows were even weaker than the average human's. However, he couldn't see that. He couldn't see how weak his attacks were, and how little they affected Thunderbird. Or maybe he did realize it, and just needed to place his frustration somewhere. After a few dozen more punches aimed at Thunderbird's face, Raiden backflipped away to regain some distance. Immediately, he dropped to one knee; his costume fading away. The clothing that guardians were able to summon took at most, one percent of actual energy to sustain. The fact that he could no longer keep his costume on meant that his energy was critically low. Something that his father would be able to take note of.

"I'm not going to fight you. I'm only here to talk, wičháȟpi." Thunderbird attempted to calm his son down. The attempt failed miserably.

“You don’t get to call me that! Not after you abandoned me! What gives you the right?” Hania screamed at his father; his mocha colored knuckles tightened so hard that his fingers turned a shade of pink. A vibrant aura of lightning surrounded Hania, and he dashed off towards his father. Hania cocked his fist back and threw a wild haymaker aimed at his father’s chin...and passed out mere inches before the blow connected. Thunderbird sighed gently, before cradling the young guardian in his arms. The task should have been difficult, as Thunderbird was only two inches taller than Hania. Luckily, the deity was more than strong enough to lift him. Thunderbird flew off into the sky, before vanishing in a blur of blue.

As Hania’s consciousness returned to him, he felt lighter than air. He also felt a familiar sensation of water seeping into his pores. Startled, Hania’s eyes shot open and he flew straight upward. Hania recognized the golden hue pool that he had been previously floating in. It was Ichor, the healing waters of the gods. Contrary to popular belief, Ichor was not the actual blood of gods. Gods bled a violet color, and their blood had almost no magical properties once it left their body. Hania realized shortly after that thought, that his powers were back, and his injuries were healed. This was Hania’s first time within Ichor, but he had to admit its effectiveness. It just didn’t do much to solve his fear of drowning.

“Can’t swim?” Thunderbird had been sitting on the stark white tile beside the pool. Hania didn’t even notice him until he spoke.

“My father never taught me.” Hania spat out; his words like venom. “Besides, I can fly. Never had any interest to learn.” Hania added, a little less bitter than the previous answer. Now Hania took time to acknowledge his surroundings. The rather large room had white tiles everywhere that the golden pool wasn’t, with the only two other exceptions being a red door that was currently tightly shut, and a single window on the right wall. A blue sun greeted him when he floated over to the window. The blue sun signified that he was no longer in his native realm. The gods had their own realm that existed parallel to the human realm, which they were forced into as the humans evolved. Even the gods themselves were unsure how exactly it happened. Only the most powerful gods were able to travel between the two realms. These gods were referred to as lords. Guardians, such as Hania, could be brought to the realm by lords, but only within the meeting place for that guardian's specific group of lords. Venturing off into the god realm meant death for any human, even a guardian. Being a demigod meant that it would take longer for Hania to die from being in the god realm unprotected, but not by much. Demigods didn't have enough godly essence to resist the environment, and the divine nature of the area threatened to chase their souls from their bodies just as any other human. The thing that kept gods protected in their realm, was that they did not actually have souls.

"Why did you bring me here?" Hania asked his father, landing softly next to him. "And where are my clothes?" Thunderbird motioned to a tattered pair of jeans and Hania's black shirt beside the pool, answering Hania's question. Hania said nothing else but sat down; content to remain in his boxers for now. He must have burnt off part of his clothes with his final display of lightning, right before he passed out. "I'm surprised you even know what I look like." Hania muttered, staring deeply into the pool. This finally elicited a response.

"How could I forget what my son looked like?" Thunderbird looked over at Hania as he spoke.

"You don't get to call me that either!" Hania whipped around, his face showing his rage. His eyes however, showed how hurt he really was. "Not after you just up and left me and mom, you phantom."

"That's not fair. I could not stay in the human realm. No god can, not even a lord. You would have me tear it asunder to stay?" Thunderbird spoke calmly, like always. Hania definitely got his personality from his mother. Of course, he was right. The power of a god would destroy the human realm in moments. Hania knew this.

"You could have tried harder! Visited more often! Or were you too busy with your other children and women?" Hania was trembling with rage. Speaking irrationally.

“I am not like Zeus. Your mother is the only woman I have ever loved. And you are my only son. My pride and joy. And I miss you so much it aches.” Thunderbird’s eyes showed an unbelievable depth of sorrow. Hania could see he was being truthful. And yet…

“Bull!” Hania cried in defiance. “If that was true, you wouldn’t have had me wondering where my father was. You wouldn’t have let us struggle. You wouldn’t force me to lie to everyone about some imaginary business you ran that kept you too busy to see me. And for what? To protect the honor of some phantom I don’t even know? God or not, that doesn’t change the fact that I needed you, and you were nothing but a broken picture on my wall! To hell with you!” Hania’s emotional dam was breaking. His sorrow was radiating from him at this point.

“Hania, I…” Thunderbird stood up and moved closer to his son.

“I’m done talking about this.” Just like that, Hania build his dam back up. He took several steps away to avoid his father. “You didn’t bring me to a completely different realm of existence to talk about my daddy issues. What’s the real reason?” The demigod could probably teach a class on deflection.

“It’s not I. It’s we. All of the lords of lightning must speak with you. Come with me.” Thunderbird said, after a long sigh, motioning towards the door. It was Hania’s turn to sigh now, donning his costume. His costume was part of his guardian powers, and it felt odd meeting the lords without it on.

“Great. As if today couldn’t get worse.” Raiden walked towards the door. Meeting with the lords always felt like being sent to the principal’s office. They rarely ever made real contact with Raiden, although he knew they were around. When they did though, it normally ended in a lecture. The few times Raiden did meet with them, his father decided to stay in his avian form which only made the meetings even more annoying. Raiden decided those moments didn’t count as a meeting with his father. The room the lords resided in was also lined wall to wall with white tiles but was around five times larger than the ichor room. Several storm clouds floated overhead, with each lord having one as their personal chair. A skylight was in the center of the room, allowing the blue sun’s rays to shine through. Thunderbird vanished from behind Raiden, and immediately positioned himself on his own storm cloud. He decided to remain in human form, to Raiden's surprise.

"Did you have a good talk with T.B.?" The lord that Raiden recognized as Indra asked. Indra was rather tall compared to some of the other Lords, with red-tinted skin. Golden jewels adorned his body, with his jet-black hair having a strand of gold in it. Beside Indra, sat his elephant mount; Airavata.

"T.B.? Don't tell me that the phantom is a frat boy." Raiden snickered.

"Phantom?" Indra questioned aloud.

"Daddy issues." Set responded, in a near whisper.

"Ah, I see." Indra nodded in understanding.

"Tell me Raiden, what does it mean to be a guardian?" Zeus spoke, silencing everyone else. Zeus was the current emperor, the leader of all the lords of lightning. Raiden didn't particularly like the white-haired deity, but he at least was respecting his wishes by calling him Raiden instead of his actual name, or boy.

"A slave to the gods?" Raiden quipped, seeing the annoyance rise in Zeus' electric blue eyes. To the right of Zeus, Thor cackled.

"What? He is not wrong." The rather muscular warrior god added. There was a reason that Thor was Raiden's favorite Lord. He always told things how it was, and much preferred to do things himself rather than assign task to anyone, especially a guardian. Most importantly though, Thor treated Raiden like an equal.

"Yes Thor, he is wrong." Zeus shot the dirty blonde lord a look that told him to be quiet. Thor flipped him off in response but remained silent. The exchange reminded him of the first time Raiden found himself in this room, all those years ago. Gods were creatures of habit after all. "A guardian is a chosen champion for the lords and are essential. If the lords went to war with one another, or settled problems on their own, it could tear apart both realms. So, the guardians…" Zeus continued, before being cut off.

"Fight the battles for them. I read the job description already, so what's the point Santa Claus?" Raiden took to the habit of calling Zeus, Santa, because of his long white hair and beard. That and because it annoyed Zeus greatly.

"The other lords are scared of you." Zeus spoke softly, as if others would hear. He had a stern expression on his face, as though he was blaming Raiden. The young hero panned around the room and noticed the other lords had the same expression on their faces, besides Thunderbird whom looked guilty, and Thor who looked a little prideful.

"Is it my dashing good looks?" Raiden joked, after a few moments of uncomfortable silence had passed.

"Be serious, boy." Zeus snapped back, instantly annoying Raiden.

"Then why?" Raiden turned away from Zeus and asked the chimera lord, Set. The Egyptian lord had the body of a man with an animal like head and tail. He didn't get many dates, Raiden assumed.

"Because you have godly blood in your veins. A lord's blood at that." Set answered in an animalistic growl.

"All guardians are chosen from humans with no special powers, as to prevent advantage in war. You, my son, being a guardian breaks every rule we have set in place. You already had power; this guardianship just makes it worse. And so, the other lords feel as though we are trying to take over their territory." Thunderbird continued. Now it was clear to Raiden why he looked so guilty.

"That's your fault, not mine. I didn't ask you to make me a guardian." Raiden said with a mixture of anger and sorrow.

“If it were really our decision, you wouldn’t be a guardian. You would be no more spectacular than a blade of grass.” Zeus bluntly stated. “Guardians are chosen by an oracle, and we honor her wisdom regardless of if we agree or not, remember?” Zeus didn’t crack a single smile as he spoke, which was honestly nothing out of the ordinary. Deep down, even Raiden was afraid of him. This was his third time meeting with the lords of lightning, and still Zeus managed to make him want to run.

“Okay, I understand.” Raiden chose to hide his fear of Zeus. He had his best, stern face on. “So then is the fire guardian just the first who is going to come after me?”

“The fire guardian is...unique.” The shirtless Thor replied. “She was a mortal girl, a fairly normal guardian in fact. However, she was forced to eat the lord Phoenix and the rush of power has given her the warrior’s bloodlust.”

“You mean insanity.” Raiden pointed out. He felt bad about the entire situation now that he knew the truth. The moments where Laura seemed truly innocent might not have been an act. She essentially was turned schizophrenic. “How is it even possible to eat a deity?”

“It is no easy task, although eat isn’t exactly the proper term. She absorbed the Phoenix into her own body. If this had happened when her body was still growing and maturing, she might have been able to merge completely with the Phoenix by adulthood. However, because this occurred relatively recently and the process was forced by Kagutsuchi, her body is trying to reject and fight off the Phoenix like an infection. It has damaged her psychologically.” Thunderbird explained.

“Kagutsuchi…” Raiden muttered. “She mentioned him when we fought. I’m guessing he’s pulling the strings, but why?” Raiden asked.

“To get to you. To us. Kagutsuchi wants a war, Raiden. You must avoid the fire guardian. If that cannot be helped due to your unhealthy obsession with helping others, then under no circumstances can you kill her. I cannot allow a war to break out. No matter what I have to do in order to prevent that." Zeus stood atop his cloud instead of sitting like he had been previously.

"Come on Santa, I don't kill. Even the phantom over there knows that. Your toga must be too tight or something." Raiden pointed to his father as if anyone was unsure who the phantom was referring to.

"If it is one thing I've learned from humanity, it's that every human has some sort of situation where they will compromise their morals. A series of events that destroys their beliefs. Soldiers, mothers, fathers, lovers, heroes, villains, it does not matter. No matter the circumstances, even if you will die, even to save a life, even if your heart should break, a guardian must not kill another guardian." Zeus made his lack of faith in Raiden perfectly clear.

"Got it. Can I go now?" Raiden answered. Zeus eyed him down briefly before nodding his head. The whole exchange left a bad taste in Raiden's mouth. He could never take another life; the very thought was revolting to him. And yet here was Zeus, telling him that he couldn't believe that to be true. He absolutely hated Zeus. Plus, he wanted to leave before he remembered a mission that he had for Raiden. He got one around once a year, and so far, he hadn't gotten one for this year.

"I'll take you home." Thunderbird offered, but Raiden shook his head.

"No thanks, you just stay up there on your little cloud. Thor, can you transport me back to the human realm? You know where New Mexico is right?" Raiden asked.

"Yes, I do." Thor looked at Thunderbird, as if asking for permission to fulfill Raiden's request. Once he saw Thunderbird had nodded, he appeared beside Raiden and clutched his arm. The two began to glow and then suddenly, Raiden found himself hovering above his home state.

"Thanks man." Raiden yawned and gave Thor a fist bump, before watching the god vanish back into his own realm. "Time to head home for a well-deserved nap." Raiden spoke to himself, as he flew off into the morning sky. At least, that was what he had planned to do. He found himself stopping and staring at what could only be described as a vaguely human shaped fire. "I just want to go take a nap…" Raiden muttered as he descended. The closer he got to the ground, the larger and more human shaped the fire seemed to become in his eyes. Once he landed, he realized the fiery being stood nearly seven feet tall. The fire-man had no pupils or eyeballs, but had angular shaped eye sockets which glowed a vibrant red. At his side sat a nodachi, which was equally on fire.

"Have a nice little meeting?" The creature asked; its voice deep contained what could only be described as a backdrop of crackling firewood. Raiden was put on edge as he looked at the being; the name Kagutsuchi rushing into his brain. Once he noticed the crown shaped symbol on what Raiden could only imagine was his forehead, he knew that his brain was correct. The emperor of fire had been making a house call.

"You know, if you'd stop listening to my mixtape, you wouldn't be on fire anymore." A silence fell over the two. "Get it? 'Cus my mixtape is fire. That means really good." Raiden explained the joke, hoping to get a laugh. The gods never laughed at his jokes.

"Do you ever shut up?" Kagutsuchi's flaming…well, everything seemed to grow more intense to match the annoyance in his voice.

"I tend to ramble when I'm dealing with psychopaths. Wanna tell me what you're doing here and why you're trying to kill me?" Raiden crossed his arms and scowled. He really wanted to lean on a tree or something, but they were resting on one of the few places in the San Juan Basin without trees. Probably a good thing, with the whole fire situation that he was currently dealing with.

"Don't take it personal." Kagutsuchi shrugged or did some sort of motion resembling that. His flames seemed less like a wildfire than before, and he appeared more humanoid, so Raiden assumed that meant he was calming down.

“It’s kind of hard not to.” Now Kagutsuchi decided to chuckle, causing his body to pulsate. Raiden failed to see the humor in his words.

“The gods are afraid of you. Out of all the guardians, you are the only one who has godly blood coursing their veins. Ever since you were named guardian, the other gods have been wary of the lords of lightning. I’m just taking advantage of their fears.” Kagutsuchi explained.

“But why?” Again, Kagutsuchi found humor in Raiden’s words.

“Because I’m tired of sharing this world with the other gods. Life wouldn’t be possible with fire, so why should the other gods get equal parts to what we made possible? So, while they’re busy scrambling over you and your issues, I’ll uproot their power from right under their noses. You’re simply a means to an end.” Kagutsuchi had no mouth, which made it difficult to tell when he was done speaking or if he was taking a breath.

“I’m not your puppet. Neither is your guardian. Leave us out of your affairs. Besides, the other gods would never allow that to happen. Once they find ou-” Raiden was cut off.

“Oh, they know.” Kagutsuchi admitted to a bewildered Raiden. “You think I’m the only one to feel like this? Us gods are arrogant creatures; lords especially. Power is a dangerous thing, you see. Creatures desired to stand above all the rest, and thus gods were created. Gods found out that there were others like them and wanted to gain even more power, thus creating lords. Lords created emperors from their pursuit of power, and so on and so forth. The guardian program was created specifically to balance each other out so that no one group could block another out of the human realm.”

“I’m guessing you have a way to block the other lords out then. Just so that you can have more power than the other lords.” Raiden had started to understand what was happening here. The guardians were a failsafe to prevent the lords from trying to seize power from one another, but there had to be others in place. Kagutsuchi was using the infighting as a distraction.

“I like you, son of Thunderbird.” Kagutsuchi decided to remain tight lipped about whatever he was planning.

“Enough to leave me alone and not try to take over the realm?” Raiden suggested.

“Don’t push it.” Kagutsuchi cackled.

“I don’t quite get it though. How are you going to get power over the other lords?” Hania knew that Kagutsuchi was using him...but there was something more here.

“You read too many comic books. Why would I tell you my plans and give you a chance to thwart them?” Kagutsuchi had a point. Even Hania admittedly knew that it was a long shot when he asked.

“Well then...what’s to stop me from beating you down?” Hania’s arms crackled with lightning. He had a habit of doing this whenever his emotions got the better of him.

“Interesting…” Kagutsuchi mused. “Let’s see you try.”

Kagutsuchi

The tension in the air was practically tangible. A human...well, demigod, facing down a god? Let alone the emperor of fire? This would end poorly for the guardian, and he knew it. Raiden's nerves were shot; unsure when Kagutsuchi would strike. Instead though, he noticed that Kagutsuchi just stood there. He wasn't agitated in the slightest, judging from the fact that he still appeared like a vaguely human shaped flame. The emperor of fire didn't even see Raiden as a threat.

"You better be taking this seriously!" Raiden declared, before converting to lightning and charging at the deity. Lightning was faster than fire, and that was probably his one advantage. Raiden had been using his go-to move; converting into lightning until he was directly in front of his opponent and striking him with a decisive blow. The attempt went rather poorly; as soon as Raiden materialized, Kagutsuchi delivered a blow directly into his stomach and knocked the air out of his body. Recovering quickly, Raiden shoot a point-blank bolt of lightning at the god, who simply swatted the attack away with his sheathed nodachi.

"Are you done?" Kagutsuchi dropped his nodachi and crossed his arms.

"Not even close." Raiden responded, using his cockiness to cover the absolute terror that was running through his mind. Kagutsuchi could easily kill Raiden, like a child ripping through a Christmas gift's wrapping paper. His only chance was to score a lucky blow that would floor the deity. Raiden charged at Kagutsuchi and feinted towards the fire god's torso, which luckily worked. The instant that Kagutsuchi raised his arms to block, even if it was a subconscious action and not due to necessity, Raiden converted into lightning. He zipped behind Kagutsuchi, went into the air, and delivered a kick to the back of Kagutsuchi's fiery head right as he materialized. Kagutsuchi went flying several feet away and was struck with a bolt of lightning before he had a chance to halt himself. "Are you done?" Raiden used Kagutsuchi's words against him, although Raiden's sounded much more like a plea rather than Kagutsuchi's demand. His answer came in the form of clapping, as Kagutsuchi walked back into striking range.

"Little lightning lad, I'm impressed. The more time we spend with one another, the more I must admit that I like you. If only you were chosen to be my fire guardian…" Kagutsuchi stopped clapping once his movements ceased. He seemed genuine...which frightened Raiden even more. The only lords that really seemed to like Raiden were his idiot father, and Thor. Sort of Raijin as well, but that's only because of Raiden's chosen name. He didn't have the heart to tell the god that the name was just some Japanese word that he thought was cool, and not a homage to the Japanese god of lightning.

"The feeling might be mutual if you'd call off your guardian and stop your plan to take over the realms or whatever you're doing. That's a pretty sweet deal, right? Not everyone gets to be on the 'gods that Raiden likes' list." It was a long shot, but Raiden had to try.

"Sorry, but no." Kagutsuchi stated, before suddenly rushing Raiden. "Why don't you sleep now so I can go back home." Before Raiden could fully react, Kagutsuchi punched him with such force to his gut, he lost all the air in his lungs. Instantaneously, Raiden passed out.

"Eyes up, boy." A woman's voice called out. Raiden's eyes found himself looking at someone all too familiar.

"Oya? What are you doing here?" Raiden wiped some drool off his mouth and stood up. Oya was a beautiful goddess, with skin several tones darker than Raiden's own medium-chocolate. Her pupil-less eyes glowed white, while white streaks fell down her cheeks onto her jaw line. Her brown micro braids were shoulder length.

"I'm not here, golden eyes. You're very much unconscious and I am visiting you through your mind." Oya helped Raiden stabilize on his feet, before hugging him. Oya was two inches shorter than Raiden, but the presence she gave off was as though she were eight feet tall. She was clad in a long, crimson skirt with a split up the side, and a golden sash around her waist. To cover her top portion, she wore a simple red piece of cloth that revealed everything from the middle of her ribs to her waist.

"Oh…" Raiden only then noticed that the two were standing within an empty void. Their voices even echoed slightly. "Well, that makes more sense." Normally, the knockout would have been a major hit to his pride, but he was facing a god. Plus, it had been quite a while since he last saw Oya. The goddess was like a second mother to the demigod, even if he departed on slightly bad terms.

"You're sloppy." Oya's Yoruba accent helped to drive home her stern personality.

"I am not. I was fighting a god!" Raiden grunted as he spoke.

"Yes, I am well aware, golden eyes. I've also been watching you lately. How does one of the fastest people in this realm get hit so often?" Oya's nickname for Raiden was golden eyes. In conversation, she normally referred to her protege as "the boy with the golden eyes."

"That doesn't make me sloppy. Lately, I fought some child of Judas, another guardian, and a god. I hate to say it but give them some credit." Raiden retorted.

"You trained with a goddess about how to use your abilities to not be hit. Or do you doubt my training? What is fact is that since fighting those weaker than yourself, you've gotten sloppy." Oya continued to push the issue.

"I told you, I have not gotten sloppy!" To Raiden, the situation felt like a mother coming down on their child for poor grades. He was immediately put on the defensive in the conversation, and that made him feel a mixture of annoyance and shame.

"Prove it. Don't let me hit you." Oya suddenly charged at Raiden and attempted to poke his forehead. The demigod ducked and backflipped away, only to see Oya already behind him. "Where are you looking?" Raiden converted into lightning right before Oya's finger could poke him in the back. He zipped behind the goddess and pushed her, but she recovered as gracefully as she always moved. One thing about Oya was that she moved as though she were dancing. Even when she was fighting, it was beautiful and elegant, yet powerful and ferocious. Oya twirled until she was upon Raiden and attempted to poke his stomach.

"Told you I'm not sloppy." Raiden mused as he jumped backwards to avoid the poke and falling for Oya's feint. Suddenly she lunged forward, and thwapped the demigod on the head with her freehand.

"Three moves and I caught you. When you were training with me, it took me twenty. You are growing sloppy." Oya walked over and gave her student a hug. "Stop with that shameful look. You've had to hold back when fighting all these humans, so it is to be expected. But now is the time to let go of that mental bondage."

"I'll try, Oya. I've missed you…" Raiden returned Oya's embrace. Oya was technically not a lord of lightning. Each group of lords partnered with a war god and nominated them as the paladin for that particular group. Oya was the paladin of lightning and was only permitted to enter the sanctum which the lords resided when she was training a guardian. Since technically, Raiden's training was over, it meant that the chances to visit Oya were significantly lower.

"I've missed you too, golden eyes. Now though, you have to wake up." Oya's form immediately faded, as the world around Raiden disappeared. His eyes snapped open, and he was back in the conscious world.

"It doesn't come off…" A park ranger had been tugging at Raiden's hood, before being startled by his eyes snapping open. Kagutsuchi had left the area, but he left a cloud of smoke that would attract any decent human being to investigate. The park ranger had jumped several feet backwards once he noticed Raiden's eyes snap open. "Erm...are you okay? I found you passed out here from the smoke…"

"I'm fine, thanks. And no, my hood doesn't come off. Don't try that again though." Raiden warned. His costume was magic, and the hood hid his identity, but the hero was sure that a powerful tug would eventually break down the magic that kept it up. "I was investigating the smoke, and I guess the fumes got to me." Raiden felt it was best if he didn't mention Kagutsuchi. To the rest of the world, he was just an irregular. Actually, anyone who had superhuman gifts were simply labeled as an irregular. Adding godly status to that, was probably not for the best.

"Well...this seems like something I can handle. Why don't you go rest?" The park ranger, like most of New Mexico, had a fairly high opinion of Raiden. At the very least, he respected the young hero. Maybe not enough to stave off his curiosity of discovering Raiden's true identity, but there was respect there, nonetheless.

"I'll do just that...good work." Raiden rubbed his eyes. They had shifted back to brown, now that he had calmed down. The fact that his eyes shifted from gold to brown was no secret to the world, but Raiden had noticed that the shifts were becoming more frequent. When he was younger, his eyes only turned to gold when he was using a large portion of his power. Lately though, he had caught his eyes shifting to gold from his emotions as well. For Raiden, this wasn't too much of a concern. However, if his eyes shifted colors during his civilian life as Hania...well, it would be far less subtle. Instead of harping on the issue however, Raiden simply flew into the air and pushed towards his apartment. The park ranger was right; Raiden needed some rest.

Happy Birthday

A few weeks had passed since Hania met with the lords of lightning and Kagutsuchi. As hard as he looked for Phoenix, he couldn't find a single trace of her. Wherever she went, it wasn't anywhere in New Mexico. That was fine with him, since he wasn't sure how to handle her anyway. She needed help, but even with his major being psychology he wasn't exactly qualified to help someone affected by a deity. Plus, he had to do things carefully as to not play into Kagutsuchi's plans. Crime was relatively normal at least. A few attempted bank robberies and car jackings were definitely a lot easier to deal with than a crazy eyed hunter or a deranged guardian. Hania decided that he had laid in bed long enough and it was time to get up. He was officially done with classes, which allotted him extra time to sleep. He had told Kylie he'd meet her before heading to his mom's house though. They finally had gotten back on good terms, after Hania apologized for the conversation they had when he met Phoenix. About a dozen times.

"First, time for some practice." Hania walked over to a rubber mat he had placed in the center of his studio apartment and took a deep breath. His form flickered from his normal human form to a being of pure lightning, before staying as such. "Keep focus, keep focus..." The living bolt of lightning uttered as Hania struggled to keep his thoughts from racing. Whenever Hania turned himself into lightning, it supercharged his brain and kept him from focusing his thoughts. It made battle strategies useless and if he was going to continue to fight stronger enemies, that was a weakness he had to fix immediately. Hania had been practicing every day since he first fought Hunter toward the end of March, and yet the improvement he made wasn't enough. *"Focus...I want ice cream, I miss my dad, this isn't working, did I buy milk, dodge!"* The thoughts came rushing through Hania's head all at once. "Screw it!" Hania shouted; grunting in frustration as he returned to his normal form.

Hania had just finished slipping into a navy-blue polo shirt and matching jeans, when he heard a knock on his apartment door. He automatically was put on guard; considering there were only a very small group of people who knew where he lived. "Who is it?" Hania called out, only to get no response. Slowly, Hania crept over to the door and flung it open. "What are you doing here?" He questioned, seeing the familiar face standing at his door.

"May I enter?" Thunderbird asked. Hania sighed, but motioned his father in.

"Let me give you the grand tour. That's the kitchen, and there's everything else." Hania half-heartedly showed his father around the studio apartment.

"How...quaint." Thunderbird struggled to say.

"It's a piece of crap, you can say it. It reminds me of you. Now, why are you here?" Hania's body language was very off putting as he spoke; his arms were crossed, and he gave off an unapproachable aura.

"Right. I came to bring you a gift. Tomorrow is the 17th of May, is it not?" Hania's father pulled out a small wooden box and presented it to his son. Hania managed to soften his expression slightly.

"You remembered my birthday?" Hania was legitimately surprised. It was his twenty-first birthday tomorrow, but considering he only heard from his father for about two of his birthdays, total, he never expected much. Especially not a gift.

"Of course. The birthday of twenty-one is important in this realm correct?" Thunderbird managed a smile that Hania couldn't help but match, even if he immediately returned to his scowl.

"Yeah...it is. Thanks." Hania took the wooden box from him and that was when he realized that Thunderbird must have carved the box himself. The craftsmanship was good, but not good enough to have been bought. Plus, he couldn't imagine a god having human money. He slid the box open, revealing a small knife. Hania recognized the ceremonial knife as being similar to the one his mother owned, except the handle was designed to look like a bird. It was also a little bigger, being closer to the size of a dagger. When he unsheathed the weapon, he noticed symbols were etched into the weapon that Hania identified as Norse runes. His time hanging around Thor had passed the talent onto him; although he only knew a few. He knew the top one was Eihwaz and represented strength, but he wasn't sure of the bottom one.

"The runes were Thor's idea, but I thought it made a nice addition. They mean strength and inheritance." Thunderbird pointed out as he watched his son thumb over the gold blade. "I gave your mother a knife like this when she was first pregnant with you, to match my own that I carry. And now I want to give you one of your own." Thunderbird continued explaining.

Hania swung the knife in the air a few times, before slipping it into the back of his pants. He had received a little bit of blade training from Oya when he was first made a guardian, so swinging the weapon felt rather natural. "Thank you..." Hania managed a small smile. He legitimately didn't know how to react. He didn't particularly like his father, but the gift was touching. Plus, it was a nice gesture, even if his father was still eighteen gifts in debt. His father patted him on the shoulders, snapping Hania out of his thoughts, before turning towards the door.

"Enjoy yourself, son." Thunderbird said, as he walked out the front door. Hania ran over to the door once his father walked through it, but he had already vanished without a trace.

"Of course, he's gone." Hania let out a rather aggressive sigh. Still, he couldn't be too angry considering his father bothered to see him. *"I better hurry so that I can meet Kylie."* Hania thought to himself, before locking his door and taking off into the air; being sure to fly high into the clouds so that no one could spot him. It was his usual method of travel, ensuring that he wouldn't be seen. He just found a nearby building to land on top of, so it looked like he had walked to his destination. He had a few close calls, but so far no one had ever caught him. Getting down from the top of the buildings sometimes proved challenging, but there was no such thing as a fool-proof plan in Hania's mind.

It didn't take long for him to arrive at Kylie's house. He actually arrived ten minutes ahead of schedule. "Huh...who is that..." Hania thought to himself as he approached her front door. Someone had been walking away from the house; someone whom Hania didn't recognize as part of Kylie's family.

"Oh...hey Hania. Happy birthday dude." The male whom had been leaving spoke in a jittery voice. Now that he was closer, Hania recognized the pale faced stranger as someone from one of Kylie's classes. Hania had hung out with him a handful of times but he was more so Kylie's friend than his.

"Hey...Ben, right? It's tomorrow but thanks anyways man." Hania smiled at Ben, although he was still wondering why he looked so nervous. Thinking back, Hania thought that Ben always looked rather nervous whenever they were around each other. Sure, Ben was rather short for a male and was a little on the skinny side, but Hania wasn't exactly the most intimidating either. Ben ran a hand through the sandy mop top he called his hair and grabbed his keys out of his pocket.

"My bad. Well, enjoy." Ben spat out, before doing a light jog down the remainder of the steps and around the corner.

"Weird guy..." Hania muttered under his breath, before continuing up to Kylie's front door. She opened on the first knock; a little out of breath.

"Oh Hania, you're early." Kylie looked around before motioning Hania inside.

"Yeah, I can't stay too long. I have to finish packing and go meet my mom at her house since we're leaving tonight." Hania couldn't help but notice Kylie's house was empty. Normally her parents or little brother would have bolted down the stairs to greet him. After all, Hania and Kylie had grown up together. In many ways it felt like Kylie was his only friend, aside from his mother. Sure, he had a large amount of acquaintances, but not too many people he really could be himself around. Well, himself minus the whole demigod, avatar of lightning thing.

"Oh okay. I was going to cook you something, but I understand. I'm so jealous that you get to go to Brazil!" Kylie swooned while gathering her hair into a ponytail. It had looked particularly wilder than usual, Hania noticed.

“Calm down there as told by gingivitis, I’m only going there for a week.” Hania’s redhead joke earned a playful slap from his friend. It was true though; Hania was very excited about going to Brazil with his mother. He had never been out of the country before, despite being able to literally defy the laws of physics. It was part of the reason he had been busting his ass to stop so many crimes since the month started. Did the superheroes in other areas go on vacation? He wasn’t really sure considering he never met anyone else in this line of work. A couple existed...just not in New Mexico.

“Earth to Han.” Kylie whistled in Hania’s ear to snap him back into reality.

“Sorry, zoned out a bit. Started thinking about all the gorgeous Brazilian women in bikinis I’m going to get to see.” Hania quickly covered his thoughts. It wasn’t exactly a lie anyway. Whenever Hania’s mind wasn’t on his duties as a superhero, the well-being of his mother, college, or his crippling depression, women were at the forefront of his mind. Kylie rolled her eyes, before gesturing over to a small gift bag on her dining room table.

“Maybe I should go exchange that for a thong you can give to one of the girls you’ll be chasing.” Kylie spat out. Hania knew he better ignore her tone, because as soon as he commented on it, an entire can of worms would open that he wasn’t ready to deal with. Hania knew that occasionally old feelings would surface with Kylie. To be fair, occasionally he also had a fleeting thought of trying to get back together with her. His thoughts, however, were much less frequent than hers. She definitely made it more apparent as well, although Hania usually pretended not to notice. Instead of addressing the elephant in the room, he walked over and opened the bag; withdrawing a very nice, digital camera. Kylie normally had more money than Hania, because she lived at home. Both of them had gotten scholarships and grants to pay for college, but whereas Hania had to use the extra money to live off, Kylie was able to keep it for herself.

“Thank you!” Hania zipped over and hugged his friend, before sticking the camera in his pocket.

"Don't mention it. Now go finish packing and don't forget that camera. I expect a lot of pictures on that thing for me to look at." Kylie shooed Hania out the front door, before giving him one last hug. Hania felt the entire thing was a little rushed and that Kylie was taken a little by surprise when Hania appeared at the door. It was strange, considering she was the one who invited him over. Hania decided to leave it alone and began to walk around the corner. He always took off and landed from the exact same spot when visiting Kylie; a dark alleyway with perpetually broken streetlights. Just to be safe however, since it wasn't quite nighttime yet, he transformed into Raiden.

"What the…" Raiden muttered under his breath as he reached into the back of his waist. The small ceremonial knife that his father gave him had mounted itself horizontally along his gold belt; the handle pointing towards his right hand for quick drawing. The rune for inheritance had been shimmering bright enough to show through the wooden sheath, although the glow slowly faded after a few seconds. Normally most of the things that he had in his pockets or person vanished when he put his costume on. He had to actively remember to take his cell phone out of his pants when he summoned his costume, but it looked like his knife was enchanted with similar magic that his costume possessed. He'd have to do a little more training with his weapon once he got back from Brazil. Raiden then took off into the air; heading back to his apartment so that he could hurry and meet his mom. Their flight was leaving in two hours, and his mom insisted that they drive to the airport instead of letting him fly them both there. He lied a little bit to Kylie; he was already packed; he just had to get his stuff and go. Sometimes it was hard to keep up with the actual time frame that it would take him to get to his mother's house by Uber.

"Did you get everything?" Hania's mom asked as soon as she saw her son land in front of the house. The biggest advantage of where his mom lived was that she had nearly no neighbors; living at the end of a road. A few houses were about half a mile up the street, but the inhabitants rarely came down in the direction of his mother's house. Hania had called ahead to tell his mom he was on the way, so she had been loading the trunk of her car upon his arrival.

“I think so.” Hania answered as he dumped his suitcase beside his mother’s three bags. “Suitcases are unsurprisingly not aerodynamic. Maybe I can invent one, become famous, and we can just live in Brazil.”

“You do realize that would only appeal to people like you, right?” Ms. Hawke pointed out, before getting into the driver's seat of the car. “Now let’s go. We’ve got an hour and forty-five minutes to get through security and board the plane. Let’s go!” Hania’s mom started the car just as Hania jumped in the passenger seat. The airport was twenty minutes away and honestly, they were cutting things pretty close.

“I could always just fly us there you know.” Hania offered as his mother hit ninety down the road.

“Can you carry me, your suitcase, and my three bags? You have super strength, not multiple arms. Plus, where would you land without being seen?” Hania’s mother continued to poke holes in his plan as she kept her eyes on the road.

“You could always try...not packing half of the house.” Hania’s retort earned a chuckle from his mom.

“We’re going to Brazil, wičháȟpi. Your mom has to look her best, at all times.” She smiled widely as she spoke. “We’re almost there. Once we stop, we have to hurry up and get in line.”

“Okay, that’s fine and all but if you meet someone, I’m not going to call him dad.” Hania teased.

“You’ll be twenty-one in a few hours; I really wouldn’t expect you to. Besides...you already have a father, and I don’t plan on trying to replace that.” Hania’s mom tiptoed around the subject per usual. Hania knew that deep down, his mother was still very much in love with Thunderbird, even if he didn’t deserve it. He tried pushing her towards other men, but nothing really worked.

"Speaking of, the ole phantom came to see me today. Even gave me a gift for my birthday." Hania noticed that they had arrived in the airport parking lot and his mom was desperately searching for a parking spot.

"I know. He stopped to see me too. I'm glad you're getting along at least a little better." Naira pulled into a parking lot, motioning her son to get out the car. The duo jumped out, with Hania grabbing all his mother's bags as well as his own suitcase. He hated to admit it, but she was right. There was no way he could have carried all the luggage, plus his mother.

"Wait, why the hell is he still visiting you? Mom, you've seriously got to make him pick between his...job and us." Hania had to be careful talking about his father now that they were in public, even if they were hurrying along. Hania's mom used that as an excuse to ignore his question; instead moving a bit faster toward the security gate. Hania attempted to bring it up again as they were in line to go through the metal detector but gave up after he saw that his mom was adamant on not speaking to him about it. Not only that, but the gate took a little longer than they expected to get through and they ended up being more pressed for time than either of them would have liked. In fact, the two had been so frantically sprinting down the airport hallway, that Hania ran smack into someone's back.

"I'm so sorry! Are you okay?" Hania helped the gentleman up, as his mom came to a sliding halt beside the two.

"I know that voice. Staying out of trouble, Hania?" Chief Valo questioned, once he was back on his feet. It was rare to see the chief in civilian clothes. Even if he was dressed in a tan suit with a red tie. Of course, it was red.

"I get in trouble one time, and you act like I'm public enemy number one." Hania rolled his eyes. Hania had to pretend of course, that he didn't see the chief on a semi-regular basis. His work as Raiden often involved saving the police chief or one of his men.

"Ms. Hawke; always a pleasure." Chief Valo ignored Hania once he saw Hania's mother. The two were friends, although they weren't extremely close.

They had a mutual interest around Hania's well-being. She smiled and nodded, before quickly explaining that they were running late for their flight. The mother and son duo excused themselves, although Hania was admittedly much more aggressive with his departure. By the time they got to their gate, the two had to run directly onto the plane.

"Do you want window, middle, or aisle?" The two had gotten seats near the back of the plane so they could sit next to each other.

"Middle is fine. I'm kind of used to the view you get from flying." Hania allowed his mom to sit down in her seat before plopping down in the middle. "You know, I'm pretty sure I could get us there in eight hours, instead of sixteen." Hania pointed out, once the plane had taken flight.

"Yes, probably. But you're officially on vacation. I don't want you lifting a finger, you understand?" Naira had been reading a book, and barely looked up to answer her son. Without looking, her hand moved to his head and she rubbed it in a nurturing fashion. "You do more than enough for not only me, but the world. You deserve some rest." Hania shrugged, defeated. He decided to listen to music as their flight continued, knowing he would soon fall asleep. Knowing that by the time he woke up, he'd be nearly in Brazil.

Guardian of Nature

“I can’t believe we’re really in Brazil!” Hania had been standing in the lobby of the hotel he and his mother were staying at, wearing his swim trunks. The plane had landed about three hours ago, and since it was officially his birthday, they checked in and went straight to dinner. "I also can't believe you're already going to bed." Hania added, looking at his yawning mother. It was about eight at night, but the sun hadn't really started setting yet, and wouldn't for another hour. Even so, Hania had enough energy to stay up for another ten hours. Maybe even twelve or fourteen if he really pushed it.

"Well not all of us slept fourteen hours on the plane. I slept about two, so I'm tired. The beach can wait." She yawned again as she answered her son. Naira had a serious fear of flying, and so she spent the entire flight jumping at every bit of turbulence that they encountered. Hania on the other hand, passed out almost as soon as they took off. Hania lived a double life, equally balancing a social life and a superhero life. Something had to suffer, and sleep was the thing that was missing in Hania's life. His body finally gave out on him once the plane took off; lulling him to sleep like a newborn baby in a rocking chair.

The weather in Rio de Janeiro was just under eighty, but the view was absolutely spectacular, and he just had to run out on the beach. “Alright, well we can meet up for lunch then." Hania grinned at his mom and gave her a hug, before leaving towards the beach.

Hania had found himself a comfortable spot on the beach, looking out at the water. He couldn't really go far into the water since he couldn't swim, but he was perfectly content with the view, and feeling the warm sand beneath his feet. He had pulled his dark brown dreads into a small ponytail, with a strand or two falling on the sides of his face. He was mistaken for a certain dread headed rapper from Washington D.C. twice since he had been there, which was strange since the only real similarities Hania thought they had in common was their hairstyles. Hania had his brand-new camera in his hand, and was snapping pictures of the view, when he noticed two females out of the corner of his eye.

The smaller, slimmer one of the two had a complexion that reminded Hania of autumn leaves. Her hair was gathered into a sloppy ponytail, with the back half of her hair dyed a bright green; offsetting the rest of her dark hair. To Hania, she seemed like the type of girl who would be first in line for a pumpkin spice latte the very first day it was back in season. She wasn't the one who caught Hania's eye, however.

The woman who had caught Hania's eye was a shade or two darker than his own mocha skin tone. The woman's box braids hung down to the middle of her back, while she had a collection of braids draped across her shoulders as well. Her curves were highlighted in her bright blue bikini; a rather ample bust, wide hips, and relatively thick stomach with thighs to match. Hania knew a dozen females who were shaped similarly to her that would have let beauty magazines convince them that they should be wearing something more concealing, but she wasn't one of them. It was that aura of confidence that radiated off her which attracted Hania so much to the women. He started to wonder if she had caught him gawking at her, because she started to walk over to him.

"Hey, do you mind taking a picture of me and my friend over there?" The woman requested in her husky, yet attractive voice. She had been holding up her cell phone, waiting patiently for his answer. Hania looked into her dark brown eyes and returned the smile that she had on her face. Maybe it was the fact that they were on vacation, or maybe it was the shot of tequila that was still making his body feel like he was sitting in a hot tub, but for some reason he felt even more confident than his usual self.

"Sure, but I've got two conditions." Hania smirked as he started to stand up; his voice brimming with confidence per usual. Her head was at his chest level, even though he was only five foot ten. She took a step back and crossed her arms, but she didn't drop her smile.

"Oh yeah? What conditions?" She looked back briefly at her friend, whom was looking just outside of earshot.

"First; I want to know your name. I'm Hania, by the way."

"Okay Hania, I'm Alicia. And your second condition?" Alicia shook her head. Hania couldn't figure out what she was thinking but he knew he already was too deep to change his mind.

"You meet me for breakfast tomorrow morning. You can pick where though, since I did kind of put you on the spot." Hania put on his most confident face that he could muster. She paused for several moments, as though she were weighing her options.

"You're an arrogant ass, you know that?" Alicia pointed out. Hania considered complimenting her alliteration but decided that was just proving her point. Hania's mom always said that he needed someone in his life willing to put him in his place every once in a while, so this was already a good sign. She rolled her eyes, before smiling. "Fine. Take our picture and when I decide where I want to eat, I'll text you where to meet me."

"How do I know you'll actually text me?" Hania asked, even though he had already taken her phone to enter in his number.

"You don't. You better impress me with your photography skills. And hope I don't oversleep." Alicia snickered as she walked back over to her friend; deliberately slower to tease Hania. It wasn't like Hania was some type of ladies' man or that he was particularly popular with the opposite sex. He had a handful of girlfriends in his life, although they never really worked out long term. His relationship with Kylie was probably the longest one he had ever been in, and even that only lasted three months before he realized that he didn't see her in that light. Still though, that didn't stop him from trying to woo any female that he felt was attractive. He wasn't easily discouraged, that's for sure. Plus, his relatively attractive face combined with his toned, athletic body certainly helped his chances. He wasn't exactly a supermodel or anything like that, but he was often considered above average on the attractiveness scale. Until he opened his mouth, at least. The entire time that Hania was taking pictures of Alicia and her friend, he was praying that she'd text him.

Luckily for Hania, she did. He was worried that she had already deleted his number and moved on with her life, but while he was sprawled out on top of the satin sheets of his hotel bed, she sent him the directions to the restaurant in her hotel building. It was already three in the morning by this point, so he needed to force himself to sleep as not to miss his date. That was the plan at least, until he looked out his window and saw thick smoke in the distance. “I’m on vacation.” Hania spoke to himself, as though he actually believed that lie. Heroes never take vacations. He stood up and allowed his costume to appear on his body; taking special note that the knife his father had gifted him was still by his side. Raiden managed to open his room's window much to his surprise, as he knew that a great majority of hotels wanted to prevent people from jumping out of them. Then again, this was Rio de Janeiro aka the happiest place on earth...in his opinion anyway. Did they even have suicides here? Raiden shook his head to regain his focus, as he flew out the window.

Even at night, Brazil was a beautiful place. Raiden flew past the beach, counting the footsteps and abandoned sandcastles as he moved further from the mainland. “You’ll get sand in strange places!” Raiden shouted as he flew over a secluded section of the beach and was forced to avert his eyes away from a young couple whom, if he was a bit more naive, he might have thought he scared the pants off of. He pushed further out, watching the waves rise and fall as he continued flying towards the suffocating smoke in the distance. He had already imagined stumbling upon a boat engulfed with flames as it sank into the crystal-clear water being the culprit to the sudden appearance of this smoke. As it turned out, he wasn’t even close to being correct.

A couple dozen miles away from the beach, he had stumbled upon a rather small island, covered in what could only be described as a rainforest of epic proportions. Raiden wasn’t exactly the best with geography, but he was pretty sure that this island wasn’t supposed to be here. The center of the island had been burning trees down, but it seemed like for every tree that fell, another took its place. Raiden stood in awe at the scene for a few moments, before flying closer towards the scene of the crime. At the very tip of the tree that had just magically grown several years too quickly sat a frantic looking boy that made Raiden’s shoulder tingle just by entering his line of sight; the telltale sign that he was looking at a guardian.

Granted; it wasn't much to look at. The boy could easily pass for an athletic Brazilian preteen girl with how slender and delicate he appeared perched upon that treetop. He had his obviously dyed hair cut into a slightly asymmetrical bob that made it look more like someone spilled an entire tub of white out on him. He looked up as he saw Raiden approach, and stood up from his crouched position. If it wasn't for his chestnut skin, he would have screamed Greek with the tree bark colored chiton he was wearing. He definitely needed to stop by his nearest target immediately and pick up some more modern-looking clothes. Still, he had to have been a powerful guardian if he was capable of summoning entire trees in an instant. Which only made the fact that his emerald colored eyes seemed to be screaming "help me" even more baffling. Until it was all made clear by another guardian rising from the forest.

"Phoenix!" Raiden cried out as he watched the guardian of fire pause in the middle of launching another fireball into the forest below. She turned and looked at Raiden as though her eyes took a moment to register who he was. She then snarled in a way that could only be described as animalistic.

"Raiden! What are you doing here? This isn't New Mexico! Wait...is it New Mexico?" Phoenix's voice shifted between anger and oddly soothing to form a rather strange speech pattern.

"I take my job of preventing forest fires very seriously. Only I can do it, y'know? At least that what I was told. More importantly, what are you doing here? I thought you were my villain! You aren't cheating on me, are you?" Raiden questioned in mock sorrow. He felt bad knowing that Phoenix might not be entirely in control of her own actions. If he could avoid a fight, he wanted to. Plus, he hated fighting women.

"What? I would never! You know you're the only hero for me!" Phoenix mocked Raiden right back, before throwing an easily dodged fireball at him.

"Phoenix, stop! I know that you absorbed...well, Phoenix, and it's destroying you inside. Let me help you!" Raiden was taking a gamble, but he had to try and convince Phoenix to let him help. He was worried that the guardian whom Raiden could only assume was some type of earth or forest guardian would launch a sneak attack, but he seemed content with staying put and watching.

"Did you mean I absorbed myself, the deity, or the city in Arizona?" The fire guardian replied, sounding genuinely confused.

"What did you think I meant? In what realm of possibility did you actually need to question which of those I meant? I'm going to have a brain aneurysm one day and I want you to know that it'll be seventy percent your fault." Raiden's mouth just started flowing before his brain could catch up. Patience wasn't exactly his selling point.

"No need to be rude!" Phoenix replied as she kicked out a wall of flames at Raiden. Clearly, this battle was going to take place if the mixed-race hero wanted it to or not. Raiden zipped up into the air to dodge the wall of flames and retaliated with a volley of lightning bolts from his hand. He expected Phoenix to just tank the hits like their first fight but was caught off guard when she rushed between them by turning her body into fire. She closed the gap rather quickly between the two and delivered a kick that would have shattered most of Raiden's ribs if he didn't block. Even then, it nearly broke his arm.

"*She's gotten stronger...*" Raiden thought to himself as he delivered a few punches to her torso. Phoenix opened her mouth wide, which Raiden noticed and followed her lead. A powerful stream of fire and lightning, respectively, came out of the two warrior's mouths and slammed into each other. The stalemate caused a miniature explosion to go off in midair and blanket the sky with smoke. Not only had Phoenix gotten stronger, but she seemed smarter too, compared to their last battle. She had been using the smoke like a veil to conceal her movements; a technique that was working frightening well.

"On your right!" He who sits on trees, as Raiden had dubbed him within his own head, shouted just in time for Raiden to counter the charging Phoenix's blow.

"This is an A and B conversation, so C your way out of it!" Phoenix yelled down at Raiden's newfound helper, preparing a ball of fire to launch at him.

"Oh lord, you really are older than me. You didn't go to school with my mother, did you?" Raiden mused while summoning a bolt of lightning from the sky to strike Phoenix before she could attack the other guardian.

"That hurts, dammit!" Phoenix spat.

"Language, young lady! Do I have to rinse your mouth out with soap?" Raiden teased. In truth, he really didn't know why he was teasing Phoenix so much. Of course, Raiden naturally teased people all the time. It was the sarcastic, arrogant asshole in him. But he normally teased criminals on purpose to get them angry. Angry criminals made stupid decisions that didn't fit with a normal, rational mind. Well, humans in general were like that. But Phoenix was too unhinged for it to affect her. Her mind already worked in an irrational fashion.

"I came here on vacation! Now I have to find an entirely different vacation spot and it's all your fault!" Phoenix launched three fireballs in a row at Raiden, whom responded by zipping in between them.

"Do you always burn down trees on vacation?" Raiden launched a kick at Phoenix side. When she caught the kick, Raiden escaped by shocking her. Their fight was going nowhere fast.

"Only when I'm bored." Phoenix stopped moving. "Like now. I'm supposed to be on vacation from fighting you. I'm not in the mood to fight you right now." Phoenix shooed at Raiden as though he were no more than a fly.

"You know I'm not going to just leave you like this right?" Raiden folded his arms and looked on at Phoenix.

"Why not? I haven't done anything." Phoenix shrugged her shoulders.

“You attacked me in New Mexico.” Raiden pointed out.

“Stop taking everything so personal. I also kissed you, so I think that evens it out.” Phoenix statement caused the guardian below them to snicker. That very snicker faded once Raiden shot him an angry look.

“No, that doesn’t. And you attacked all those innocent people in the middle of the battle.” Raiden continued with his list of evidence.

“But did they die? I don’t think so. Did some of their stuff get burned? Sure. But materialistic things are only holding them back from enlightenment.” Phoenix was pushing Raiden’s buttons, and the worst thing about it was that it wasn’t even on purpose.

“That’s still arson.” Raiden’s tone was laced with his growing annoyance. “Even if I ignored all of those things, you were literally burning down a forest like five minutes ago.”

“You can’t prove that. I don’t have anything on me to start a fire with.” Phoenix pointed to her costume, and her lack of pockets. That was definitely a design flaw, Raiden had to admit to himself. His costume had pockets in the pants. Even Speaks with Trees down there had what looked like a carrying pouch dangling from the belt of his chiton.

“You’re the FIRE guardian!” Raiden practically screamed.

“...Sema-” Phoenix began, before Raiden interjected.

“Say semantics! I dare you! I double dare you!” Raiden was prepared to unleash the full might of his powers on her if she even dared to say the word.

“You’re really tense, you know. You should go on vacation. Want a shoulder rub, big guy?” Phoenix mimed giving a massage in the air. It was too much for Raiden to handle. He thrust his hands into his face and let out a muffled scream.

"Go. Just go. I can't do this today, not while I'm on vacation. Go literally anywhere but where I am for the love of every god that we collectively know. I don't even care anymore. We can fight another day." Raiden sounded absolutely defeated. It wasn't like him to give up, or let villains get away, but he was already getting a migraine from dealing with her.

"Well if you're sure…" Phoenix grinned at Raiden, whom was very clearly at his wits end. She blew him a kiss, before flying off in the opposite direction. Raiden had no idea where she was flying to, and he couldn't care less at this point. He needed a strategy to deal with her and earplugs to drown her out; neither of which he had at the moment. After floating in the air for a few moments to regain his composure, he floated down towards his new friend.

"Sorry about that. I feel like it was partially my fault she attacked your magical trees. You okay?" Raiden asked the guardian, who was perched on the top of a tree. He responded with a nod and caused the tree he was on to extend a branch out for Raiden to sit on. "Thanks. Oh, by the way, I'm Rai-"

"Raiden. I definitely know who you are." The guardian had a huge, genuine smile on his face. Raiden couldn't help but envy the fact that his teeth were so white, someone probably accused him of painting them. "I'm Juan Silva, the guardian of nature. Huge fan of your work!" Juan spoke with such excitement that he slipped into an accent. He didn't sound native to Brazil like he previously did when he was speaking normally. It had a Puerto Rican flare that overtook his Brazilian accent.

"Juan? That's an odd alias. I personally think you should change it to Walks-with-Trees or something like that." Raiden's response made Juan burst into laughter.

"No, Juan is my actual name. I'm not a superhero or anything like that. Actually, I'm a pacifist."

“Really? Not that there's anything wrong with that, but why?” Raiden had never met an irregular who didn’t fight. Granted, Raiden could count the number of irregulars that he knew on a single hand, but that wasn’t the point.

“I only care about nature. I don’t really enjoy dealing with people, normally. They’re too complicated and it’s just not worth it. So why fight? Plus, I hate the sound of my fist hitting people. That grating sound of bone against bone…” Juan shuddered. Raiden sensed that there was something deeper within that answer, but it wasn’t worth exploring if it wasn’t freely offered.

“That makes sense.” Raiden nodded his head in agreement. This was his first time meeting a guardian who wasn’t insane, so he couldn’t help but have a smile on his face. The two had immediately started to chat about life as guardians, and various other things. It just felt so natural; like a pair of old friends reuniting after several years apart. Raiden even revealed his actual identity to Juan, which was usually a closely guarded secret. Besides the two supervillains who had figured it out, of course. They had never known each other but it was like the bond was old as time itself.

“Okay, weirdest girl you’ve ever dated? For a week, I once dated a girl who would walk like a crab whenever she was excited. I bet you can’t top that.” Raiden mused.

“I’ve got something to tell you…but I don’t know if I can. I don’t want you to hate me.” Juan was staring down at his shoes, as though making eye contact with Raiden would physically hurt him.

“Shoot.” Raiden had started to make a joke, but he saw the look of anguish that was smeared all over Juan’s face. Even he knew when it was time to be serious. Whatever the conversation they were previously having was irrelevant at this point.

“I’m...gay. I should have told you, but I was scared, and it had been so long since I spoke to anyone, so I didn’t.” Juan spoke as though every word was being forced out of his mouth, but once he was finished, he had been wincing. As if he were preparing to be struck and was just unsure where the blow was coming from.

"Oh…" Raiden smiled as he talked, although Juan couldn't see that. "Is that all? Don't scare me like that, I thought you were about to confess that you didn't like tacos or something else life-altering." Juan looked up and looked absolutely baffled by Raiden's acceptance. Raiden could tell just by looking at his face that Juan lived a hard life. As a minority, Raiden knew all too well the face of someone who was discriminated against.

"You really don't care?"

"Nah man, why would I? Love is love; it doesn't matter who you love. Besides, that just means less competition for me." The superhero teased. Raiden was happy to see Juan smiling again, even if he wanted to trade teeth with him. Such perfectly white, perfectly shaped teeth. Sure, Raiden's teeth were okay, but Juan's teeth sparkled. He was tempted to sing a song about how his teeth twinkled, but he rejected the idea.

"You're very kind. I can see why Demeter speaks so highly of you." Juan's comment threw Raiden for a loop, since he had never met Demeter. Did the gods sit around and watch the human world like some type of TV? "Growing up was…pretty rough honestly. I used to be teased at school, in my neighborhood, hell even at my own house. Sometimes things got physical and well...honestly, I don't think I like people very much. Crazy I know, talking to a man of the people about that."

"You're zero for two. I definitely get the whole not liking people thing. I'm starting to think it's a requirement for becoming a guardian to not like people to some extent." It was the first time Raiden had admitted that out loud, but it felt so natural. Maybe it was because he was relating to Juan, or maybe it was because deep down inside, he had known that for years now. He didn't hate people, but he had definitely seen some of the darker acts that humans were capable of.

"Even you?" Juan's question sent Raiden in a trance; getting lost in his own memories. The hero saw himself when he was younger being teased by the other kids in school that he didn't have a father. Tears streaming down the face of a young boy who didn't know why the other kids thought it was funny to tease him. He remembered being called a stereotype, before he fully understood what that meant. He remembered a mother who tried her best to dry his tears but didn't know how. The main memory that flooded in his mind was that fateful day in third grade where one of the kids went one joke too far, and Hania had punched him in the chest so hard that the boy collapsed. The boy went to the hospital, and Hania was expelled...yet he didn't care. Hell, he didn't even bother to remember the kid's name.

"Especially me." Raiden let his mind return to present day; back to his friend who smelled like sunflowers. "I know just how cruel people can be. I mean, I know that even I have the capacity to cause a great deal of pain. But I also know that humans have such a large capacity to love, to do good, and that's what pushes me to keep protecting everyone. Plus, I think having that small bit of hatred inside of us helps us serve as the bridge between the humans, the elements, and the gods." Raiden let himself be vulnerable for a brief, rare moment.

"You just make me like you more and more, dear." The voice tingled the back of Raiden's neck. He whipped around to see a woman standing behind him. Raiden had no idea how long, or even how the woman with wheat colored hair had gotten behind him, but he felt oddly calm. One look into her deep brown eyes and he knew that she was someone on his side.

"Demeter, hey!" Juan ran over and hugged the tanned goddess. Raiden recognized the small, golden crown symbol that was on the center of her forehead as being like the one that Zeus had. It was the symbol that identified an emperor or empress. It was hard to believe someone, so kind was on the same level as Zeus. It was even harder to believe how close she was to Juan. She had returned his hug with no hesitation. There was a sense of pride that reminded Raiden of the same look his mother often gave him. Juan's birth parents were both very human, and very much alive, but during their talk he did mention that he ran away from home when he was twelve. Demeter must have been watching over him for the past five years.

"I always wished I could have two guardians. That brother of mine doesn't treat you right at all." Demeter smiled, as she smoothed out some wrinkles in her pure white dress.

"I think we just became best friends. If you want to tell your brother that a few dozen times, I wouldn't mind." Raiden joked, at the risk of being hit by a sudden bolt of lightning by an angry Zeus.

"I'm just glad you and Juan are becoming friends. I always told him that out of all the guardians, you were the one who I respected the most. I hope you forgive me for eavesdropping on the conversation, but I simply had to meet you face to face." Demeter's voice was so soft and soothing, it felt like the model that every mother should base themselves off. Unlike Hera, whom Raiden unfortunately had met and felt as though her voice as closer to a shrieking harpy.

"That means a lot. Thank you, Demeter." Raiden gave a slight bow to the goddess, whom responded by curtseying.

"It's my pleasure! I better take my leave for now, before the other lords of nature realize I'm gone. They still aren't too keen on taking orders from a mere goddess of harvest." Demeter explained; stretching her arms out as though she were preparing to exercise. Demeter was built like an Olympic gymnast, with a more lean and muscular build compared to some of the more...delicate goddesses such as Hera.

"I was wondering about that. How did you beat out the other gods and goddesses to become the empress? I know Zeus barely beat out Indra and Thor didn't feel like competing, but I figured Aja would have been leading the lords of nature. No offense of course." Raiden quickly added. Demeter stood motionless for a moment, before contorting her face into a grin that would make the Cheshire cat envious.

“Have you ever performed the Piledriver?” Demeter asked; her voice as flat as what the ancient civilizations thought the world was. “I’ve performed a Piledriver. On every other lord who dared to challenge my right to rule.” The harvest goddess flexed her biceps to show off her muscles. Raiden made a personal note to remain on Demeter’s good side.

“Oh crap! What time is it?” Raiden suddenly shifted the subject, noticing the sky had grown from pitch black to a nearly blue hue. Dawn was coming, and he had to meet up with his breakfast date within a few hours. “I’ve gotta go! I have a date in the next few hours and I need to sleep. You’ll be here later right, Juan?” Raiden began talking quickly, as though he were pushing the words out his mouth.

“I can be. I created this island, and I normally just collapse it and move on to another place. I can wait here a little longer if you’ll be in the area.” Juan nonchalantly answered.

“Okay, so when I have a little more time, we’re going to talk about how you just casually add entire landmasses to the world. I’ll be back later tonight!” Raiden called out; flying in the air towards his hotel. He’d have to set two or three alarms to ensure he’d be up in time for his date tonight. Still, excited didn’t begin to describe the feeling he had in his heart.

The one who can see the fate of the world

"You look dead tired. What, did you have too many dates to bother sleeping for ours?" Alicia tapped her fingers against the table; glaring at her half-asleep date sitting across from her.

"I was awake with anticipation, that's all. You look nice." Hania attempted to let out a private yawn but failed. His dreads were collected into a ponytail with a few dreads framing his face; a hairstyle he had begun embracing a lot lately.

"Well thank you." Alicia answered, a small smile forming across her face. She had gone simple for their date; dressing in a sleeveless blue shirt with black shorts. Luckily, Hania didn't feel out of place. He was wearing a pair of black joggers, and a white tank top. If he had muscles, they would be absolutely showing right now. Unfortunately, super strength didn't always mean super physique. Sure, Hania was toned, but he was definitely more on the lean side.

"You're welcome." Hania managed to yawn out. The two had sat and made small talk, although Hania could tell she wasn't nearly as interested in their date as he was. He did learn that she was older than him, and that she lived in California. Other than that, the conversation between the two of them seemed dry; stale even.

"Do you believe in palm reading?" Alicia had finally come out and asked. It was probably the most excited she had been all morning, much to Hania's annoyance. He sighed a bit, hoping she didn't see, and folded his arms.

"In all honesty, not particularly. But I'll try it if you know a spot." Hania admitted. It seemed strange for him not to believe in things like that, considering he was a demigod. Perhaps that was the exact reason why he didn't believe in it though. It's hard to trust cold readings, when you know beings that could literally predict the future.

"No, no, no. I do it. I have to admit; something drew me to you the moment I saw you." Alicia admitted. Hania sat for a moment, before sighing and rolling his eyes. She wasn't interested in going on a real date with him, she was only interested in reading his palm. She'd probably charge him for it too. "I'll do it for free, of course." She added, as if she could read his face.

"*Well if it's free...*" Hania thought to himself. What was the worst that could happen? He remained silent, but he placed his hand out. Her hands felt remarkably soft, he couldn't help but think, as her fingers gently traced the lines on his palms.

"Let me see.... you have a deep connection to your mother." Alicia began; closing her eyes as she felt up and down his hand.

"Just another cold reading. I already mentioned I came here with my mother, that's pretty obvious." Hania thought; deciding to remain silent as she continued.

"You are distant from your father...he has been in and out of your life." She continued, to the still silent Hania.

"*Still not a big deal. I haven't made any mentions of my father this entire time, and she knows that I only came here with my mother. She's probably seeing if my hands are going to sweat or twitch, so she can use body language as clues."* Hania continued to dissect her mentally. Outwards though, he chose to remain stoic.

"You have an aura of...power around you. As though not all of you is from this world." Alicia spoke almost in a trance.

"*Just...a coincidence. She's probably about to hint at some type of past life or something like that."* Hania was getting a little nervous now.

"You have a great destiny awaiting you. Your journey is going to be filled with heartbreak, but you must press on. You are stronger than you know, Raiden, son of Thunderbird." Alicia gasp and covered her mouth as soon as she finished speaking. Before she could pull her hand away from Hania's though, Hania let out a tiny spark to shock her.

"Listen here; who are you? Seriously. There's no way you should know that information. Who are you working with, and what is your endgame?" Hania switched from stoic, to serious without missing a beat. He had already had his identity known to two villains, and he wasn't going to tolerate this upward trend. He had to nip this in the bud now. He softened his expression though, when he saw the fear in Alicia's eyes.

"I'm not working for anyone, I swear! I don't know who I am. I don't even know what I am! I just know I've had these...gifts." Alicia's hands were shaking as she spoke. Hania was inclined to believe her. Now that he wasn't being so skeptical towards her palm reading, he could sense a sort of different air about her than normal humans.

"Okay...calm down. I believe you. How long have you had these...gifts, and what exactly are they?" A memory flung into the forefront of Hania's brain as he spoke; a child version of him sobbing in his room alone, calling himself a freak while sparks of electricity wreaked havoc on his walls. His mother jumping in, throwing on a pair of rubber gloves and plunging towards her son. She was fearless; tanking electrical burns as though she were the ones with superpowers to embrace her son. The pair cried together; just a scared second-grader and a concerned parent. Nothing else was relevant in that exact moment.

"Did you hear me?" Alicia's voice snapped Hania back to his senses. He shook his head no and motioned for her to repeat herself. "I said, I've had this ability for as long as I can remember. Something just...comes over me, and I can see glimpses into a person's life. It's mostly just things that call out to me."

"Like telepathy?" Hania may have been a demigod, but this was admittedly a subject he wasn't very familiar with. Contrary to what one might believe, the world of magic didn't exactly run side by side with his experiences as a demigod. The magic he knew of was limited to the fact that his costume was endowed the magical energies to come and go at will.

"Not quite. I can't read people's minds or thoughts...I can't even really see images. It's more like...words appear in my head, and they're generally right.

Usually it's just things that happened before to them, or bits about their character, but occasionally it's something to do with a future event. I guess it's more like fortune telling." Alicia was slowly letting the fear in her voice and being subside; replacing it with what Hania had noticed was her normal, laid back self.

"You can start a hotline, mon!" Hania teased, in his best Jamaican accent.

"No thanks, I don't want to be sued." Alicia snickered. "Can you help me?"

"I can try, as long as I'm not fighting anymore redheads or anything. Are your parents' irregulars?" Hania hoped he wasn't peering too much into her personal life, but he had to get whatever information he could. He didn't think she was a demigod, but it couldn't hurt to ask. It left a bad taste in his mouth to have to use that word though. irregular was used in such a vile way sometimes, by the rest of society. Not to mention the fact that he hated how everyone was lumped into one category anyway. There really needed to be some sort of class system associated with the irregular moniker.

"As normal as could be. The weirdest thing about them is that my dad wears long sleeves in the California heat, and my mom can drink an insane amount of liquor without getting drunk. Those don't count as superpowers do, they?" Alicia pondered.

"I'm going to wager, no. Well then...I'm stumped." Hania stroked his chin, before an idea flew into his head so fast, he might have gotten whiplash. He whipped out his phone and scrolled through his contacts until he got to the most recent addition; Juan. "I'm using a lifeline." He stepped out of the baffled Alicia's earshot. She could do nothing but stare and wait for her audience to return. "Do you have anything planned for the day?" Hania asked upon returning.

"Not really...my friend is sleeping off a hangover." Alicia admitted.

"Great! Let's head to your hotel room." Hania grinned, although Alicia crossed her arms.

“You’re not exactly unattractive, but I’m not interested in you like that.”

“What? Wait no, not like that. If my confidence recovers from that rejection you just handed out, I need to fly us somewhere, but I can’t quite just take off in the middle of a bunch of people. “Hania quickly explained.

“Your confidence will be just fine, I’m sure. If it makes you feel any better, it’s more so because I’m seven years older than you and not sure if I can keep up with someone who could fry me in an argument and not because you’re revolting or anything. You definitely don’t make me want to throw up. That’s more than I can say for my past few dates.” Alicia admitted to Hania. It was a little depressing knowing that there was never any chance for the two to be anything more than…. whatever they were now, but Hania could understand her reasoning.

“Well I’m glad I don’t give you an upset stomach or anything. “Hania rolled his eyes a little but smiled.

“And my hotel room windows don’t open...like most hotel room windows.” Alicia added on.

“Wait, my hotel room window opens.” Hania realized.

“Then your room is probably haunted, or old. Hotel room windows don’t usually open so people can’t commit suicide by jumping out of them.” Alicia began looking around for a place where it didn’t seem like someone would see them fly off. She would never admit it to him, but she was excited to experience flight without an airplane.

“I feel like that’s not exactly true, but I don’t want to argue and be proven wrong.” Hania made a mental note to investigate that later. The thought had crossed his mind, but he didn’t think that it was the legitimate reason. Alicia grabbed his hand and dragged him towards a collection of large rocks on the side of her hotel. Realizing what she was hinting at, Hania looked around to make sure there were no peering eyes, before donning his Raiden garb.

“Alright, that’s awesome.” Alicia admitted, before being scooped up by Raiden. Sure, she was only five feet, compared to Raiden’s five foot ten, but it still wasn’t exactly something she was used to. Raiden noticed that she smelled like strawberries, so at least that experience was mutually pleasant.

“Let’s go.” Alicia wrapped her arms around her pilot’s neck for safety, and Raiden zipped off into the sky. She didn’t ask any questions about where they were going; instead just trying to take in all the sights. She seemed almost disappointed after they landed on Juan’s private island, fifteen minutes later. Once they safely touched down, Juan swung down from a vine to greet them.

“Took you long enough.” Juan spoke, before introducing himself to Alicia.

“Look here Tarzan, it’s not my fault you decided to move the island.” Raiden allowed his hood to fall, since the two both knew his identity.

“I sent you directions!” Juan countered.

“You sent me longitude and latitude lines! Who just casually knows those on the top of their head?! You could have sent a gps signal or something!”

“What did you expect me to tell you? Turn right at the large body of water but if you’ve passed the dolphin you went too far? Not exactly a lot of landmarks up here, hermano. Stop scrunching up your face, it makes you look unattractive.” Juan teased; looking to Alicia for confirmation.

“Very unattractive. Stop brooding.” Alicia joined.

“Please, I’m fabulous. Now if we’re done with Juan’s poor directions, let’s get him up to speed.” Hania opened the floor for Alicia to tell her story.

“It’s not much to go off, hermana.” Juan spoke, once Alicia was finished talking. He was very attentive when she was speaking unlike Raiden, whom zoned in and out of his own memories.

“Hermana? I thought you hated people.” Hania teased. That year of Spanish he took was paying off.

“She’s not people. She’s Alicia. I like her.” Juan stated, as though the fact were just as obvious as the color of the sky. “Well, I don’t know for sure...but it sounds like you’re a Magi.”

“What’s that?” Alicia and Hania asked in union.

“Okay, Alicia, I understand you not knowing, but how do you not know, Han?” Juan was met with a shrug from his fellow guardian. “Magi is an umbrella term for those who are magically inclined. Sort of like...demigod. There are a bunch of different types, with their own abilities. I don’t know too much about them, as far as their differences and their abilities and anything like that. All I know is the names of the different types. Wizards and Witches, Sorcerers and Sorceress, Djinn, Magicians, Oracles, and Shaman. I think those are all the types. Beyond that, the only thing I know is that most Wizards and Witches are descendants of Circe.

“Wait, she saw stuff from my past. She’s probably an Oracle.” Hania pointed out.

“Not necessarily. That’s a basic skill for Magi. It requires touch, and it only works on certain people. Oracles are a whole different ball game. Skilled ones can literally control fate. It doesn’t rule it out completely, but don’t just go on that.” Juan corrected Hania.

“Well...how do I find out?” Alicia asked.

“Google it? Oh wait, I’m sure there's a personality quiz or something you can take. “Hania mused. “I’m being ignored, aren’t I?” He was.

“I don’t know. For demigods, like him, it’s ingrained in your very soul. Whether you want them to or not, your powers and heritage will surface.” Juan looked over at Hania, whom was grumbling under his breath. He nodded his head in agreement. “And for guardians, like both him and I, you’re chosen. It’s presented to you and you have to accept the role and powers; mind, body, and spirit.” Juan motioned to Hania again.

“It’s a very painful process. But so far, he’s definitely telling the truth.” Hania put in his two cents, before letting Juan continue.

“But for Magi, I believe it’s more of a journey of self-discovery. At least that’s what I learned from our oracle.”

“Wait, you’ve met your oracle?!” Hania questioned, rather loudly. He knew that each group of lords had their own oracle, but he didn’t think guardians were permitted to interact with them. That’s what Zeus had told Hania after all.

“Hush, hermano. Apparently, there are a lot of Magi in the world who never actually awaken their skills. It comes naturally, as they go through life and begin to know themselves. Really know themselves. What do you do?” Juan asked.

“I’m just a cashier.” Alicia admitted. She wasn’t exactly embarrassed about it, since it paid the bills. Still though, it made her seem so insignificant when she was in the company of a superhero, and someone who could create a literal mountain.

“What do you WANT to do?” Juan emphasized.

“I…” Alicia began to talk, but quickly stopped. What did she want to do? She was on her way to being manager at the store she worked at, and sure that would let her live comfortably. In fact, if anyone else had asked her this prior to this exact moment, that would have been her answer. But for the first time, she hadn’t known the answer to that question.

“I’d start there. And be open to change.” Juan mentioned.

“So, does this mean that we could be Magi?” Hania asked, genuinely curious.

"Maybe. But we'd never discover our gifts. I run from change and from things that don't go my way. And you fight it. We're like the tides when it comes to life, you and I, crashing and retreating…" Juan started.

"And Magi have to be like the surfer. Riding the waves, adjusting to them but never trying to change them." Alicia realized.

"Sounds like you've got it figured out." Hania smiled at Alicia.

"I do. Thank you both, for all your help." Alicia gave Juan a hug and made sure the two exchanged numbers.

"What, no hug for me?" Hania pretended to pout.

"I'm leaving him. You're my ride. I'm not leaving you." Alicia explained. "It's hard to believe that Juan is the younger one sometimes." Juan grinned at Hania when Alicia added the last bit on. To be fair, Juan was surprisingly mature for a seventeen-year-old.

"Come on, while I can still resist the urge to drop you into the ocean." Hania went to scoop Alicia up, but this time she leaped into his arms. He let the hood from his costume cover his face once more, since he knew that they would be headed towards the public. The two flew off and sped away from the island; noticing that Juan had been collapsing it as they were leaving. It seemed like he was also leaving on his own journey. Raiden had to wonder just how Juan could be so cheerful and upbeat despite the overwhelming aura of loneliness that radiated off him. "I meant to ask him if the fact that you smell like strawberries would be a clue." Raiden remembered on their flight back.

"I don't smell like strawberries. I'm not wearing any perfume today. I probably smell like sweat, or sand." Alicia sniffed herself. She had determined she didn't have much of a scent today.

"Your natural scent. You smell like strawberries, with a hint of desert sand. Juan smells like sunflowers, which fits him. Phoenix, the fire guardian that you might have heard about since you aren't too far from New Mexico, she smells like firewood. Again, that fits. My mother smells like a mixture of notebook paper and lilac. That fits too because of her job and personality. My poor mistake of a dad smells like summer rain and a bird coup. All those smells fit. So, I'm assuming yours does too."

"You ever think that has something to do with you, as well? I mean I don't think it's normal to be able to smell like that. You can do that for everyone?" Alicia pointed out. Raiden had never given that much thought. Whenever he mentioned it, people did look at him strange. He had just assumed he had a sharp nose. Could it be something more? He could even determine his own smell; a mixture of sparks and an unfortunately familiar summer rain.

"I don't know." Raiden admitted. As far as he knew, his father didn't have that ability. If Juan had the ability, he hadn't mentioned it so far to Raiden. Could he have developed an unforeseen power? Like Zeus loved to point out, he essentially was a weaker, carbon copy of his dad when it came to his powerset. Granted, they were amplified by his guardian status, and he couldn't shapeshift, but those were the only exceptions.

"Well, let's figure it out together." Alicia said, once they landed. They were forced to land a short distance away from either of their hotels to avoid being spotted. Raiden let his costume fade, and the two walked out into the public eye. Their hotels were in opposite directions, and it was time to part ways. She gave Hania a kiss on the cheek, as well as a hug.

"Wait, selfie!" Hania whipped out his camera. He had taken one with Juan too, and wanted evidence that this trip really did happen. Alicia smiled into the camera but waited until after the picture was taken to point out the lipstick marks on Hania's cheek.

"I'll be in touch, demigod." Alicia spoke softly so no one would overhear.

“You better be. Goodluck, magi.” Hania called back in a similarly hushed tone, as he watched her walk away. He knew that this wouldn’t be the last time they would be meeting. If nothing else came from this trip, Hania felt satisfied that he gained two friends that he could discuss all aspects of his life with.

The challenge

"Mom, I'm here!" Hania announced as he flung open the front door to his childhood home. They had been back from Brazil for three weeks now, and this was his first time stopping by since then. The young hero had been working overtime as Raiden, as if he had to make up for lost time. In fact, he almost felt guilty being away from his city for longer than an hour. He had been in regular contact with both Alicia and Juan, although he had some trouble with Juan considering he was international. Alicia was back in California, but Juan was somewhere near the Caribbean Islands. Still though, it was a little liberating to be able to talk about his dual life with someone other than his mother.

"You have a key; you don't have to announce yourself every time you come in. This isn't a sitcom." Naira walked out the kitchen just as Hania was closing the front door. She always got on him whenever he did anything that made him seem like a stranger. Even though he had his own apartment, she always wanted him to consider this as his home. Once his scholarship ran dry, it probably would be his home again anyway. It wasn't exactly an easy thing to balance college with being a superhero, and he couldn't imagine it would be any easier to do with adding a job to the mix. His mom had never wanted him to move out in the first place, but Hania wanted some personal space. Mostly, so if something were to happen and he had to return injured, his mother wouldn't worry.

"I know, I know." Hania plopped down on the couch, while his mother sat down on the loveseat. The tv was on, albeit mostly serving as background noise. Like his mother, Hania never really watched much tv. They had been catching up with what was going on in each other's lives the past three weeks; mostly Hania talking about the criminals that he had busted, when Naira's house phone rang.

"Hello? Oh, hi Kylie!" Naira looked over to see her son shaking his head and putting his finger to his lips. She stared, not so much because she didn't understand the gestures he was making, but because she expected an explanation. "No, I haven't seen Hania. He's probably asleep somewhere. I'll let him know you're looking for him." Hania's mother glared at him. She wasn't one to lie, but normally she was a little more understanding when it involved Hania's superhero life. This didn't seem to be the case. "He hasn't returned your text messages in three days. You're right, that's not like the social butterfly that he is. I'm sure he's okay though." She hung up the phone and looked at her son. Hania hated that look; that motherly look that spelled disappointment.

"It's not like that, I swear! I'm just sore from all the fighting and I need a little time to recover." Hania explained. It didn't seem to satisfy his mother, however.

"What you're doing is cruel, you know? I get that you need a secret identity to protect the people around you, and yourself more importantly. Trust me, I do understand that. But if you keep pushing people out of your life, eventually you won't have anyone." Naira continued to lecture her son, much to his dismay.

"You don't even like the thought of us together." Hania's retort made Naira chuckle softly under her breath.

"I don't. I think you need someone who can live as part of your world, and I do not think Kylie is it. But that is not the only way that someone can be in your life and care for you. A lover should be someone who can stand beside you, but you could use a friend that can help keep you grounded. Isolating yourself isn't protecting anyone." She gave Hania a hug that he reluctantly returned. She was right, per usual. Before he could reply though, something caught his eye on TV.

"Wait, mom. Turn that up." He whirled his head past her.

"Don't think you can get out of this."

"Mom! Please…" Hania convinced his mom. She reached for the remote and turned the television up so that the two could hear.

"Hunter…" Hania recognized the figure on tv. He was standing in what appeared to be a public park, with a rather terrified news anchor beside him.

Clearly, she was being threatened to remain there and give him the mic. To the other side of Hunter, however, was someone whom Hania didn't recognize. The figure was rather lanky and looked generally out of place standing next to the more built, Hunter. The male wore a suit as white as the snow with short sleeves, although his arms were so pale, they nearly blended in. On the chest of his shirt was a blood-red scourge and he bore a helmet that matched that very same hue. The armored helmet covered the mysterious fighter's complete skull and face, with curved horns sticking out. In the center of the helmet, however, was a small rainbow that seemed to have a slight glow to it.

"Is this the guy you were telling me about?" Naira's words fell on deaf ears. Hania was too focused on the TV to even acknowledge her presence at this point.

"My name is Hunter! You lot won't know me, but Raiden does." Hunter spoke into the microphone, while his associate remained silent. Hunter was back to using his fake British accent, which was a great source of annoyance to the young hero. "Raiden, I hope you're listening. I'm sure you are. I'm proposing to you a challenge; Me and my partner, against you! If you come, there will be no harm to the citizens here! If you don't however...well, I think you know how good of a shot I can be." Hunter's cross-shaped eyes peered into the camera. "Tik-tok, my prey."

"You know it's a trap…" The young hero's mother turned to her son. His fist were clenched tightly in anger. Without a word, she knew that he would be leaving. It was hard for her to separate the two; Raiden, the hero whom served the people, and Hania, her son that she would always try and protect.

"I know." Hania answered, after a few moments of silence passed.

"You have to go, don't you?" She knew the answer. Hania knew that she knew the answer. His costume warped its way around Hania's form in a brilliant display of light and lightning.

"I can't let anyone get hurt because I was too afraid to face an issue that I caused." Raiden spoke, before his mother embraced him tightly.

"You better make it back safely, wičháȟpi." Raiden nodded, before opening the front door and flying quickly into the sky. "Kick their asses, son."

Raiden zipped through the air, quickly approaching the area that he had gathered his enemies were. If only there was a way to lure them away from the public...at least he could feel better knowing that no one else was involved in their fight. It was his fault, indirectly, that Hunter was here in the first place. Sure, Hunter took some sick pleasure in chasing down supernatural creatures, but had Raiden not made such a name for himself....

"This isn't my fault." Raiden told himself. This wasn't his burden to bare. Besides, he had no idea who this other person was that was helping Hunter out. He didn't give off the same presence as his fellow villain, that was for sure. Hunter was more theatrical and methodical whereas this new guy seemed content to sit and watch from the shadows.

"There's the man of honor!" Hunter enthusiastically cried out as Raiden landed in the center of Roosevelt park. The young hero made sure to take a glance at his surroundings as he landed. Trees; numerous trees circled them which would give Hunter plenty of vantage points if he decided to start sniping. Juan would have been ecstatic to come here.

"All this fuss, just for me? You shouldn't have!" Raiden let his eyes linger on Hunter's associate. He didn't have the same supernatural eyes like Hunter, so at least he wasn't a descendant of Judas. Then again, if he were, at least Raiden would know what to expect. "Did you just snarl at me?" Hunter's friend looked at Raiden in a way he had never seen. His gray eyes, the only thing visible from his helmet, seared with hatred and contempt for the hero.

"Forgive my associate, he just absolutely loathes you." Hunter spoke in a southern drawl that was very clearly forced. Raiden had heard his normal voice and placed him having come from somewhere on the east coast. Not quite New York...maybe Delaware?

"Rainbow bright over there have a name?" Raiden motioned to the rainbow on the guy's helmet.

"Roy G Biv." His voice cracked a little as he finally spoke. Roy G Biv sounded nervous.

"Seriously? Yeah, you definitely belong with Hunter. I'm not sure whose name is dumber. So, Roy, my boy. I'm happy to take your supervillain virginity and all, but I can't promise I'll be gentle." Raiden's mocking seemed to get under Roy's skin. Hunter motioned for Roy G Biv to remain silent however and looked directly into the camera. Raiden had hoped that the news crew would have used the chance to move like everyone else, but they seemed to care more about the story than their own lives. No wonder they had such great ratings.

"You and I are a lot, alike aren't we?" Hunter had caught Raiden's attention, as well as the attention of the news crew and everyone in the area.

"How do you figure?" Raiden questioned.

"I am a descendant of Judas, the ultimate betrayer. This power that I have is the result of my cursed bloodline. You and I are the same in that regard. After all...that power of yours also comes from your cursed blood." Hunter had stirred the crowd. Murmurs had begun, although Raiden couldn't fully make out what they were saying. He was too busy trying to figure out what Hunter's purpose was for doing this. Raiden knew Hunter well enough to figure out that he never did anything without purpose.

"He's trying to get the city to fear me…" Raiden spoke his realization under his breath. Right now, Raiden was rather beloved by pretty much everyone. But he knew that they questioned his actual origins. In general, no one really knew much about irregulars. It was still a new concept in the world. Usually it was just treated like a mutation, but everyone wasn't convinced. This wasn't exactly the way to reveal his heritage to the world, but Raiden's hand was forced. He was definitely in check-mate. "Me and you are nothing alike! I am a demigod...the son of Thunderbird. He did not betray the world like your ancestor." Raiden decided it was better off to admit a truth than try and lie. But would it be enough? He still could hear the murmurs from the crowd, even though they had retreated to a safe distance. Raiden could not lose his city to some scumbag with a Zaroff complex.

“Semantics.” Hunter shrugged, earning a growl from Raiden.

“Enough of this talk. Let’s just skip to the part where I’m throwing you both in jail.” Raiden looked between Hunter and Roy G Biv whom both stared at him. The news crew had finally taken the hint and put some distance between the fighters and themselves for safety. “Let’s start with you, Crayola!” Raiden took off towards Roy with his fist cocked back. He wasn’t exactly sure what his abilities were, so he figured it would be better to knock him out before he had the chance to team up with Hunter.

“Red is the color of...rage!” Roy’s starch white suit turned a vibrant shade of red, as his lanky physique rapidly morphed from its nearly stick like frame, to an overly muscular figure that didn’t seem humanly possible. HIs biceps alone swelled several times larger than Raiden’s head.

“Aw sh-” Roy connected a punch with Raiden’s cheek that sent him flying across the grass hard enough to knock the wind out of his lungs. By the time he sat up, Hunter was nowhere to be found. Hunter was in his element, with all the available hiding spots within the park. A bullet whizzed by Raiden just as he took a step, causing the shot to graze his shoulder.

“Gotcha!” Roy used the brief moment the demigod was distracted to jump high into the air and come down overtop of Raiden with a hammer fist. It wasn’t the most graceful back roll, but Raiden managed to flop away just before the blow smacked into his head. Instead, the sheer power of Roy’s attack unearthed part of the ground.

“You’re messing with taxpayers’ dollars!” Raiden explained as he charged; connecting a whirlwind kick into Roy’s ribs. The hero proceeded to use the opening to pummel Roy’s torso with punches that had him reeling back. The rainbow might have been super strong, and the added muscle mass might have afforded him with extra defense, but he was still only human. Sort of. Raiden wasn't too clear on that at this point. Roy roared in anger and threw a powerful haymaker that Raiden attempted to block with his left arm. Big mistake. He was forced to quickly braced his left arm with his right just to avoid his limb from snapping in two. He was sent flying several feet away with a slight fracture to his left arm. "Fight through the pa-" Raiden told himself as he recovered, only for a harpoon to pierce his shoulder. "Mother of Zeus, that hurts!"

"Thar, she blows!" Hunter mocked from his perch, tugging Raiden in close to him. His long sword was drawn; allowing him to slash at Raiden once he was in striking range. The demigod was barely able to block the sword with the knife that was gifted by his father. Once again, he thanked Oya in his head for training him.

"Did you just call me fat?" Raiden knew he couldn't beat Hunter in bladed combat. As stubborn as he was, he had remembered their last encounter. Raiden could still move his left arm, but it wasn't as strong as it normally was. Hunter knew that and seemed to be directing his swings to force him to try and swap his weapon to that hand. Instead, Raiden jumped back and launched his knife at Hunter to create some distance. Raiden flew out the clearing, with Hunter trailing behind.

"Violet is for royalty!" Roy announced once Raiden returned to their battleground. His body deflated back to its normal size in a slightly nauseating display, before his body began to glow with violet streaks. "Kneel, peasant." Raiden thought that was kind of cocky considering he was a few totems up on the food chain, but his thought process was interrupted when he immediately crashed to the ground. The hero quickly deduced that this power involved some type of gravity manipulation.

"Sorry, last time I checked you weren't royalty." Raiden teased, before opening his mouth and shooting a beam of lightning directly at Roy. It hit Roy square in the chest and this time it was Roy's turn to be sent flying. The effects of his powers wore off immediately, and Raiden jumped up to face Hunter. "Are those sticks?"

“They’re called Tonfa, you uneducated dolt.” Hunter had been using two tonfa and was prepared to attack his opponent.

“You used to be so nice.” Raiden mocked, throwing a right jab once Hunter was in range. The older fighter dodged the blow easily and responded by hitting him in his arm. Raiden took a brief step back, before following up with two punches to his opponent’s gut. Both blows were blocked and responded with a knee to his chin.

“You’re strong, lightning rod. I’ll give you that.” Hunter had dropped his forced accents and spoke in a gruff whisper. All the while, dodging and countering all of Raiden’s blows. “But you’ve got no style. You’re sloppy and untrained; relying on your gifts to protect you. Sure, that speed and strength and bravado might be well and good against regular opponents...” Raiden had attempted to shoot lightning at Hunter, but he used his Tonfa to nudge his arm into the sky and cause the lightning to miss its mark. “However, against someone like me, that is nothing. My only purpose is to fight.”

“Shut up!” Raiden shot lightning into the ground in order to force some distance between Hunter and Raiden. He was irritated, more so because everything that Hunter said was true. Even though he had been trained by Oya, it was only for two years. Considering that was years ago, he was considerably out of practice. Oya was right; Raiden had gotten sloppy. He needed to concentrate and remember at least some of the things that he was taught. The only thing he seemed to retain was his swordplay, and that a distracted opponent was an easy one. Behind him, he noticed that Roy was now glowing green and clutching his ribs. That had to be some sort of healing power, since he was sure he broke nearly all his ribs with his kick. He’d be back up soon. Meanwhile, his own arm was mending but still wasn’t up to its full power.

“Show me some more of that demigod power!” Hunter charged at Raiden, interrupting his thoughts. Hunter attacked with his tonfa, but Raiden quickly weaved out the way. Several more of Hunter’s attacks missed as he zipped out the way to avoid them. It was true that Hunter was a much better fighter. Whatever this cursed blood of Judas was, it was no laughing matter. It was making him closer to a war god than an actual human, and Raiden knew one personally. But Raiden was stubborn, and much more than just a human. It was high time he started to use his abilities, even if he was holding back to avoid seriously wounding Hunter. When Hunter aimed for Raiden's head, he saw his chance. Quickly converting into lightning, he zipped behind Hunter in the middle of his strike and delivered his own lightning-infused backhand to the middle of his back.

"*Rubber...*" Raiden thought to himself as his blow connected. Hunter had added rubber to his clothing after their last encounter. It wasn't as if that would completely stop Raiden's attacks, but it certainly was helping. Hunter had crawled away from Raiden during his distraction.

"Now!" Hunter cried out, just as Raiden noticed Roy was back in his eyesight.

"Orange is the color of heat!" Roy's body began glowing with orange streaks, as he pointed at Raiden. The air around him superheated at once, before Raiden was consumed in flames. "Burn in hell, where you belong." Roy was much different than Hunter. Hunter seemed to enjoy fighting Raiden, and the two had much more banter. Even stranger, Raiden had a bit of respect for Hunter. At the very least, he was a man of his word. But Roy G Biv, was filled with nothing but malice and contempt for the demigod. All he seemed to focus on was Raiden's death, by any means necessary.

"Hell's flames are hotter than this." Raiden walked towards the duo, nearly unscathed by the fire. Raiden absolutely had never been to hell, but he thought the line was pretty badass. And he fought Phoenix who put him through hell, and her flames were hotter than Roy's. Close enough, he told himself. "Are we done here?" Raiden asked, scanning to gauge the reaction of the crowd. He was still on camera, even though the entire crew was hiding safely out of harm's reach. Hopefully mercy would let them forget that he was no longer just Raiden, the superhero in their eyes. Thanks to Hunter, he was Raiden, proof that gods existed.

"Not even close!" A familiar voice sounded from the sky.

“No. No, no. No, no, no, no, no!” Raiden quickly uttered, as he watched Phoenix land not too far away from the group of fighters. Hunter and Roy together were a challenge, but it was manageable. The three of them teaming up together, was an entirely different story.

“You don’t sound happy to see me, Rai-rai. You’re going to hurt my feelings.” Phoenix blew Raiden a kiss.

“Am I ever?” Raiden retorted.

“Comments like that are why we’re divorced now.” Phoenix held up her vacant ring finger.

“We were never married.” Raiden bluntly stated. The cameras were still on the group, and he didn’t need that rumor flying around.

“Sem-” Phoenix began, before Roy let out a bloodthirsty scream.

“Red is the color of rage!” Roy swelled back up to his unnatural physique. Raiden prepare himself for the charge, trying to figure out how he would defend against all three of the villains. “I’m going to kill you with my bare hands...Phoenix!” Roy shocked everyone, as he made a beeline directly towards Phoenix.

Three Way struggle

"Didn't see that one coming." Raiden muttered as he watched Roy throw a punch at Phoenix.

"Do I k-" Phoenix began, before the fist smacked her dead in the face and sent her flying into a nearby tree. Raiden winced after seeing the blow. She may have been his enemy and all, but he especially hated fighting women. Hunter also looked on with disdain from his spot; apparently deciding to remain out of the brawl between Roy and Phoenix. "Rude." Phoenix chastised as she got up from the tree, and then burned it to the ground. "Raiden, your friend is rude." Phoenix pointed at Roy, which only seemed to irritate him more.

"Yeah, not quite my friend." Raiden was tense. He had no idea what was about to happen next, and he had no idea how to get out of this situation.

"Oh, good. Because I plan to burn you all into a cinder!" Phoenix cried out; charging at Roy. Hunter had withdrawn a pistol from his right thigh and began shooting at Phoenix but failed to hit as she burned the bullets before they got there. Raiden quickly put himself in between Roy and Phoenix, which earned him a punch directly into the center of his back from Roy. Phoenix followed through by kicking Raiden into Roy and toppling them both over. Hunter leaped over the jumbled mess on the floor and pulled out a small knife to try and stab Phoenix. Raiden had to wonder how many pockets Hunter had to store all these weapons, and where he could order some clothes like his. Two pockets seemed practically useless when Hunter had about eighty. He felt like some sort of peasant.

"Watch out!" Raiden grabbed Hunter's leg and threw him backwards. Phoenix's attack narrowly missed its mark. "You guys have to leave! I can't protect you both and fight her!" Raiden exclaimed as he scrambled to his feet. Roy swung at Raiden again, but this time Raiden used his momentum against him and tossed him back onto the ground. Without missing a beat, Raiden shot a bolt of lightning towards Phoenix and hit her square in the chest. Hunter fired two shots for good measure at Phoenix. It caught his eye that Hunter was no longer attacking

Raiden, which was great.

"Yellow is for gold!" Roy shouted as he popped up. His entire body transmuted from its nearly translucent skin, to a vibrant and shiny gold hue.

"That's just inaccurate. How can yellow be for gold? Gold is a color, isn't it? Unless you mean the met-" Raiden began mocking Roy up until the point where Roy's metallic fist connected with the side of his face. Raiden went down; hard. "Yellow is for gold. Gotcha, big guy." Phoenix came flying in towards Roy and kicked him in his arm so hard, her own foot wrapped around it like a lasso; sickening, bone-snapping sound effects following. The scene was so horrific, it even made Hunter hesitate, and Raiden felt sick to his stomach.

"Well, that hurt." Phoenix flew back with her foot dangling, and bone exposed. Roy took the brief repose in fighting to vomit. For all his talk about wanting to kill the two guardians, Roy didn't have the stomach for it. Phoenix placed her arms around the injury, and it became consumed with flames. Within a few moments, her ankle was right back to normal.

"Well...damn." Hunter said under his breath. Raiden felt as though Phoenix had grown stronger since the first time they met, but he had no idea that it was on this level. Her healing was at least ten times as fast as his own at this point. Roy snapped out of his panic and charged towards Phoenix; running directly through the flames that she began spewing out of her mouth.

"Well it's not copper but…" Raiden closed his eyes and concentrated. As a guardian of lightning, he had the ability to connect with lightning itself. Shooting electricity from his body was something he could do on his own, even before he became a guardian. It was just enhanced by the magical energies that his body was embedded with. Manipulating the weather on earth, however? That was only made possible because guardians borrowed a portion of godly power. As soon as Roy was within range of Phoenix, Raiden called down a bolt of lightning from the sky that hit Roy directly. He was using Roy to amplify his own attack against Phoenix by bouncing the blow off him and towards her. The result was both villains being blown back. Roy was knocked out of his golden form, whereas Phoenix just rose back up. She shot a fireball directly at Hunter, surprising him. Raiden barely managed to place himself in front of the two; taking the full force of the hit. Raiden kneeled on the ground to recover, while shooing Hunter away.

"Why would you do that?" Hunter asked.

"No one dies on my watch. Those are the rules." Raiden managed to say between pants. He was going to need some time to recover. Hunter however, simply pulled a sword from his back and held it at Raiden's throat.

"You're an idiot. Now I can simply lob your head off and let those two duke it out." Hunter whispered. Silence fell between the two as they eyed each other down. Raiden screamed at himself internally but remained calm on the outside. He had a pretty good judge of Hunter's character by now.

"You could. But you won't." Raiden called his bluff. It was risky business in all actuality. Hunter hesitated for a second, before removing his sword from Raiden's neck.

"This isn't over. But I respect you too much to kill you if I didn't wound you myself. I'm not getting involved with those two either though. I'm content with watching until I find a chance to make my departure." Hunter admitted. Whenever he spoke to Raiden in private, he dropped the fake accents.

"Likewise." Raiden had to admit. His eyes snapped back to the battle just in time to see Roy, now in his red rage mode, tackling Phoenix to the ground and continuously beating her while she laid on her back. He had no idea why Roy hated her so much, but this was taking things way too far. At this rate, he might kill her. Raiden cursed under his breath as he zipped over to intervene. "That's enough." He grabbed Roy's arm and watched as he paused for a brief moment. Whatever the reason why he hated Phoenix, it was clearly a personal vendetta. It was almost funny to him. Raiden could easily see himself on Roy's side of things. That thought changed almost instantaneously though, when Roy threw Raiden on the ground beside Phoenix, and began hammering away at the both of them. Raiden felt his ribs giving out on him faster than a groupie's legs when they're invited backstage by their favorite musician. He had to get of this. Using all his might, he sprung up and wrapped his legs around Roy's arm. He looked over to see Phoenix had done the same. The two sat up and delivered a punch simultaneously that sent Roy flying into a tree. Raiden was out of breath, but Phoenix seemed...irritated. That was never a good sign.

"I'll kill you!" She screamed. Raiden had to lead her away from here and separate her from everyone. Without looking, he knocked her to the ground with a swing of his fist and zipped next to Hunter.

"Time to go." He threw him over his shoulder and then zipped over to Roy, throwing him over the other. Luckily, he had reverted to that green hue that Raiden figured was for healing. He had a strange bit of powers, that was for sure.

"Put me down!" Roy struggled, as Raiden took off into the air.

"Shut up, just pretend that I'm trying to be romantic." Raiden countered, making sure that Phoenix was following him before he began to fly faster. At this point, speed might have been the only advantage he had over the fire guardian.

"Separate, if you're trying to get away. She'll only be able to catch one of us." Hunter called out from Raiden's shoulder. He seemed more so desperate to be put down than to escape Phoenix. Still, he had a point.

"I'll make sure it's me." Raiden agreed with Hunter's plan.

"You're running?" Roy asked. His powers were healing him, but he accidentally healed Raiden as well. It must have been something to do with proximity.

"A cornered animal is the most dangerous thing you could face. A cornered, deranged animal is something you probably won't live to tell about. I like living, so it's time to fold 'em." Hunter spoke in a strange, southern drawl now. Raiden had figured this meant that Roy didn't have any idea what he sounded like or really looked like. Granted, Raiden still hadn't seen the bottom of his face either. It was like he was some sort of ninja who was known for covering their face or something but needing his special eyes for combat.

"Consider this partnership dissolved then!" Roy quipped. Hunter just laughed.

"This partnership dissolved faster than sugar in water, the second you decided to go all vengeance on the firespitter. "Hunter's words made Raiden consider dropping him. It was bad enough that he was speaking in this fake accent, but he drew the line at cowboy quips. "Fly near that lake." Hunter pointed below. Raiden dipped down and as soon as he was low enough, Hunter flung himself into the water. Luckily, Phoenix kept chasing the two. She either wanted Raiden or Roy.

"Your tu-" Raiden began, before Roy punched Raiden in the throat. The sudden blow made Raiden drop Roy.

"Blue is for sky!" Roy shouted, before his entire body began to glow the aforementioned color. He flew away; catching Phoenix's attention. Up until Raiden shot a bolt of lightning at her, however. Her attention shifted back to Raiden, as the two zipped along in the air. He just had to lead her far enough away that she would get disorientated, and then lose her. She was like a goldfish it seemed, or a child. If it was out of sight, it seemed to be out of her mind completely.

Phoenix followed Raiden for a while, which was his every intention. "We should be near Colorado by now…" Raiden wasn't the best at geography, but he knew he had been flying for a while now. He had passed a wide variety of mountains, and figured he had to have been out of Utah by now. The mountains that the duo were approaching were snowcapped; a telltale sign that he was somewhere in Colorado. It should be safe to ditch her now. Raiden stopped in midflight and turned to face Phoenix.

"Have you finally stopped running from me? You know I'm just itching to kill you." Phoenix grinned.

"It doesn't have to be like this, Phoenix. Kagutsuchi has poisoned your mind, but I'm sure we can get you help. Maybe even separate you from that deity inside of you. It's killing you, Laura." Raiden tried to reason with her. She seemed to actually be considering this.

"I've never felt more alive." Phoenix answered, before charging at Raiden.

"Worth a shot." Raiden transmuted into lightning and zipped out of the way before taking to the sky and bolting away. Phoenix didn't even attempt to follow, Raiden saw, but instead floated there shouting. He might have turned Phoenix loose on Colorado, but hopefully she just attacked the Broncos or something. That way, at least Raiden would have one small victory. Still though, he felt like he was doing an absolutely horrid job at being a superhero. He had three supervillains now, all gunning for him personally, all three of which he lost track of. And he knew that Phoenix was not going to let him get away next time. He needed to handle things one step at a time for now on, which was hard for him. First things first, however. Raiden needed to get home and get some sleep.

Father and son

Hania was inside of his apartment, punching his wooden practice dummy. It had been a week since his fight with Hunter, Roy G Biv, and Phoenix, and the trio were long gone. Hunter and Roy left no trail to follow at all, and he had lost track of Phoenix somewhere near Denver. He was pretty sure she wasn't sane enough to cover her trail, so all signs pointed to one of the fire lords helping her out. It was bad enough that he couldn't defeat and capture the three of them, but Hania couldn't even manage to track them down. Plus, Hunter's mocking had engraved itself in his brain. He was trained by Oya, even if it was only for two years. Hania was better than this.

He picked up the pace as he continued his assault on the wooden training dummy. Hania was trying to remember his training with Oya. "Use your gifts to your advantage. Do not try and use brute strength against your opponents. You are as swift as the lightning itself; your hands can make any man feel like they are up against a militia. Your feet can make it seem as though you are in every place at once. Your thoughts are so rapid, when contained, it is as though you are sitting in a war room calculating every move your opponent uses. The art of combat is just that; art. Do not attempt to replicate another's style, instead do what works best for you." Oya's voice was in his head, repeating words he had already heard. He could hear her every word clear as day. Too clear to be a memory…

"Oya?" Hania called out; now moving around the training dummy as he struck. He received no answer, but he could feel her presence lingering in the air. She was watching, or at least she had been watching. It was a shame too considering he rather liked Oya, but she was more reclusive than the other gods he knew. It was rare that she would make an appearance twice in such a short timeframe. She came around when she wanted to and left just the same. The wooden training dummy had now been spinning after every strike, forcing Hania to concentrate not only on his own fist, but dodging the "arms" that were attached to it. He had to move faster than he had been to combat Phoenix. He had to hit harder than he had been to break through her healing. He had to think several steps ahead of her to stop her from hurting others. He could do it…

Whack! One of the arms caught Hania in the side when he wasn't looking, causing him to stumble. He caught his balance and quickly converted to lightning; zipping around and striking the wooden dummy with more malevolence and frustration than anything else. For each strike, he would return to his human form, before transmuting into lightning and moving again. *"You're failing everyone, but what else is new? You should be better, but you're not. No one is going to trust you to be their hero now that they know what you are. You couldn't even convince your father to stay with you, what gives you the idea that you can convince an entire city to keep their trust in you. Your form is sloppy."* Hania's thoughts came rushing into his head. All the thoughts that he had kept locked away. He let out a frustrated grunt, before quickly donning his Raiden garb. With one fluid motion, he turned and withdrew the knife that his father had made for him and lobbed off the area that would have been the wooden dummy's head, and let his costume and weapon fade away.

This only frustrated Hania more, once he realized how long he had to save up to buy the practice dummy in the first place. Superhero life didn't exactly pay, and he hated asking his mother for money. His income consisted of his scholarships, which were close to running dry, and tutoring students around his campus. He got good grades in his psychology classes, sociology classes, and anything involving mythology, but it wasn't exactly easy to tutor while saving people from burning buildings and petty theft. Once you add in three supervillains to that list, well his social life and financial security were dwindling down at an alarming rate. "No use dwelling on it." Hania muttered to himself, as he pushed the training dummy back into the closet. Luckily, no one ever came over but Kylie, so he didn't have to explain why he had the thing in the first place. Come to think of it, did he even know anyone besides Kylie? Not that it really mattered, considering she hadn't been over in a while. The more he thought about it, the more he realized Kylie had been acting strange. She had been spending a lot of time with Ben, not that it really bothered him. Normally though, Kylie invited Hania along whenever she went to hang out with friends. Granted, he normally said no since he was always busy, but the gesture was appreciated. Plus, Hania had ran into the two of them twice while he was out and both times Kylie looked like she didn't expect to see him. It would probably help if he stopped avoiding her phone calls though. He made a mental note to give her a call soon. Not today of course; he had already decided to go visit his mother.

Hania opened his door and make sure no one was looking, before taking off into the sky. Eventually, Hania knew that he would have to find a different place to take off from. The more often he did it, he felt like the higher chance he'd get caught. Flying around his mother's house was always easy however, as she lived in the outskirts of town. Even though she had neighbors, there was such a huge space between them that they barely qualified. He ran up to his mother's house but hesitated to open the door when she heard her voice.

"Sweetie stop making me laugh. I'm going to start crying." She managed to force out in between her hysterical laughter. Whoever was her company spoke softly; too softly for Hania to fully make out. It was a male's voice though. Hania couldn't help but grin. For years, he had been trying to convince his mother to start dating again. All he wanted was for her to be happy, and not stuck waiting for someone who didn't give a damn about her. She had dated once or twice, to Hania's memory, but it had been so long ago that he was sure she had given up. He didn't want to be rude and interrupt, but he couldn't help but be nosy. He'd come in and act surprised, get a quick glance of what her new man looked like, and then roll out before things got awkward.

"*Solid Plan.*" Hania thought to himself, before using his key to open the door. "Hey mom, just here to visit!" His grin quickly faded once he stepped inside the house. "What is he doing here?" Hania locked eyes with his father, who gave a rather sheepish wave.

"Don't be like that, Hania. It's nice to have the family back together." Naira's attempts at reasoning with her son quickly went out the window.

"Since when did he decide to include himself in our family? This is the first time he's come to see you in years!" Hania felt himself getting aggravated all over again. Of course, he knew that Thunderbird had visited his mother on Hania's birthday. But that barely counted; after all, that was the first time in years, and it was only a few weeks ago. Or maybe it was just his aggravation still carrying over from earlier today.

“Don’t talk to me like that, Hania. I’m your father.” Thunderbird, for once in his life, decided to stand up to his son’s verbal lashing. Today though, Hania had time to argue.

“Since when? Since you decided to leave me in the dark for years about who you really were? Or when you decided a visit once every few years because giving up your godhood would be too hard? Or maybe when you missed all my birthdays and holidays. You weren’t there when I was learning how to be a man! You weren’t there to wipe the tears off mom’s face either! I was! So, tell me again, since when did you decide to become a father?” Hania gradually grew louder as his speech went on.

“Since I held you in my arms, seconds after your birth. Since I named you myself, Hania Abel Hawke. Since your seventh birthday when I used all my power to stop the thunder and lightning so your party wouldn’t be canceled. Or perhaps when I began to weep daily, as I could only watch you grow from a distance. I’ve been your father since the start, just like I’ve watched over you from the start.” Even though it was clear that Thunderbird was irritated, he still spoke slowly and calmly.

“Enough.” That was all Mrs. Hawke needed to say. Immediately the tempers within her son and her lover had faded away.

“Fine.” Hania relented, after a few moments of silence. “That doesn’t change the fact that he has no right to waltz in here like this isn’t the first time he’s seen you in practically forever.”

“No, it’s not.” His parents said in unison. Hania’s annoyance quickly turned into confusion.

“I don’t mean on my birthday. Before that, it was years.” Hania clarified. He was left stunned again, when both of his parents shook their head in disagreement.

“Maybe you should tell him everything, my love. I think it’s time.” Naira addressed Thunderbird. She then patted the cushion beside her on the couch and beckoned Hania to come sit. He was still confused but decided to sit beside his mother. Thunderbird sighed a bit, before turning to face his son.

“You know that gods cannot go down to the human world on a whim, correct?” Thunderbird started. This was common knowledge to Hania at this point. Lords were able to go down to the human world for brief stints of time, but they couldn’t use their powers. Otherwise they could risk tearing the human world apart. Most other gods would face the wrath of the other lords if they did so or weren’t even able to go down at all. The only exception were the war gods that were aligned with a group of lords. Like how Oya had aligned herself with the lightning lords. That was the reason why they needed guardians in the first place; to do their bidding. Hania nodded and motioned for Thunderbird to continue. “The exception to that are lords, however. Lords are able to seal their godly presence in weapons and items which we call divinities. Thor’s hammer, my knife, Zeus’ thunderbolt; all these are examples of them.” Thunderbird was still doing that rather annoying thing where he closed his eyes as he talked.

“Makes sense, I guess. I do constantly see you guys walking around with those things.” Hania had tried to hold Thor’s Mjolnir before and it nearly shattered his arm, so he figured it had been more than just a weapon. “Still though, I don’t see what that has to do with us.”

“Sealing our godly essence allows us to enter the human realm without tearing it apart, but there is a problem with that. All we have ever been is divine. When you take that essence away from us...we have nothing. In order to exist in the human realm, without the very thing that makes up our being, we need a tether. Something to ground us to this world.” Thunderbird averted his gaze away from his son.

“Something like what?” Hania had a feeling he knew what was coming next.

"Guardians. We rely on a guardian's lifeforce in order to exist in the human realm. It's the reason why we do not pick a guardian from birth, but rather until they are at least a teenager. It is also why we try to retire our guardians when they reach the end of their lifespan, if they do not fall in battle. Every second we spend within this realm; we take a little of our respective guardian's lifespan." Thunderbird looked guilty when he spoke. It wouldn't save him from Hania's wrath, however.

"So, you've been playing with human lives for years! Without having the decency to even tell us!" Hania bellowed. His mother attempted to grab his hand, but he jumped up from his seat. "Mom, how can you still be in love with this man? He's killing me!" Hania had to constantly remind himself that now was not the time for tears. But he was hurt, and he was furious. He felt betrayed by both of his parents. By Thor, whom he had grown fond of. Was Oya in on it as well? What about the other guardians?

"It's not like that, son. That is the reason why all of us, especially me, try to avoid coming to the human realm as much as possible. Ever since you became guardian, I have made it a point not to allow any of the other lightning lords to take frivolous adventures to the human realm. I remained out of your life for so long, because I want to ensure that you have a full one. Your godfather has helped me on this endeavor, but it hasn't been an easy task." Thunderbird's words calmed Hania down. He seemed genuine, at the very least.

"Wait, I have a godfather?" Hania's attention shifted for a second.

"Thor. You didn't know?" Naira smiled sweetly at her son. Hania had returned to his seat now, allowing her to embrace him. No wonder why Thor had taken such a special interest in Hania throughout the years.

"You two still should have told me." Hania snapped back to his original point. He was a little less angry now, but he still felt hurt.

"I couldn't tell you. We made it a point not to tell any of the guardians, but especially not you." Thunderbird earned a quizzical look from his son. "The reason why the other lords fear you...why they have grown untrusting towards us, is because you're my son. As a demigod, you have a stronger lifespan than the average human. You're more likely to remain in your prime longer and live longer than the average human. Strictly speaking, we are able to enter the human realm for much greater periods of time, and more than one of us could come at a time."

"They think you lot are plotting something." Hania had put the scenario together now. "So, what they did to the fire guardian...they weren't trying to make her stronger than me, specifically. They were trying to enhance her lifespan." Thunderbird's nod made him realize that he was accurate with his assumption. Indirectly, he's responsible for Phoenix's current condition; both the deity and the actual guardian. The trio sat in silence for several moments. It was a lot of information to take in, and Hania was unsure of how to feel about it. For years, he resented his father because he abandoned both him and his mother. Only now to find out that his father left so that he wouldn't shorten Hania's own lifespan, and that his mother was in on the entire ordeal. His head was spinning, trying to process exactly how he should feel now.

"Are you okay?" Naira broke the silence. Hania turned to look at his mother, and her warm smile instantly erased any anger he had towards her.

"Why are you here, Thunderbird?" Hania asked, instead of directly answering his mother. The truth was, he wasn't sure if he was okay or not. He wasn't ready to work through over a decade of emotional baggage to figure that out either. But Thunderbird never made social visits; something that he just confirmed himself.

"I have a mission for you, actually." Thunderbird mentioned in his rather sheepish tone. Hania stared for a second, before sighing. It had been a while since he had to go on an actual mission for the lords of lightning, but that didn't mean he was looking forward to it. The last time they sent him on a mission, he ended up fighting a Zhenniao. Given that for some reason, Raiden was extremely sensitive to drugs, poisons, intoxication, and hypnosis, saying it was an unpleasant experience was putting it lightly. Even with his advance healing, or maybe it was because of his advanced healing, Raiden ended up bedridden for a week after the mission. He even missed thanksgiving that year.

"Of course, you do. Can I use some time off and skip this mission? Let's give it to another guardian instead. Is there a rock guardian? Or maybe a water guardian?" Raiden was rather ignorant to the other guardians. He knew that there were a handful of guardians out there, but he only could confirm the ones that he had met.

"This mission is of...personal interest to you." Thunderbird admitted. Hania really hated talking to Thunderbird. His father always spoke in riddles; not even in a stereotypical way. It was just annoying as all hell.

"I highly doubt that." Hania shrugged.

"I thought you would like to know why this...what did he call himself? Roy G Biv was after you. Or rather, why he suddenly has powers." Thunderbird always spoke in a soft and calm manner. It was as though he had one constant mood. Naira was a little more excitable than her lover, but neither of them possessed the sarcastic and blunt personality that their son exhibited. Although, Naira did admit that her personality was a little closer to Hania's when she was younger.

"You've got my attention." Hania was hoping that there would be a way to blame the gods for this entire situation somehow, but he wasn't exactly the luckiest person in the world.

"Anuenue was captured by someone; whom we do not know." Thunderbird looked at his son, who made it rather clear that he had no idea who that was. "Rainbow goddess." Thunderbird added. Now it was clicking why that was relevant to Roy. His powers and his costume were very reminiscent of a rainbow.

"So, we basically have to track Anuenue down, and once we do, we just bring her back and stop whoever took her?" Hania questioned.

"More or less. We already know where she is. We just don't know what to face. But after seeing your battle, the other lords decided to let us handle it. It's very likely that this person you fought is connected to whoever took Anuenue." Thunderbird squeezed Naira's hand when he spoke, which made her smile. As much as Hania hated admitting it, his father did make his mother very happy.

"Alright. I'll address how creepy it is that you guys sit around and watch me do my thing later. Tell me where to go and I'll take care of it." Hania stood up and shifted into his Raiden costume.

"Not this time. I'm going with you." Thunderbird stood up and went over to his son. Raiden started to argue but decided at the last minute not to. Now, more than ever, he just wanted to get this over with. The duo walked towards the door and left towards whatever area that Thunderbird had not yet revealed.

What lies at the end of a rainbow?

"You really didn't have to come with me. I can handle myself." Raiden spoke, as he flew beside his father. Thunderbird had morphed into his avian form, in order for him to keep up with his son. His diminished powers had reduced the god's speed tremendously.

"This is a great opportunity for us to bond." Thunderbird naturally spoke slowly, but he always spoke extremely methodically when approaching his son. It was like navigating a minefield; one false step and he'd activate his son's explosive temper.

"You're about twenty-one years too late for that." Hania retorted back. Although it was a snarky remark, it was said with significantly less venom than that same statement would have contained several months ago. Hell, several days ago at this point.

"Gods do not see time in the same way that mortal beings do. It comes with being ageless." Thunderbird earned a stare from Raiden. Partially because it seemed like a cop-out excuse, but also because his choice of words was particularly interesting.

"Ageless...not immortal?" Raiden thought to himself. "How convenient." Raiden retorted after removing himself from his thoughts.

"Besides...we have high reason to believe that another god kidnapped Anuenue." Thunderbird's statement caused his son to pause in midair.

"Hold on. Another god?! Here on earth? I thought gods can't use their powers in this realm." Raiden had felt a twinge of anger swelling up in his chest. There was no way another lord was involved in kidnapping a god...was there?

“Shouldn’t. Not, can’t.” Thunderbird emphasized. “Any god can come and go to the human realm, with some extraordinary amounts of effort. The problem is that, without being associated with a guardian, and the magics that allow us to link to their souls, their power goes unchecked. They can come to earth full force, and the longer they remain on earth and the more they use their powers, the more they begin to warp the realm itself. Eventually, just a god's presence will destroy the entire realm.”

Raiden couldn’t help but chuckle. “So basically, you’re saying that, any god could decide they’re pissed off at humanity and destroy us just by taking a vacation?” Saying it out loud really made Raiden feel like everything he was trying to do as far as his hero thing, was basically for nothing. What good would saving the world do, if it could be destroyed in a matter of hours?

“In theory, but then the gods themselves would cease to exist. Gods only retain their powers and undying bodies, so long as they have mortals who are aware of their existence. It is that sole reason that we have made great efforts to continue inserting ourselves in modern society. In schools, in books, in children's games, the list goes on. As long as we are being referenced, we continue to live on.” Thunderbird responded. Raiden had remained still for a moment to listen, before deciding to continue on with their flight.

“So if someone were to write a book about my life, it would benefit you all because of all the mentions of gods it would have within it.” Raiden looked at his father, who nodded. “Let’s hope no one decides to publish a book about me then.” Raiden’s remark baffled his father, but nonetheless decided they should keep going. “So, which god is holding Anuenue captive?”

“We aren’t exactly sure.” Thunderbird admitted. “But we do not foresee any other being possessing the power to kidnap Anuenue.”

“Do you do everything else half-assed, or is it just parenting and information gathering?” Raiden glared at his father. Sure, he wasn’t exactly the world’s greatest detective, but he could at least manage to do the basics of figuring out what exactly he was up against.

"I've upgraded to half-ass parenting, have I?" Thunderbird was grinning, which looked exactly as terrifying as one could imagine a thirty-foot bird grinning would be. Raiden looked away; he hadn't even realized his leniency until his father pointed it out. Even more so, he hadn't realized that his father was starting to become more comfortable with him. This was an entirely different side of Thunderbird that Raiden was not ready to deal with.

"Shut up, before you end up as a bucket of fried chicken." Even Raiden had to admit, his response was weak. He decided to speed up, hoping that his father wouldn't be able to reply. It worked; or the deity had simply lost interest. "How much further do we have to go?" Raiden questioned. They were approaching what he could only assume were the Black Range mountains, but his father hadn't really said a word as far as how close they were.

"They're somewhere in this set of mountains." Thunderbird murmured.

"In the Devil's mountains, huh?" Judging by the look Thunderbird gave Raiden, he figured he hadn't heard that nickname before. It made sense though, considering his father wasn't even from this realm. "Hey, ugly duckling. Morph back into your...whatever form. The human looking one. People might be hiking around here or something, and it'll be harder for us to be spotted if there isn't a rotisserie chicken big enough to end world hunger floating in the sky."

"I am not a chicken; I am the Thunderbird." It was odd, seeing the deity pout, but clearly the chicken jokes were taking a toll on Thunderbird's psyche.

"I don't give a damn if you were made by Ford or if you do those really cool airshows; change your form. Now!" Raiden snapped, causing Thunderbird to rapidly switch to his human form. Of course, the real reason for this was that he had already been hearing people around the state express their concern over his origins. People generally still loved him whenever he showed up, but over the last few days he caught a look on a few people's faces that he wasn't used to: fear. Sure, criminals generally seemed irritated whenever he showed up. And to be fair, he did see a look of fear in some criminals' eyes when he showed up. But that was fear of being caught, not fear of Raiden in general. Raiden didn't want to give people any more reason to fear him, or to think that he was going to bring about the apocalypse or something.

"That was a bit out of character." Thunderbird had moved closer to his son and placed a hand on his shoulder.

"Yeah, because you've definitely been around long enough to be considered an expert on my character." Raiden swatted his father's arm away and continued to fly into the mountains. Thunderbird followed, making sure to keep a pace behind his visibly annoyed son. The two had just passed behind a rather tall mountain peak, when they both came crashing to a halt. In front of them, the entire area had looked like a Picasso painting. Some of the mountains were floating in the sky; while others appeared to be upside down. A river flowed from a cloud into a tree, that seemed to have purple leaves. Occasionally, the sun would flicker to an all too familiar blue tone, before switching back to normal. "What the hell is going on…" Raiden landed on the side of a mountain, which was somehow entirely untethered from the ground.

"This is what happens when we use the full extent of our might. Cataclysm. Soon enough, that sun will stop flickering, and this entire area will merge with the god realm." Thunderbird shook his head at the sight. Out of all the lightning lords, Raiden had to admit, he loved the human realm more than any other god.

"How do we stop it?" Raiden's voice was laced with disbelief and fear. His precious planet was going to be warped into something dark and twisted, for something that the entire realm had nothing to do with.

"We have to find Anuenue, and whoever kidnapped her. Once we do that, I can force them back into our realm." Thunderbird looked nearly as worried as Raiden did.

"How?" Raiden was scanning the area, hoping he would be able to locate the rainbow goddess somehow.

"It's part of our power when we become lords. We can force beings back to the god realm if we're able to get our hands on them. "Thunderbird held his palm out, and it shimmered the same blue hue as their realm's sun, before returning to its normal tone. Raiden nodded his head in understanding. They just had to get whatever god that was invading earth to sit still long enough to be grabbed. Raiden turned towards his father; grinning. He then sucked in a large amount of air in his lungs. "What are y-"

"ANUENUE! WE'RE HERE TO RESCUE YOU AND KICK THE ASS OF WHOEVER TOOK YOU! WHERE YA AT?!" Raiden bellowed at the top of his lungs, allowing the mountains to carry his voice.

"Do you really think that's going to work?" Thunderbird had covered his ears in the middle of Raiden's yelling. He was answered with a simple shrug.

"Wait...is that a rainbow?" Raiden was squinting at something in the distance. Sure enough, a rainbow had appeared, and appeared to be going directly into one of the floating mountains.

"I don't believe it…" Thunderbird joined his son in squinting into the distance.

"It must be Anuenue! She heard me! Don't ever doubt me again, featherhead." Raiden grinned while pointing at the rainbow. "Let's go get our pot of gold." Raiden spoke in a horrible, fake Irish accent. "Get it? Because leprechauns are known for being at the end of rainbows. Wait, are leprechauns real? Is that racist? Oh no, I've been around Hunter too long."

"Ahem. Yes. I get it. Yes. Yes. Who? In that order." Thunderbird answered, before flying towards the rainbow. Raiden followed close behind initially, but he quickly overtook the deity with his diminished power. Without halting or missing a beat, as soon as Raiden closed the distance between him and the mountain, he transmuted into lightning and crashed directly into the side of the mountain.

“Lucy, I’m home.” Raiden teased once he returned to his normal form. The inside of the mountain seemed to have been hollowed into a rather damp cavern. Although, the skylight that Raiden created did illuminate the area a bit. His father landed right behind him; flying gently through the hole. The end of the rainbow led directly to a woman whom was tied up on the ground. She appeared to be a cute, but plain looking Polynesian woman; her doe eyes constantly shifting between the seven colors of the rainbow. In the light, Raiden could see that he was only a shade or two darker than her and that she had bits of rock from being on the ground entangled in her thick, long black hair. “Anuenue, is that you?” Raiden had already known that it was. Not only was her rainbow colored, flowery dress a dead giveaway, but her name flew into his head once he focused on her.

“You’ve got to get out of here.” Anuenue had a light, almost high-pitched voice that matched perfectly with her petite frame. Raiden had started to question why she was so nervous, but he felt the hairs on the back of his neck stand on end. Reacting quickly, Raiden flipped forward and rotated 180 degrees; just barely missing a blow aimed at his neck. Once his feet touched the ground, he withdrew his knife and was barely able to block a sword strike from his assailant. His attacker moved in a blur; kicking him in the stomach before his eyes could register their form. Raiden was thrown back by the force of the blow but recovered to watch his father now locked in combated with the opponent.

“Nemesis…” The winged goddess’ name appeared in Raiden’s head once he finally was able to get a good look at her. She wore a pure white toga that hugged her muscular physique yet flowed in the wind towards her ankles. Her tanned arms were exposed through her sleeveless toga, however her facial features were hidden behind a silver, armored mask. Her mouth and chin were the only parts exposed on her face, although bits of fluffed, black hair extended out the back of the mask. Raiden had wondered how she was able to see without having her eyes exposed, but now wasn’t the time to argue about logistics.

“Nemesis! You need to return to our realm. Now!” Thunderbird bellowed. Although his knife was much shorter than Nemesis’ double-edged sword, he was still able to push her back. The goddess of vengeance flapped her large, white wings and flew directly in front of her captive. Raiden turned to face her once more, with his father appearing next to him.

"I refuse. Not when there is such a thirst for revenge lingering in my champion." Nemesis had a rather gruff voice for a female. Raiden turned to his father for clarification.

"This is how Nemesis operates. She gets drawn to individuals whom are particularly invested in revenge. The way her powers work however, is that she cannot give another being her powers. Instead, she has to take some of the powers of another god and warp them so that they are purely focused on what her champion needs to enact their revenge. Normally though, she doesn't stay in the human realm when she does this." Thunderbird never took his eyes off Nemesis as he spoke.

"I don't get it. Who is so hellbent on revenge that you'd go this far?" Raiden's answer came in the form of an all too familiar face suddenly appearing at Nemesis' side. "Roy?" Raiden questioned once his form fully materialized. It was apparent that Nemesis had summoned her champion to her side. Raiden knew that Roy hated both him and Phoenix, but he didn't think it ran this deep. After all, Raiden had done absolutely nothing to Roy G Biv before he got his powers. He didn't even know who he was.

"Son. Nemesis' champion will be more powerful as long as he is by the side of Nemesis. I need you to hold him at bay, while I try to force Nemesis back into our realm." Thunderbird spoke in a whisper. Meanwhile, through the skylight that Raiden had created, the duo could see that the area was still being affected by Nemesis and Anuenue's presence. Clouds warped above them into mushroom clouds, which was sure to scare quite a few humans if they happened to gaze into this area.

"How much of your power are you able to access?" Raiden spoke in the same hushed tone that his father had initiated.

"About thirty percent, without unleashing my divinity and damaging this world. That's about the average for all lords. The emperor, Zeus in our case, can use about sixty while in the human realm and not cause any damage. But thirty is plenty for Nemesis. She actually isn't all that strong compared to most gods. She's only dangerous in the way that she fights and that she can empower other beings." Thunderbird explained; still making sure not to take his eyes off his opponents. Roy suddenly shifted completely orange and unleashed a stream of air at the two. They split just as the area around them combusted into flames.

"He normally has to call out his powers!" Raiden shot lightning at Roy, whose body stopped glowing orange and began glowing blue instead. The villain flew into the air and charged towards Raiden. Meanwhile, Nemesis had charged Thunderbird and the two deities had been locked in a vicious blade battle.

"His powers will be stronger due to Nemesis' close proximity." Even in battle, Thunderbird was calm and collected when he spoke. Thunderbird ducked a slash from Nemesis, and his right hand began to glow blue. He moved to touch Nemesis, but at the last second, she cut a piece of her toga, and dropped that in Thunderbird's path. The second the cloth touched Thunderbird's palm, it immediately vanished from sight.

"I know exactly how a lord's powers work, Thunderbird. If you don't physically touch me, you can't send me back into the god realm! I will not go until my champion's vengeance is complete, and that boy of yours is dead!" Nemesis flew back out of Thunderbird's reach as she spoke.

"I don't get it. I don't even know you, dances under rainbows. Why are you attacking me? Is it my good looks?" Raiden teased, shooting out a bolt of lightning at Roy. The villain quickly dropped down from the sky and began glowing violet. With a tug of his hand, he increased the gravity of the air around Raiden and sent him plummeting towards the ground. As soon as he was in range, Roy quickly shifted into his red rage form, and delivered a powerful right hook that launched Raiden towards the back of the cave. At that exact moment, Nemesis had overpowered Thunderbird and launched him towards the back of the cave as well. However, Thunderbird recovered first. As his son came barreling towards him, he extended his hand; catching his offspring's hand. With a quick motion, the deity whipped his son right back at their foes. Raiden palmed Nemesis' head on his way back towards Roy and dragged her body along the ground; punching Roy with his free right hand as soon as he was back in range.

"Hold her!" Thunderbird bellowed, as Raiden came to a halt. Nodding, Raiden proceeded to put Nemesis in a full nelson. Lightning flew directly at Nemesis; leaving her smoldering from the intense blow. Even Raiden felt his skin tingle, so he knew the blow had to have wounded Nemesis. Before Thunderbird could close the distance however, Raiden was tossed away. The two sides regrouped with one another.

"You and that damned fire witch, took everything from me!" Roy cried, while Nemesis grinned at his side.

"I don't understand! I didn't do anything to you. I don't even know you!" Raiden had been trying to convince Roy that he had the wrong guy. Or maybe, he was trying to convince himself.

"Liar!" Roy shouted. His body began glowing an indigo hue, although it wasn't easy to immediately tell the difference between this form and his gravity form. That was, until a third eye appeared on his forehead. Roy charged at Raiden, easily dodging the wild haymaker that Raiden threw at Roy. Raiden attacked again, only for his blow to hit air. The instant that Raiden lifted his right foot to kick Roy, the rainbow-themed villain was already out of the way.

"Is he reading my moves?" Raiden thought to himself, as he felt Roy grab Raiden's now extended leg. Out of pure reaction, Raiden let lightning surround his body and shock Roy. Right when he released, Thunderbird leaped over his son and kicked Roy directly into Nemesis.

"We work better as a team." Thunderbird told his son. As much as Raiden hated to admit it; he was right. The two had a natural chemistry that allowed them to react to each other without words. They were in near perfect sync. Nemesis drew closer and Raiden reacted by blocking her blow with his knife. Thunderbird delivered a blow to the hilt of her weapon, causing her to drop it. Fluidly, Raiden grabbed the weapon before it touched the ground and slashed at Nemesis' wing.

Her own weapon embedded itself into Nemesis' wing, and Raiden shot a stream of lightning out of his mouth. The lightning hit Nemesis square in the chest and pushed her directly into her champion. Crack! Lightning fell from the sky at Thunderbird's command and hit his two enemies from the hole Raiden created in the mountain.

"Had enough yet?" Raiden teased, once the smoke cleared from the father-son combination. "Or are you at least ready to tell me why you hate me? I'd settle for who you are, really. Or we can just squash this and go grab some tacos." He was directly addressing Roy at this point. Roy said nothing, once he had recovered from the blow, and instead removed his horned mask and tossed it on the ground. For the first time, Raiden had been gazing upon Roy G Biv's actual face. His face had the same Casper white skin as the rest of his body, and his cheeks were significantly sunken in. His shaggy brown hair screamed "emo," or the younger days of that singer from Canada that Raiden absolutely hated. For the record, he hated the singer before he started peeing in buckets. A sort of, hatred hipster if you would. Still though, underneath the mask, Roy G Biv did look familiar to Raiden.

"Do you remember me now?" Roy shouted at Raiden. Thunderbird and Nemesis both stared at Raiden, awaiting his response.

"You're that one guy!" Raiden exclaimed; clearly stumped.

"Your boy irritates me to the point that I want to kill him myself." Nemesis directed her comment at Thunderbird, whom simply shrugged his shoulders.

"Yeah well, I feel that way about myself too sometimes." Raiden slipped. "I don't know who you are, Roy G Biv. I'm sorry, but I really don't." He quickly started his next sentence, before anyone could register what he originally said. He was sincere in his apology to the villain, but that didn't exactly mean it was appreciated.

"Phil! My name is Phil! And I lost everything thanks to you and that woman, Phoenix! I even broke my leg!" Roy G Biv announced his real name, before putting his mask back on. Suddenly, the gears in Raiden's head began turning and piecing everything together. He did know who Phil was. Sort of.

"You lived in the apartment complex that Phoenix burned down. You were the one who jumped from the window and broke your leg. I remember…" Raiden felt extremely guilty now. Because he saved everyone and tried to go after Phoenix, he didn't get a chance to check in on everyone. He knew a few people had broken their legs, and he knew that none of the apartments were saved. Raiden had told himself he would go back and check in on everyone...but he never did. The news had reported that the city was assisting in relocating everyone, so Raiden left it to them. Maybe that wasn't the best option...

"I lost everything! Everything I owned was destroyed in that fire! I was too distraught to work, and my job fired me! My girlfriend left me when she realized I had nothing!" Roy G Biv shouted at the top of his lungs. Raiden had to resist asking how he even managed to get a girlfriend while he was a decently looking superhero and was perpetually single.

"I'm sorry. I'm truly sorry. But you have to know, I didn't plan for any of that to happen." Raiden decided apologizing was the best course of action. It wasn't as though he didn't genuinely feel remorse or anything for the guy. But it was weeks ago, and Raiden really tried his best to do everything in his power to save everyone. Saving everyone's things just wasn't exactly heavy on his mind.

"You think your apologies mean anything? I lost everything because of you. You and Phoenix. So, I won't stop until I take everything away from you." Roy G Biv spat, before transforming into his red rage form. Raiden looked at Anuenue for a moment, and then to his father.

"This world is going to be permanently corrupted if we don't get the two gods out of here." Raiden told his father. Not only were the gods warping the world, but he was feeling the effects of Thunderbird's prolonged fighting in this realm.

“You’re feeling the effects of my presence here.” Thunderbird noticed, right as Hania thought it. He had been in the human realm for a while now. Ordinarily, Raiden probably wouldn’t have noticed. But the combination of the length of time and the fact that he was fighting in the realm was taking its toll. “I should have sent Zeus. He can at least remain in this realm with his own power for a limited amount of time.”

“Don’t piss me off more than I already am. You know that I hate Zeus. Now shut up and listen; we still have the advantage here.” Raiden whispered. Thunderbird looked at Raiden for a moment; trying to decide if he wanted to point out that Raiden hinted at not actually hating the avian god. He decided to let it go.

“We do?” Thunderbird kept an eye on their opponents, unlike Raiden.

“Yes. They don’t know that I’m holding back. If I blitz Nemesis, I can probably surprise her. Then you swoop in and get her back into your realm, along with Anuenue. With Roy G weakened, it’ll be easier for me to take him down.” Raiden explained.

“Okay, I’ll watch your back until you make your opening.” Thunderbird couldn’t help but smile at his son. He really was quite proud of him. The moment was killed however, when Roy came lunging at the duo. The villain cocked his massive fist back to throw a punch, but Thunderbird immediately stepped forward to counter. With his left hand, he deflected Roy’s punch while simultaneously sending him flying with a well-placed punch from his right. Nemesis ducked Roy’s body, only to find Raiden had hidden himself behind Roy.

“Tag.” Raiden kneed Nemesis in the stomach, before zipping around behind her and knocking her away. Thunderbird moved beside his son and without looking, the two shot a stream of lightning from their hands directly at Roy, who was in the middle of another charge. Raiden converted into lightning and got behind Nemesis, transmuted back into his human form, and threw Nemesis to the ground. “Now!” Raiden beckoned his father. Nemesis tried to move from the ground, but Raiden let loose a continuous stream of lightning to hold her down. Thunderbird moved swiftly, allowing his hand to glow as he grabbed Nemesis’ wing. In an instant, she was enveloped in a blue light, and vanished. Raiden was impressed with his father's ability, as he had never seen it in action. Whenever he went on missions, he simply had to vanquish the supernatural being. "Can she come back?" Raiden asked his father.

"Not easily. It is rather difficult for supernatural beings whom aren't lords to pass into this realm. Especially after having already been here, and considering I sent her into Tartarus." Thunderbird calmly explained.

"You mean hell?" Raiden could see that Roy G Biv was recovering in the corner; clearly surprised by his now diminished power. Raiden himself felt a little worn out though, and slowly made the connection that when Thunderbird banished Nemesis from this realm, it took a heavy toll on Raiden's own body. It's entirely possible that other guardians may be knocked out just from the strain.

"No, I mean Tartarus. While hell is a section of the underworld, it isn't the entirety of it. Tartarus is a small section of the underworld that serves as a supernatural prison for our more powerful foes. She won't be forced to remain there forever, but I expect that she'll be stuck there for a few decades or so." Thunderbird moved towards Anuenue after he spoke. "I offer sincerest apologies that you were drawn into this." With one fluid motion, Thunderbird cut Anuenue out of her restrains. She stood up, and smiled at both Thunderbird, and Raiden.

"Oh no, my loves. I'm just glad you're both okay." Anuenue spoke from her spot, before she was suddenly beside Raiden. Her hand extended out and stroked his cheek. The action made Raiden blush harder than he'd care to admit. "Such a sweet boy. Thunderbird love, are you still in love with the human? We would make beautiful children just like your son here." She smiled at Raiden, who didn't exactly know how to feel towards that statement. While it was technically a compliment towards him, it also felt like an insult towards his mother. Plus, anyone hitting on Thunderbird just felt morally wrong.

"Yes, very much so." Thunderbird grinned. Raiden rolled his eyes, while Anuenue sighed. They both sensed that he was being genuine.

"How lucky for her. I'm sure she is a beautiful soul, to have given birth to someone as gentle as Raiden love." Anuenue rubbed Raiden's cheek again, before walking back over to Thunderbird. "Shall we go, Thunderbird love? My presence here strains this beautiful world, and your presence here strains this beautiful boy. Perhaps in more ways than one." Anuenue was surprisingly perceptive.

"Son. Will you be able to handle Nemesis' champion if I leave?" Thunderbird questioned. Raiden hated that he never referred to him by his superhero name. He was so much more than just Thunderbird's son.

"Yeah, I've got this. Just go." Raiden couldn't hide all the irritation from his voice. Probably because he was too busy hiding his uncertainty.

"I've got to send you back the old fashion way, Anuenue." Thunderbird admitted. Raiden braced himself, after seeing Anuenue just nod and smile. Thunderbird's hand began to glow, and with that, Anuenue was gone from this realm. The lord magic exhausted Raiden even more, but he refused to show that. Thunderbird turned to say something, but Raiden simply shooed him away.

"I'm busy." Raiden pointed at Roy G Biv; Now fully up and functional. The lord actually looked a little sad but nodded in understanding. Thunderbird floated into the sky; his entire body shimmering in the same blue light that formed whenever he banished another god. He then faded from view, leaving Raiden and Roy staring each other down. "Just you and me now. Why don't you make this easier on the both of us, and just give up? Let me help you. I mean I don't exactly make any money doing this, but we could set up a crowdfunding account or something, right?" Raiden really didn't want to fight Roy anymore. Not only because he was exhausted, but because Roy G Biv just needed help. Phil just needed help. "Phil…"

"Don't call me that!" Roy G Biv screamed. "I don't want your charity now. You're too late! Orange is for heat!" Roy's transformation was much slower now that Nemesis wasn't in such close proximity. Raiden halfway hoped that his opponent's powers would fade once Anuenue was free, but it seemed that wasn't the case. The air heated up around Raiden all at once, but the fire that resulted felt rather dull compared to what he was used to.

"Okay, I'm sorry. But I don't want to fight you. "Raiden waved the flames off of himself and continued to stare his foe down. "If you don't want me to help you, that's fine. But that means I'm going to take you to jail. I'll personally speak to ask that the judge goes easy on you, and we can get you the help that you need." Raiden tried to be as calm as possible. Essentially, the exact opposite of his usual personality. Roy G Biv simply scoffed.

"Indigo is for perception!" His body morphed to its indigo form, with his third eye opening. Only now did Raiden fully study it and realize that the third eye was also a dull shade of indigo. "Don't make me laugh. I've noticed it, ya know. You're tired and weak. You can't beat me in this form! I'll win! I'll make sure you suffer, just like I have!" Roy screamed. Raiden felt bad for Roy, but he had offered up every possible way to help him. "I can see your every move, you know."

Raiden sighed. "I'm going to rush you as fast as I possibly can, and I'm going to hit you in your stomach just hard enough to knock you unconscious. No tricks, no fakes, just a straight rush. I'm sure you can see it. And I'm sure you know that there is no way you can react fast enough to block me. And if you try to block now, I could just break your arms on my way through to your stomach." Raiden knew full well that Roy G Biv was even less trained than he was at fighting. In his indigo form, he was no stronger than the average human. Actually, he was a little weak. Raiden tapped the toes of his foot against the ground. "Ready?" Raiden transmuted into lightning and was upon Roy G Biv in an instant. He reverted into human form and delivered a swift punch to Roy's stomach. Just as he said he would. Roy slumped over into Raiden's arms; unconscious. At the last second though, Raiden could have sworn he saw a smile on Roy's face.

"Yo! Chief Valo!" An hour or so later, Raiden had flown back into Albuquerque and was descending to the police station. He had Roy G Biv under his right arm; his mouth gagged with some type of cloth. The police chief had been standing outside having a smoke break with two officers when they spotted the hero. Immediately, the three withdrew their guns and handcuffs. Once he landed,

Raiden turned over custody of his foe to the police. “Don’t take that out his mouth. His powers are voice activated.” Raiden made sure to point out, right before the two officers had went to remove the makeshift muzzle. “His real name is Phil…. something or other. Johnson? He looks like a Johnson.” Raiden shrugged.

“Your detective skills are incredible.” Chief Valo sarcastically uttered.

“Give me a break. I was too busy dealing with him and his freaky rainbow powers to stop and ask for some ID. He lived in the apartment complex that Phoenix burned down a few weeks back, so if you can get a list of everyone involved then you’ll be able to figure out his last name.” Raiden watched the chief pull a notebook out and write down the information. Roy G Biv woke up and began trying to speak to Raiden, but his words were incoherent. “It’s okay. I’ll stop him before he gets a chance to use any of his powers if he tries anything.” Raiden motioned for the officers to remove the mouth restraint temporarily.

“I’ve seen it.” Roy G Biv chuckled. “Your face warped in the same thirst for revenge that mine is. I only wish I could be there in person to watch you lose it all. You’ll suffer just as I have. I only pray I get to see the instance it happens.” Roy laughed loudly, before another officer ran out of the police station with a muzzle to cover his mouth once more. Raiden remained silent at Roy’s words.

“Take him away.” Chief Valo waved his men and their new prisoner away. “Hey.” Chief Valo grabbed Raiden’s arm right before he started to fly away. “I know you’re a good kid. And you’re plenty capable. But if you find yourself in a bind, I hope you understand that you can turn to me.”

“Thank you. I can handle myself though.” Raiden lied. The truth was, Roy’s words had him a bit shook up.

“We may not be in the exact same situation, but I know what it’s like to have the weight of the world on my shoulders. Twenty-one isn’t exactly an age where you have a wealth of life experience either.” Chief Valo pointed out. Raiden froze in his place and stared at the Chief for a moment.

“How long have you known?” Raiden figured that Chief Valo wasn’t just making a blind guess about his age.

“I figured out who you were about three months after you went public. Your mannerisms are the same as when I arrested you and Kylie for deciding to...acquaint yourselves better at the mall a few years back. You were just as impulsive back then as you are now. But you’ve always been a good kid at heart. Your secret is safe with me, so long as you never give me reason to come after you.” Chief Valo patted Raiden on the shoulders.

“We were in a car. In a parking lot. At night. Don’t make it sound so sleazy.” Raiden had put the situation behind him long ago. It took a lot of sucking up for Chief Valo to let him take all the blame. His mom nearly killed him when she found out but settled on grounding him for eight months and forcing him to do community service. Sixteen was a strange year for him. “I appreciate you looking out for me, Chief. If something comes my way that I can’t handle...I’ll consider involving you.” Raiden was a little more sincere this time. He then flew into the air, and away from the station; choosing to be alone to contemplate Roy G Biv’s cryptic message.

To catch a firebird

Things had been going suspiciously well for Hania over the past two weeks. Phil, whose last name was Zackerman and not Johnson, had been the definition of compliance in prison. Even with his muzzle removed, he made no attempts to use his powers, and only requested to watch the news every day. Even when attacked by someone much bigger in prison, Phil took the beating and simply smiled. He either was a truly broken man, or a truly satisfied one. Raiden had been to see him once to make sure he was staying in line, but all the supervillain did was look at him and utter a single word.

"Soon." Phil's words remained in Raiden's head for several days after the event. Still though, he was behind bars. Neither Phoenix nor Hunter had shown up over the course of the last few days, which Raiden decided to count as a win. Thunderbird made no attempts to contact him over the past two weeks, minus a message he found under his door following the incident with Anuenue and Nemesis. Apparently, the gods had gotten together and decided that Nemesis would remain in Tartarus for five years, and Anuenue wanted a selfie with him. Did gods even have phones or cameras? As far as crime was going, it was the usual. Some petty theft here and there, and a single bank robbery that Raiden managed to stop before they even left the door. Even Hania's social life had improved; managing to find time to tutor a couple freshman to put some money in his pocket. Phil's omen had faded from his mind at this point, because life couldn't be going smoother.

"Hey mom, let's go to Mexico next year." Hania had been at his mother's house. A pile of college books had been scattered along the floor, with Hania lazily plopped down in the center of them. He had decided to get a head start on the fall semester, having finally picked his courses.

"Is this your way of asking me to make you tacos?" Hania's mother had been sitting in her recliner, reading a book. She barely looked up from it when her son spoke, but he knew that she was actively listening.

"Mom, you never have to question if I want tacos." Hania pointed out. He had pushed aside his psychology book and began looking at his sociology book. He wasn't exactly thrilled about minoring in sociology, but Hania was notoriously bad at math. Plus, he had finally decided that he would rather be a psychologist instead of a psychiatrist. The fact that math was not as heavily involved with psychologist work was a major factor in that decision. It wasn't that he explicitly hated math, but it was more along the lines of preferring to shovel up cow manure while dismantling bombs than actively doing the subject. So maybe it was hatred.

"Fine, wičháȟpi. I'll make tacos tonight." Naira was too engrossed by her book to look up at her son. She seemed to be nearing the end of her story, after spending the last few weeks reading it. His mom was a bookworm, but her busy work schedule normally meant that she would be reading the same book for months on end.

"Glad to see that you're working hard to keep that title of best mom." Hania mused, before feeling his phone vibrate against his thigh. He had half hoped that it would have been Juan or Alicia calling; both of which he hadn't heard from in a while. Still, seeing Kylie's name pop up on the screen wasn't exactly a disappointment. "Sup fire crotch. Nothing, just chillin' at my mom's house. Nah, I can come over for a bit and be back for dinner. Alright, see ya soon." Hania ended the short phone conversation.

"How are things between you two?" Naira peered up from behind her book. This was her first time doing so since Hania got there an hour ago.

"Me and Kylie? We're better...yeah, I'd say we're good. I get the feeling that she's hiding something from me though." Hania admitted. Her behavior over the last few weeks had been rather strange, and now that he wasn't dealing with supervillains every few days, it was tapping the back of his brain.

"Probably because she can sense that you're hiding something from her." Naira placed her bookmark, a white feather with a red tip, inside of her book and shut it. Apparently, this conversation warranted her full attention.

“I don’t know if she’s that perceptive.” Hania was a little worried. The number of people whom involuntarily knew about his secret identity was growing at a rate that he wasn’t comfortable with. Hopefully, she was wrong.

“She might not know what you’re hiding, but don’t go underestimating us women. When we care about someone, we can pick up when they’re feeling or acting different.” Naira pointed out.

“I get that, mom. But what am I supposed to do? Just walk up to her and reveal who I really am?” Hania knew he had his mom’s point disproven. It wasn’t anything he could do about hiding things from Kylie.

“Yes.” His mom’s answer threw Hania for a loop. “Kylie is your friend. She may not have been the most ideal girlfriend, although I’d like to point out that you could have been a better boyfriend, but she is certainly a wonderful friend to you. I like her having that role in your life.”

“What if she gets hurt?” Hania asked.

“What if I get hurt? Or Juan? Or Alicia? The people who have gravitated towards you want to be part of your life, no matter what. If you explain to her the risk, I guarantee she will be as careful as I am. If you don’t want to tell her for your own personal reasons then that’s one thing, but that means you should tell her that you can’t be her best friend. Best friends wouldn’t keep things from each other. Same goes for significant others, while we’re on that subject. Besides, you have such a warm and honest heart. I don’t want to see that heart corrupted trying to keep up a lie.” Naira was right, as usual.

“I promise, that I will consider what you said. Is that a fair compromise?” Hania was still trying to sort through his mess of a mind to figure out his feelings towards his father and trying to figure out what Kylie was hiding from him. Adding this heavy decision on his mind wasn’t making things any better for him.

"That's all that I can hope. I'm just offering you some advice, but it's your life. Now go catch up to your friend and tell her I said hello. Dinner should be done by the time you come back." Naira walked over and hugged her son tight.

"I love you mom. Thank you. Now go finish reading your book, so you can be done before I get married and put my children through college." Hania teased as he walked towards the door.

"I love you too, Han. And I'll have you know that I will be finished this book tonight!" Naira called out as she watched her son open the door, look both ways, and fly off into the sky.

"I would have picked you up, ya know." Kylie mentioned once she opened her front door. Hania had made sure to fly a little slower than usual to account for travel time. It took him about forty-five minutes to get from his mom's house to Kyrie's, which in all honesty was still a little too fast.

"Oh, it's okay. My mom's neighbor does Uber, so I caught a ride instantly." Hania really needed to get a car. At least for appearance's sake. Once Hania walked into Kylie's living room, he plopped down on the couch. He had noticed a blue cap sitting on the table, which was odd considering he knew that Kyrie's dad hated blue. He considered pointing it out, but he didn't particularly care that much. It was just something that caught his eye.

"Have you picked your classes?" Kylie was a biology major, so she always took the classes that he hated. She happened to take a psychology class and mythology class to pad her GPA a little.

"For the most part, I guess. If I'm being honest, I'm really not feeling school this semester." Hania had to admit. Trying to keep up with his social life, his superhero life, and his school life was exhausting. But he wasn't some billionaire playboy with childhood trauma, and he didn't have any companies to inherit or some other cliché. Somehow, he'd need to make money to survive. Charging for his superhero services just felt...wrong though. Sure, he did have some money saved up from his college scholarships, but it wasn't a large amount. Eventually, that was going to run dry.

"You're not going to drop out, are you Han?" Kylie sat next to Hania on the couch.

"Nah, my mom would kill me." Hania wasn't exactly telling a lie. "Something drastic would have to happen to make me drop out. Like someone removed my heart or something." Hania stared at Kylie when he spoke, for an extended amount of time. It caused her to raise an eyebrow at him. "Are you hiding something?" He didn't even mean to say it out loud. No taking it back now though.

"Are you?" Kylie retorted. The room fell uncomfortably silent at that point. Should Hania just open his mouth and tell her his secret? That this entire time, he was both a superhero and a demigod? Could he protect her when things went south? She already was identified as someone close to him by one of his villains, but he did manage to stop him. "That's what I thought." Kylie's voice snapped Hania out of his thoughts. "Whatever it is, is either too important for you to tell your best friend…or we've just grown further apart than I thought."

"Kylie…" Hania began, but Kylie shook her head.

"You don't owe me any explanation. Plus, I don't want one. Not like this. It'll just feel forced. Whatever it is, just know that I worry about you, and you can tell me when you're ready." Kylie turned on the television after her statement. Hania sighed a bit of relief. He really wasn't sure if he was ready to tell Kylie that he was Raiden, so at least this way he could think on his decision more.

"Wait, what about you? You think you're slick, don'tcha?" Hania mused.

"I'll show you my secret, when you show me yours." Kylie barely looked up from the TV when she spoke. A smile was clear on her face though.

“Isn’t that how we lost our virginity?” Hania’s joke made Kylie pick up a book that was planted on the coffee table and smack him with it. “Oh! That’s the same book my mom is reading.” Hania realized, once her assault had stopped.

“Is it? I figured mama Hawke would be into this. I just kind of started it though, so it’ll be awhile before I actually finish it.” Kylie pointed out. Hania could tell from a glance that was true based on how close her bookmark was to the front. He started to say something else on the manner, but the basketball game that was on TV being interrupted by an anchorwoman claiming breaking news distracted him. The volume was down all the way, but he didn’t need it. The anchorwoman immediately cut away to the heart of Albuquerque; Phoenix flying overtop throwing fireballs at random citizens. Kylie covered her face in disgust, but Hania had to remain as calm as possible, even if he felt the flames of anger welling up in his chest. He had to think of a way out of this situation, without making Kylie catch on.

“Think...think...” Hania was struggling, when his own personal deus ex machina reared itself. His mom must have saw the news and immediately called his phone. “Yeah mom, I see it too.” He picked up the phone and began piecing his plan together. “Mom, you didn’t have to send an uber to get me. I know you’re worried, but Kylie isn’t too close to there.” This had absolutely nothing to do with what his mom was talking about on the phone, and Hania felt bad for having to ignore her cries to be safe and to not fight her if he could avoid it. “I know you feel safer when I’m home with you during these things. I’ll go jump in the Uber right now. I’ll see you soon.” Hania hung up the phone and looked at Kylie. “You know how she is.”

“Yeah, I do.” Kylie smiled before hugging Hania tightly. “Get there safe and be careful, okay?” He felt bad telling her that he would be, considering he was going right into danger, but he nodded anyway.

“Stay inside and lock the doors. I’ll call you a little later.” Hania bolted out the door and down the street, searching for a safe place to take off from. He ended up ducking behind an abandoned house on the corner, summoning his Raiden garb, and taking off into the air.

"Phoenix! Stop!" Raiden had gotten to the where Phoenix was, just as she threw a fireball towards a building.

"Raiden! There you are!" Phoenix had nearly snarled at Raiden when he arrived. She was completely animalistic at this point. "I'm going to kill you! Then burn this entire city to the ground!"

"If you want my attention, you could have just called me." Raiden teased, trying to stall for time so that the stragglers underneath them could get away. They weren't very high up in the sky, and collateral damage was high on his list of things he tried to avoid. Followed shortly by peach cobbler, due to childhood trauma in the form of severe food poisoning.

"No jokes!" Phoenix charged at Raiden and kicked him directly in the ribs. She followed up with a ball of fire launched point blank at his head; sending him flying into the side of a nearby building. Phoenix was stronger than she had ever been. Luckily, Raiden had been training. The hero launched several bolts of lightning at Phoenix all at once, before transmuting himself into lightning and moving behind her. She was too distracted trying to swat away the smaller lightning bolts to notice Raiden until he was shooting a stream of lightning at her back. Fighting females really bothered Raiden, but she was becoming a rather sizeable threat. The force of the blow shot Phoenix like a cannon into the ground. Like the poem however, still she rose.

"Phoenix, you don't have to do this." Raiden tried to convince his foe. She just stood in place however; breaking out into hysterical laughter.

"What do you know of what I have to do? What do you know about me at all? I'm prepared to go all the way." Phoenix held her hands up and began generating a massive orb of fire. It looked like the size of a monster truck's tire; a highly compressed ball of flames. She launched the ball at Raiden, who responded with his own feat of elemental fury. A large bolt of lightning flew from the sky once Phoenix had launched the fireball and dissipated it. The young hero followed up by spewing bolts of lightning from his hands in order to strike down the tiny balls of fire that had erupted from their colliding attacks.

"You can't win, Phoenix. This is your last chance. Give up and let me find you some help." Raiden contemplated adding finding her a strait jacket to that statement but decided that wasn't very welcoming. The fact of the matter was, with Phoenix being stronger than she normally was, the fire guardian was quickly approaching equal levels with him. A drawn-out fight might result in him losing when her healing abilities were factored in.

"Kagutsuchi will not allow me to fail." Phoenix charged at Raiden, who ducked the blow and delivered a well-placed strike to her ribs. Phoenix didn't even flinch as she moved to kick Raiden, but Oya's training was returning to the forefront of his mind. A lightning quick jab to her hip stopped the kick from connecting, and the open palm strike to her chin sent her flying backwards. The one thing that Phoenix would never have over Raiden, was speed.

"I'm stronger than you, Phoenix." Raiden mocked.

"I know." Phoenix' answer threw Raiden off.

"You do?" Raiden questioned.

"Yes, I do. But it's okay." Phoenix began, before moving closer to Raiden. She ducked the kick that Raiden attempted to deliver and placed her hands directly in his face. The guardian of fire then created flames brighter than she ever had before. The intense light emissions that flew out from the flames warped Raiden's vision, until everything went completely white.

"Sh-" Raiden covered his eyes too late, and felt his eyes burning in their sockets. He was at the very least, temporarily blind. Even though he felt his body responding to the ailment and was working on healing it, this wasn't exactly an ideal situation for fighting.

“Remember; I know who you love most.” Phoenix whispered in the blinded Raiden’s ear, before laughing. Raiden tried to swat at Phoenix, but she easily moved out the way. “I can’t wait to watch them burn, my hero.” Raiden swatted again, only to have the same result. Suddenly, Raiden heard screaming from underneath him. Without his vision, he couldn’t really see what Phoenix did, but he felt the area beneath him heat up significantly. “So many people to let down. This is the life you asked for, right hero boy? Good luck.” Phoenix kissed Raiden on the forehead, just quick enough to avoid the headbutt he threw at her. Thinking quickly, Raiden opened his mouth and shot out a bolt of lightning. Phoenix, however, had already left.

“What do I do?” Raiden questioned out loud as he floated in the sky. His vision was completely gone, his loved ones were being hunted, and his city was burning beneath his feet.

The hardest choice

"Don't panic, don't panic." Raiden thought to himself, as he proceeded to panic. He opened his eyes, only to see all white. His eyes still felt like a midsummer's day on Venus, but the bubbling sensation that followed the heat meant that his healing factor was working. Still though, it wasn't working fast enough to begin saving the people underneath him. Plus, Phoenix was up to something. Someone he knew was in danger, and the next few moments had to be played out very quickly.

"Help!" Someone cried out; their voices laced with pain. Raiden couldn't just sit there and ignore them, hoping his vision would get better. Raiden clumsily plummeted to the ground, and since he couldn't figure out when to slow down and touch down gently, he smacked against the gravel hard. While picking himself up, he tried to open his eyes again. They no longer felt like two tiny slivers of hell, but more like stepping onto the hot sand on a beach. Still though, his vision was nothing but pure white.

"Where are you?" Raiden decided to try and trust his ears instead of his vision. "Yell!" Raiden looked like he was drunk the way he was stumbling around and was sure that the tabloids would have a field day with this.

"I'm here!" The voice, apparently a younger male, sounded out. Whoever it was, had a distinct Hispanic accent. It didn't seem Puerto Rican like Juan was...perhaps Mexican? Wherever the guy was from, Raiden was determined to save him. Immediately, the hero flew towards the voice...directly into fire. Dropping from the sky and rolling to put out the flames, Raiden decided to run instead. Luckily the guy was smart enough to catch on that there was a problem and continued to sound out and direct Raiden. "Take three steps to your left!" Raiden followed the instructions. "Now, I'm straight ahead! Um...twenty feet!" Raiden leaped forward with his arms out first and was able to grab his helper in one fluent motion.

"I've got you." Raiden told the random citizen. He was solid but wasn't quite as heavy as the average adult. The way he clung to Raiden's neck also gave

Raiden reason to believe that he couldn't have been much older than sixteen. Probably closer to fourteen or fifteen.

"You can't see?" The teen questioned. Raiden attempted to open his eyes again, before shaking his head. His eyes no longer burnt with the white-hot intensity of a thousand suns, and he no longer saw pure white either. Instead, all he saw was darkness. Occasionally, a speck of light entered his eyes, but nothing that was close to actual vision. Trembling, the teen climbed over Raiden's shoulder so that he was hanging off his back. "People are dying, Raiden. If you can't see...I'll have to be your eyes." His voice quivered as he spoke.

"What's your name, kid?" Raiden was moved at the teen's bravery. It felt weird just calling him kid, especially considering the age gap between the two was probably only five or six years.

"Jose." He answered, tightening his grip around Raiden's neck. Raiden wasn't terribly tall himself, perhaps average at best, so Jose couldn't have been more than five foot six.

"Jose, I'll make sure everyone here today knows that you saved them. Not me. Now, tell me where to go." Raiden began floating above the ground, with Jose in tow. He'd have to be careful not to fly too fast with his extra passenger.

"Two people are trapped behind a wall of fire directly in front of us, maybe fifteen feet." Jose pointed, forgetting that Raiden couldn't see that.

"Got it. Hold on and I'll fly up over it and grab them." Raiden was worried to death about everyone that was close to him, but he had to focus on what he could do in this very moment. The faster he saved everyone else, the faster he could move on. So, Raiden flew, grabbing the two out of the fire as fast as he could and placing them safely on the ground. He heard them thank him, followed by the scattering of feet in the opposite direction.

"Oh god...everything is burning. Even the fire trucks!" Jose cried in horror. Raiden had wondered why there were no fire trucks on the scene. Turns out there were, they just took on their name a little too literally. There were more trucks in the distance though; apparently coming in their direction.

"Things can be replaced! Let's worry about the people! I know it's scary Jose, but I really need you." Raiden thought back to Roy G Biv and how that one fire ruined his life. If nothing else, Raiden was determined to make sure this event created heroes, not villains.

"Okay...okay. People are helping each other out of the fire now. Firefighters are on the scene helping too, and I can see some fire trucks headed this way. Go...southwest and up. There is a building that's on fire and I see someone hanging out the window. Three stories up? No... maybe five." Jose held on tightly as Raiden bolted off in the direction of the building.

"Just tell me when to st-" Raiden ran smack into the building shoulder first; nearly dislocating it.

"Stop." Jose sheepishly mumbled.

"Gee, thanks. I think I figured that out on my own." Raiden, visibly annoyed, retorted. Luckily, Jose was far enough back that he didn't get hurt. Plus, the outside of the building was hot, but not inflamed. At least not where he ran into it anyway. "Higher or lower?"

"Up about two stories and then over to your right." Jose was trying his best to sound sure of himself. Raiden had to forgive the kid. Raiden had only been doing the superhero thing for a little under two years now. Even though he was a guardian at the age of thirteen, he hadn't really done much in the way of saving people. He spent two years in training, and then a few years simply completing missions for the lords. It was only two years ago that he had gone full time hero. This was a terrible burden to place on someone like Jose. Raiden followed his instructions and was met with a woman who threw herself in Raiden's arms. Once she was placed on the ground, she ran off to what Raiden presumed was safety. By now, fire trucks were obviously on the scene.

“How are we looking?” Raiden asked.

“I think everyone is going to be okay. There’s a few people left but it looks like the firefighters are taking care of that.” Jose mentioned; using Raiden’s hood as a place to grip. Luckily, magic held the hood in place. Raiden opened his eyes, praying that his vision would return. Now, he was at the point where everything was blurry, but he could make out some general shapes at least.

“You did great. Go ahead and get down now.” Raiden turned to face Jose once he was safely on the ground. Raiden’s brown eyes still couldn’t quite make Jose’s face out. He even tried to surround himself in lightning so that his eyes would shift to gold; hoping his demigod eyes would somehow help. There was a slight change, but nothing of real significance. “Which way did Phoenix go?’

“I’m not sure…. she flew straight into the air, threw a bunch of fireballs all over the place, and then was gone.” Jose admitted. Panic and terror were setting in with Raiden now. Without knowing which way Phoenix was going, he had no way of figuring out what his next move was.

“Did anyone see which way Phoenix went?” Raiden shouted towards what he could only hope was a group of people. They murmured among themselves, but no one seemed to answer. Raiden took that as a no, which brought him right back to the edge of panic. Raiden floated high into the air and paused for a moment. “C’mon stupid. Think this out rationally. Where would Phoenix have gone?” Raiden spoke to himself, with his eyes closed. His thought process was all over the place due to fear, but he had to reel it back in and think this through logically. He didn’t interact with very many people...maybe six in general. Thunderbird, Thor, Alicia, Juan, his mother, and Kylie, was pretty much the only people in his life. Kagutsuchi seemed to be involved, and he had to assume that Phoenix knew how to find these six. How was the question, as lords could only see through their guardian’s eyes. Perhaps Phoenix tailed them in secret or found a way to look them up. It wasn’t incredibly farfetched considering Hunter implied to have known where Kylie lived as well.

Raiden felt confident that he had narrowed the targets down to those six people. “Phoenix is struggling against me, so I doubt she’d take on any gods; especially lords. Thunderbird and Zeus should be out.” Raiden continued to speak his thoughts. “Alicia and Juan are both outside of the state, and I doubt she could get to them before I could.” That left the target of Phoenix’s rage to be either Kylie or his mother. They lived in essentially, the opposite sides of town from where he currently was, so he’d have to think carefully on this decision. His mind was racing trying to make his decision, when memories flooded his mind. Kylie sitting at the table with him all those months ago, when Laura first decided to introduce herself. He remembered how Laura’s eyes briefly lingered on Kylie, a few moments before he had registered that Laura was the guardian of fire. He remembered Kylie’s bright smile moments before Laura approached, and the hearty laugh that was shared between the two during that one intimate moment. The strong bond that they had which was practically tangible. “Kylie!” Raiden made up his mind and took off flying in the sky towards Kylie’s home.

The guardian kept his eyes open as he flew; his vision becoming less blurred by the second. Without the full capabilities of his vision, Raiden was forced to move at half his natural speed to allow his eyes time to adjust to his surroundings without overshooting it. “Hold on, Kylie!” Raiden called, as he came closer and closer to where Kylie lived. His eyes had nearly returned to normal, just as he was nearing his best friend’s house. Hovering over top of her house, the scene shocked him. Kylie was standing in the doorway, talking to Ben. Both of them seemed perfectly happy; smiling and talking about something that was just outside of Raiden’s earshot. Gazing at the two, another memory charged directly into his consciousness. In vivid detail, he was back at the “date” that Laura and Hania had went on. He remembered gushing about his mother, about her accomplishments and how proud he was of her. How he had openly bashed his father and admitted that his mother was all that he had growing up. How could Raiden have been so stupid? He had chosen wrong.

“Your journey is going to be filled with much heartbreak.” Alicia’s voice echoed in his mind as he sat there, stunned for a moment. Raiden’s powers flew into overdrive to match his emotions; his eyes turning a vibrant shade of gold that restored the rest of his fractured vision. Like a bolt of lightning, Raiden took off towards his mom's house; leaving nothing but a sonic boom in his wake.

"Did you hear that?" Ben yelled; covering his ears. Kylie said nothing but gazed into the sky for several moments.

"Was something there?" Kylie yelled as well; both of their hearing apparently damaged from their proximity to Raiden's flight.

"Probably just a jet or something. Now, where were we?" Ben ushered Kylie into the house and shut the door behind them.

"You'll suffer just as I have…" Roy G Biv's prediction echoed in Raiden's mind as he made his way across the city.

"No, I won't." Raiden answered the memory, before converting himself into lightning so intense that not even a mulberry tree could ward it away. His mind was racing even more than normal as he streaked across the evening sky. Raiden was remembering his childhood with his mother. Her laugher and her voice. Her scent of notebook paper and lilac filled his nostrils. "If Phoenix does anything to her I'll k-" Something hit Raiden with the force of a ballistic missile; knocking him out of the sky and his lightning form. He was able to slow his descent enough to avoid breaking anything, but he still crashed into the ground hard. Brushing off some rubble, Raiden stood up...coming face to face with Zeus. "What are you doing?" Raiden angrily questioned the emperor of lightning.

"I cannot allow you to go on, boy. I can't risk you killing the fire guardian and potentially causing a war among the gods." As Zeus spoke, the crown engraved on his forehead began to glow blue. Raiden felt sick to his stomach. Zeus used Raiden's own life force to enter the human realm, to stop Raiden from saving his mother.

"If you would just move out of my way, I wouldn't be killing anyone! I just need to save my mother!" Raiden was on the verge of breaking.

“Fool! You’d tear this entire world asunder for the sake of one lowly human?” The crown symbol on Zeus’ head reached maximum glow after he bellowed and created a blue hued bubble with a thirty-foot radius around the area. Raiden felt his breath run shallow; a feeling he was all too familiar with whenever he was in the god’s realm.

“Yes!” Raiden’s voice echoed. “You’d use my own life force to stop me from saving my mother?” Sparks bounced around Raiden as he cried out.

“I guess that father of yours told our little secret. I’ll deal with the bird later. It matters not; I don’t need your miniscule life force to be in this realm. The emperor is endowed with the ability to bring a sliver of the god realm with them without destroying the human realm, for a short time.” Zeus informed Raiden, not that he really cared.

“I don’t care.” Raiden drove the fact home. “Move out of my way, or else.”

“Or else what, boy?” Zeus spat, before laughing. “You dare to challenge a god?” Raiden’s entire body was consumed with an aura of lightning, while he stared Zeus down.

“Whatever it takes.” Raiden answered; preparing for the hardest fight of his life.

Raiden Vs Zeus

"Don't make me kill you." Zeus warned, unfolding his arms. Even with everything being tinted in a divine blue hue due to Zeus' magic, his eyes still were as vibrant as lightning in the night sky. Raiden stared him down but said nothing. Realistically, there was no way that he would beat Zeus. He didn't have to though. He just had to get past him. The young guardian charged at Zeus and delivered a blow with all the power he could muster. The emperor barely flinched, as the attack smacked into his face.

"Move, damn it!" Raiden cried, although it sounded more like pleading than a command.

"I see I'll have to show you the difference between a god and a demigod." Zeus let an aura of lightning surround himself, right as Raiden jumped back to gain distance. Despite both being lightning users, Zeus' lightning was on an entirely different level. Without even touching it, Raiden's skin tingled, and his breath ran shallow; even more so than it already was at least. He felt an intense pressure weighting the area down, as if the lightning that Zeus was preparing to harness formed a cage surrounding him. Death felt just a constant step away. It didn't matter though. Raiden would go to the depths of the underworld to save his mother.

"Oh yeah? Well what's a god to a non-believer?!" Raiden charged as fast as he could and delivered a kick to Zeus torso. Or at least he attempted to and realized a second too late that he hit nothing but air.

"Still a god." Zeus informed Raiden of his ignorance; appearing directly behind him. The hairs on the back of Raiden's neck stuck up, as if they were trying to tear away from his flesh and run to safety. A massive bolt of lightning rained from the sky and struck Raiden so intensely, his flesh began to smoke and peel away from his bones. Like a teenager getting intoxicated for the first time, Raiden stumbled away before kneeling over and vomiting. Luckily Raiden had placed his arms up at the last second, because even with his resistance, the pure strength of

Zeus' lightning had exposed some of the bone on Raiden's forearms. Clearly, there was an insurmountable difference between a demigod and a god.

"Let me through!" Raiden opened his mouth and fired a beam of lightning. The pain that he was going through made him beg for the feeling of fire in his eyes again. It dulled in comparison to what he was experiencing now. He wouldn't give up though. He couldn't give up. Zeus brushed the beam of lightning away and folded his arms again.

"Once again, don't make me kill you. Stand down boy." Zeus spat. "Mortals die, it happens. If you so desire, I'll find you a new mother. For some unfathomable reason, Oya has grown fond of you. Perhaps she can be your mother. Just let this go." Zeus spoke the last sentence slowly, as if to drive the point home. The god was determined to prevent Raiden from killing Phoenix. Even if that wasn't Raiden's intention in the first place. The hero said nothing but sucked in a large amount of air. Raiden let his anger take over his emotions; surrounding his body with enough lightning that he seemed like the personification of a storm.

"If you don't let me go, a god will die today as well." Raiden's golden eyes flared with a rage that would not be quelled easily. His emotional flare up sent his healing factor into overtime; covering Raiden's forearms with muscle again, as well as a thin layer of skin. His arms were still raw and a bright red that offset the rest of his mocha complexion. Instantly, Raiden transmuted into lightning and zipped in front of Zeus, before bolting to the right of him. While in lightning form, Raiden moved so fast that he caged Zeus in. Zeus appeared unamused but seemed to struggle finding where Raiden was. Raiden popped up in human form directly in front of Zeus' face, causing the god to block out of sheer instinct. Exactly what Raiden was counting on. Once Zeus fell for the feint, Raiden quickly dropped and delivered a body blow; following it up with a huge blast of lightning from his fist. The attack propelled Zeus backwards, but did little to harm him. "Fall!" Raiden's assault wasn't done. With a wave of his wrist, lightning crashed down into the area that Zeus had created and struck Zeus hard enough to leave him engulfed in smoke. Raiden flew off after this; leaving Zeus pocket realm and returning into the human one. He could get away and reach his mom if he hurried.

“You don't learn.” Zeus let Raiden get about ten feet before appearing behind him; dragging Raiden back into the pocket realm. Zeus clutched Raiden by the ankle and tossed him into the ground. Hard. Raiden let out no sounds of pain as he became well acquainted with the ground, but he did yell out in frustration. Nothing that he could think of would work against Zeus. The time that Zeus could keep this sliver of the god realm swapped with a sliver of the human realm was implied to be limited. Once this sliver vanished, Zeus wouldn't be able to use nearly as much power. That was probably Raiden’s only chance at getting away. The only problem was that he had no way of knowing the actual time frame on the emperor’s magic.

“Guess I've got to fight.” Raiden murmured to himself, before he felt the air leave his lungs faster than a student leaving on the last day of school. He hadn't even seen Zeus move, yet suddenly his fist was practically caving his torso in. Raiden hit the ground and rolled backwards to get away but couldn't stop himself from hurling bile and blood onto the floor. Without giving Raiden a chance to recover, Zeus flung an arrow of pure lightning at the guardian. It struck Raiden in his shoulder and numbed his entire body for a moment, before shocking his entire being. Every cell in Raiden’s body was in pain; a level of pain he hadn't experienced since first becoming a guardian. Still, however, Raiden rose from the ground in his fighting stance.

“Do I have to completely break your body in order to make you yield?” Zeus seemed mildly impressed. Vocally, at least. His face was still wearing the permanent scowl that Raiden has grown accustomed to.

“Yes.” Raiden answered. His body wanted to collapse, and the pain was unbearable, but the thought of losing his mom kept him going. That, and the anger that he had towards Zeus that had compiled over the years spilling over.

“To keep going, facing odds that your impudent brain can't even comprehend, for the sake of saving a human life…” Zeus began, while cracking his neck. “...absolutely disgusting.” Zeus fired a stream of lightning which Raiden managed to deflect and follow up with his own stream of lightning. The sliver of god realm that Zeus carried with him seemed to be less vibrant than before, if only a little. About fifteen minutes had passed since Zeus began this fight, and Raiden was guessing that he still had another fifteen minutes before the magic would wear off. That was entirely too long for multiple reasons, with the primary two being his mother's safety and that Zeus probably would kill him during that time frame.

"I don't care if I break every bone in my body…" Raiden began, as he stared down Zeus. "...or if I lose all of my powers…" Lightning surrounded Raiden once more. This time however, the lightning was so radiant that Raiden's physical form was practically consumed. "...or if I lose my life here. I'm going to save her!" Raiden proclaimed, to an unyielding Zeus. Suddenly, he was off. Raiden appeared in front of Zeus and delivered a punch so powerful; it actually sent the god reeling backwards. He followed his assault with a swift two hit combo to Zeus's ribs, and a roundhouse kick that launched the god back even further.

"You insolent…" Zeus spat, but was cut off.

"Move!" Raiden screamed in defiance, as he condensed all the lightning that was surrounding his body into his fist and fired a massive display of lightning towards the god. Even Zeus would have trouble recovering from the blast that was large enough to engulf him. Raiden was tired though. He dropped to his knees, struggling to stand again. "C'mon body, work with me." The hero whispered to himself, rising to his feet with sheer willpower. Just in time too, as an extremely pissed off Zeus was standing behind him.

"I don't know who the hell you think you are, but this ends now." Zeus attempted to punch Raiden, but the hero ducked out the way. When the second blow came from Zeus, Raiden withdrew the knife that his father had gotten him for his birthday and slashed at the god's wrist. For once, Zeus seemed to reel back in actual pain. Something that Raiden took notice of. Like a lion on the hunt, Raiden pounced at Zeus and drove his knife directly into his torso.

"Lightning, give me strength!" Raiden beckoned the sky. A bolt of lightning struck Raiden, who redirected the energy through his weapon and through Zeus. The emperor spit out purple blood onto Raiden's hand; appearing absolutely stunned. Raiden kicked Zeus while sliding his weapon out of Zeus' bloody torso and sheathed his weapon as the god of lightning fell to the floor. Raiden looked on at this scene for a moment, before turning to fly off. That was, until he felt an unfathomable amount of pressure being placed upon his body. The air felt as though it was becoming solid. It wasn't the actual air though...it was fear. His body had reacted to the fear before his eyes had time to process what was happening. Raiden turned to see Zeus, apparently at the breaking point for his patience. The energy he was currently giving off was unlike anything Raiden had ever felt.

"Your father made you that, didn't he?" Zeus spoke in a much more menacing tone than he previously was. Before, Zeus spoke to him as though Raiden's very existence was annoying. Now...he treated Raiden like a threat. "It matters not...I'll ask him myself, while he sweeps up your ashes." The baseball shaped hole that had been in the center of his torso from Raiden's attack closed itself up immediately, in a rather sickening display. A bolt of lightning came down from the sky and landed in front of Zeus, who reached his hand inside and withdrew a rather long staff. "This is what makes the difference between a minor god and a lord. This is my divinity, the Original Bolt." Raiden had known what divinities were, but he had never been on the opposite end of one. He knew that divinities were what lords sealed part of their godly powers in to prevent it from leaking out of their bodies. Raiden also knew that if Zeus was going to use his divinity, that this would be the last few moments of the young hero's life.

"You'd kill me for trying to save my mother?" Raiden was trying his best not to be reduced to a whimper.

"No. I'm going to kill you to teach you a lesson about defying a god." Zeus corrected. Raiden started to point out that killing him wouldn't really teach him a lesson, but his voice was paralyzed by fear. His eyes were fixated on the staff, mesmerized by the finer details. The staff came up to Zeus' neck, making it nearly seven feet in length. It was a majestic gold hue, and a much deeper gold than Raiden's eyes were whenever he was using too much power. Jagged grooves ran from the center of the staff outward, giving off the appearance of a fractal scar. The very tips of each end of the staff were shaped into lightning bolts; giving a bladed edge to the weapon for when blunt force trauma wasn't enough of a punishment. The scariest thing about the staff though, was that the air seemed to crackle around the weapon itself. Raiden was definitely going to die. Phoenix would have his mother on her clutches, waiting to taunt him with her life on the line, until she realized that he wasn't coming. Maybe she'd get bored and move to torment some other guardian. Quality, positive thinking on Raiden's part. He always was a glass half-full kind of guy.

Just as he was trying to decide what was going to be written on his tombstone, a bolt of lightning crashed through the miniature realm that Zeus was creating with his emperor magic and landed in front of Raiden. It slowly took physical form, becoming someone all too familiar to Raiden. "Thunderbird?" Raiden questioned his father's appearance. His father was standing in his human form, with his back to his son.

"I'm going to create an opening for you, using my divinity. It'll drain you significantly, but you're going to have to push past that if you want to get out of this." Thunderbird didn't bother to look at his son.

"I don't need you to hel-" Raiden felt anger start to well up in his chest, before he was cut off.

"Shut up and listen!" Thunderbird's anger frightened Raiden more than even Zeus did. Perhaps it was because he had never seen Thunderbird angry before. "I need you to go save your mother. Protect the woman I love, in place of me. And let me protect my son, like I should have before." Thunderbird sounded more sincere, but the anger was clearly still present. Raiden said nothing but nodded his head to acknowledge the demands.

"Thunderbird, think clearly." Zeus' irritation matched Thunderbird's. It might have exceeded it. "Using your divinity in the human world is one thing but using it against your emperor is treason. This will not go unpunished."

Thunderbird said nothing but drew a knife that was only slightly longer than the one that he gave Raiden for his birthday. The handle to the knife was carved in the image of a totem pole, with a Thunderbird at the very top. There were no runes like on Raiden's weapon, but the weapon was clearly powerful. Storm clouds formed behind Thunderbird's back, with small bolts of lightning occasionally arcing out to his weapon. The air in front of his knife was so dense, it occasionally looked like an elongated blade connected to his weapon. Raiden looked upon it and the name of it appeared in his mind, just as the names of gods did: The storm totem. "I am thinking clearly. I will not let you kill my son." Thunderbird stood ready for combat.

"If you intend to let him go, you will share his fate. To protect this world, I will kill you." Zeus warned. Raiden had never felt this tense. Not to mention the exhaustion from Thunderbird using his divinity smacked Raiden like six semis.

"No, you won't." Thunderbird coldly announced, before flinging a bright bolt of lightning from his weapon at Zeus. As soon as the blast collided, Raiden saw his shot. Pushing past his exhaustion, he took off as a bolt of lightning into the sky, and away from the battle.

"Don't die on me." Raiden caught himself speaking aloud, looking back at his father's general direction. Raiden pushed himself faster and faster towards his mother's house. The battle with Zeus made him lose out on too much time. Based on his continuous exhaustion, Raiden could tell the battle was still going on, but it would have to stop once Zeus's magic wore off, which had to be very soon. Two divinities exposed to the real world would tear it asunder in a matter of seconds. Zeus wouldn't allow that to happen, if only for self-preservation purposes. Gods only existed if they had people who believed in them, so killing all humans would be a bit of a bad call. Raiden was knocked out his thoughts when he felt his phone vibrate against his leg, but he quickly sent it to voicemail without bothering to look. Whoever it was had to wait. "Mom…" Raiden picked up the pace when he started to imagine his mom's face. He had to save her, no matter the cost. After a few minutes of flying, he finally arrived in her neighborhood; panicking at an entirely new level once he saw her front lawn on fire.

Raiden landed and ran into the house, which was easy considering the door had a large hole burnt into it. He ran into the living room, seeing that a struggle had clearly took place. The apparently completed book that his mother was reading was on the ground, as the table it should have been resting on was split in half. The couch was inflamed, as well as the walls and part of the floor. "Mom!" Raiden screamed in a panic, running towards her bedroom. The hallway was heated to an unnatural temperature, as he pushed through. The exhaustion faded from his body; the reason being a mixture of the godly fight being over, and the levels of adrenaline coursing through his veins. He entered his mom's bedroom and quickly took in the scene. Phoenix had her hand gripping the back of Naira's neck, although Phoenix had a fresh wound on her cheek. At his mother's feet sat her cell phone and the slightly bloodied knife that was given to her by her godly husband. No tears fell from her eyes, but instead a determination that burned wilder than any flame that Phoenix could create.

"Ha-" Naira began to say her son's name, before her body was engulfed in flames. She burned so intensely and quickly, that she didn't even have time to scream. Her body was reduced to ash that crumbled out of Phoenix's hands and onto the scorched floor. Just like that, in a matter of seconds, Naira was no more. Killed before her only son's eyes.

Even if your heart should break

“Mom…” Raiden’s voice was quiet and hollow. The shock alone had knocked his body for a serious loop. Raiden’s mind was slowly fading, as he struggled to make sense of what he had just witnessed. There was surely a fake body, or some type of trick involved. Some high-level magic that caused him to see illusions. Perhaps the two rigged the ground with a trap door so that his mother would fall through it. Wouldn’t that be funny? Raiden struggled to come to terms with the fact that there was no joke, no surprise, no trickery involved. His mother was truly killed before his very eyes, because he was a few moments too late.

“Are you as flammable as your mother?” Phoenix asked, as she ran a finger along her cheek. The wound was taking annoyingly long to heal, which was surprising. Her voice never reached Raiden’s ears, however. He was lost in memories of his mother. The warm embrace of his mother wrapping her arms around him as a child and telling him that everything would be okay. The way that she smiled whenever she lectured him, as if she were trying to make sure that he knew she loved him, even when he did something wrong. The sense of pride he had when they were able to take turns walking across the stage; graduating high school just hours before his mother graduated college. How she tried to call out to him, right before Phoenix burnt her alive. Raiden wept. He wept harder than he had ever wept before. No, it wasn’t just tears. It was rain. The heavens themselves joined Raiden in crying for the loss of such an innocent soul. Phoenix looked up for a moment as she heard the pitter-patter of rain quickly upgrade to sound as though the water was trying to penetrate the roof through rapid fire.

“Mom…” Raiden spoke once again, his voice far removed from his body. It sounded feeble and weak, like someone being choked.

“If only you weren’t so slow. For someone being as quick as lightning, you sure took your time!” Phoenix mocked. Once again, her efforts were wasted. Raiden’s mind was focused on more thoughts of his mother. Of how she threatened to beat up the adults who teased him when he was younger about not having a father. The look of panic in her eyes when she found the old note that he had written her when he thought of taking his own life. How strong she seemed to be when she started going to the gym with him as a bonding experience. How she used her last moments, judging from the scene at hand, to wound Phoenix. Because if there was one word that Naira Hawke couldn't be described as, it was weak. Raiden looked at his mother's killer, and he let out a howl so fierce that Phoenix jumped backwards until her back slammed into the wall. His voice mixed in with the wind, which had picked up to match his howl. Debris flew by the window of the late Naira's house; casualties of the wind's ferocity.

"You killed her…" Raiden felt lost.

"I did. Are you out for revenge?" Phoenix mocked, although she sounded a little less in control of the situation than before. Raiden closed his eyes, as he tried to focus. He tried to push the thoughts of his mother out of his head. He blocked himself off from feeling all of the sorrow that was dragging him down. His chest felt like it was on fire. Lightning circulated his body, rejuvenating him. The sky rained down lightning near the home; occasionally shining a bright light through the windows with its fury. Lightning was never supposed to strike twice, but it struck continuously around the house. Raiden struggled to figure out what was going on with his emotions. He was pushing aside his sorrow, but he didn't quite feel numb. Something was rumbling inside him like a stampede of elephants. But what? Raiden clenched his knuckles together tightly as he thought. What was left for him to feel, now that his mother was gone? Oh...that's right. Rage.

"Revenge? No. I'm just here to show you the difference…" Raiden's eyes snapped open, revealing a set of golden eyes that seared with nothing but hatred. His eyes were sharp and intense, unlike his normal soft and kind eyes. Phoenix felt herself quiver for a moment. For once, she was truly afraid. And yet…

"Difference? The difference between what?" Phoenix immediately regretted asking that question. She hadn't seen Raiden move, yet she felt his left thumb and index finger firmly grasp her tongue. She wouldn't be allowed to speak anymore. Phoenix looked upon Raiden, whom had closed the gap between them before her eyes could even register what was happening. She no longer saw the hero, that had been so intent on trying to save everyone. She no longer saw a guardian, who was the bridge between the human world and the other deities. What Phoenix saw when she looked at Raiden, was the face of a demon. Raiden looked directly into her eyes, his face a few inches away from hers.

"The difference between a demigod and a corpse." Raiden saw Phoenix's eyes widen, before delivering an uppercut to her sternum that was so powerful, it propelled her through the ceiling. Phoenix recovered herself in the sky, and immediately found a storm had surrounded her. Gale force winds threatened to rip the flesh off her bones, while rain pelted down from each direction. Lightning streaked around her from side to side, like the wind was playing a game of godly pong. Raiden came flying up at her and threw a lightning-enhanced punch that immediately broke through her guard. The rampage continued with a flurry of blows, each of which pushed Phoenix higher and higher into the sky. Each blow was more powerful than the last. Each blow carried more of Raiden's anger and hatred than the previous attack. Phoenix recovered from the last staggering blow and released a stream of fire. Not only did Raiden dodge the flame, but he converted to lightning and zipped around it. Toying with her. Mocking her efforts.

"Stay away!" Phoenix released another stream at the demigod, but Raiden flew directly up the sea of fire, and fired a point-blank bolt of lightning once he emerged from flames. Phoenix was no longer a match for her once rival. She looked down and could see that the force of his storm had torn apart his late mother's house and scattered debris along the ground. Her eyesight was then blocked by the rage-consumed Raiden. He said nothing before easily dodging the two strikes that Phoenix made at him and grabbing her and tossing her higher into the air. Raiden slammed into Phoenix and carried her upwards again, despite the woman placing an aura of fire around her. The two traveled higher, with her flames growing weaker, until they reached the stratosphere. Her flames completely snuffed out, and Raiden paused for a moment to look at her. He hesitated for a moment, until his mind began to play back the scene of his mother's murder. Raiden raised his hands over his head and cupped them together, before delivering a double axe handle strike with so much power to Phoenix, that it sent her plummeting back down to earth. Her body had become a mixture of lightning and flames, as she went from the sky to the ground with enough intensity to form a crater. Raiden turned into lightning and zipped back to the ground, a few feet away from Phoenix's crash zone. Slowly, he walked to check on her.

What Raiden saw would have disgusted him, if he weren't so consumed with his own rage. Phoenix's body was in shambles, and it was clear from her expressionless face and shattered body, that she was dead. Raiden looked on at her with a stoic expression, as if what he had done didn't have a chance to sink in yet. Suddenly, Phoenix's body erupted into a brilliant flame that burned the same hue as Raiden's eyes, but not as intensely as the hatred those same eyes carried. When the flames subsided, Phoenix was surrounded by ashes, but her body had healed. Something was different with her though. It didn't seem by much, but she seemed...younger? The instant she opened her eyes, Raiden lifted his hand into the air and brought it down, resulting in an intense bolt of lightning striking Phoenix. She screamed in agony as her body was consumed in lightning....and then the screams stopped. Phoenix's body was smoldering as a result of Raiden's attack, and she was dead once more. Again, her body was consumed with a vibrant flame, and again her body was restored. She was definitely younger, however. The worry lines on her forehead had faded, and a certain innocence and youth leaked off her. She appeared to be Raiden's age now.

"Who are you?" Phoenix asked once her eyes snapped open. She attempted to rise, but again Raiden called down a bolt of lightning so intense that it killed her once more. She seemed to be getting two or three years younger every time she died. Raiden realized, once her screams of agony stopped, that Phoenix was reincarnating after every death. But she wouldn't be able to keep this up. The now eighteen-year-old Phoenix opened her eyes for the first and last time; just to watch Raiden bring down his hand. Lightning snuffed her life out once more. Loss and rage had turned Raiden cruel. Every time she reincarnated; Raiden hesitated. Every time he looked at her face however, no matter how young, all he could see was his mother's killer. He saw it in the fifteen-year-old Phoenix, as he killed her one more. He even saw it in the twelve-year-old Phoenix, although he closed his eyes when he struck her down. The next two times, Raiden didn't wait for her body to finish regenerating. Maybe because deep down inside, beneath the rage, he knew that what he was doing was wrong. He knew that looking upon her face, seeing that she was no longer the same person, seeing that she was a child, Raiden would not be able to go through with it. Just once more…he just needed to do it one more time.

"That's enough, son." Thunderbird had grabbed Raiden's wrist from behind once he raised his hand for the final blow. Raiden whipped around to see his dad's face, before yanking his hand away.

"That's enough?! How could it be enough?! My mother is dead! My mother is dead and it's all her fault!" Raiden screamed.

"I know son." Thunderbird couldn't meet Raiden's eyes.

"No, you don't! Because you left! You didn't love her! You didn't need her like I did! How the hell can you tell me that you know?! You don't know shit!" Raiden continued his verbal assault.

"That's not true. I loved her more than I could ever express. But she wouldn't wa-" Thunderbird tried to reason.

"Shut up! How is it fair that my mother had to die, but she gets to live!" Raiden whipped around to point at Phoenix, and for the first time set eyes on her. Phoenix was standing in the crater with tears in her eyes; the innocent tears of a lost and confused three-year-old. What had Raiden done? What did he almost do? He killed someone, again and again. It didn't matter if she reincarnated. The gravity of the situation had finally hit him now that the cloud of rage was lifted from his mind. Raiden had lost his mother, and he retaliated by murdering someone in cold blood. Over and over...he had no right to live. When he first saw his mother being murdered, something inside him snapped. He became something that wasn't even human. But now…now that he was standing in the ruins of his mother's house, which he destroyed. Now that he was looking at this little girl that he almost murdered, for something she did in another lifetime. Now...something inside Raiden had broken. He turned towards Thunderbird with tears threatening to spill over. Until Thunderbird ran over and pulled Raiden into his arms. That was the moment that Raiden began to truly weep.

Aftermath

Although only a few minutes had passed, it felt like hours since what had happened. Hania had released his Raiden garb, and was sobbing into his father's chest. Thunderbird said nothing but held his son tightly and refused to let go. Occasionally Hania would look up at Thunderbird, attempt to form words, but would return to sobbing. Everything was too much for him to handle. His mother's death. The fact that he couldn't save her. The fact that he had committed the one act he promised himself he'd never do. Heroes do not kill. And yet, that was the first thing he did once his emotions got the better of him. Plus, he felt weak. Hania hadn't cried in years, and the last time he did cry it was because of his father. Now he was crying to him. Phoenix, now the age of a toddler, also cried in the crater. No one had come to hold her though. She had no family to speak of. Little Laura, in a miniature version of the garb her adult form had worn, was alone in this world. Right now, Hania couldn't be bothered to care, however. If it wasn't for the fact that the ground between Hania and Laura began to float and flash blue, Hania would have been content with crying until his eyes stopped functioning.

"Who…" Hania looked to see someone was now approaching Laura. The figure was completely blue, and only had a pair of tan parachute pants on as coverage. That wasn't the most peculiar thing about them, however. It was the two additional faces he had; each resting where a shoulder would normally be. Agni's name flew into Hania's mind, and quickly he charged at the fire deity and attempted to strike him. The anger had returned immediately to the forefront of Hania's mind. It wasn't Phoenix's fault that she killed his mother. No, not entirely. It was gods like Agni, lords of fire, who were to blame. Agni whipped around to block Hania's fist, but the power behind it sent the two sliding back several feet.

"I come in peace!" All three of Agni's mouths spoke, creeping Hania out. There was a certain...sincerity behind Agni's voice though. Hania relented his assault but kept the scowl on his face. *"To be able to do this to a god..."* Agni thought, trying to reset the three fingers that Hania had snapped from the punch. Granted, Agni had his powers still sealed within his divinity and refused to unleash any power while he was in the human world, but still. He was both impressed, and slightly afraid of the implications.

"Agni, why are you here? You're a lord on earth under your own power. The earth can't handle that." Thunderbird pointed out; matching his son's scowl.

"I know. That's why I want to make this quick. I came for two reasons. The first reason is to offer an apology. Most of the lords of fire did not agree with Kagutsuchi's plan to kill your mother. We didn't even fully agree with sacrificing lord Phoenix for the guardian's power." Agni's three heads spoke in such unison, that it sounded like surround sound.

"Your second reason?" Hania asked. He wasn't ready to accept any apologies for what happened tonight. Nor was he ready to offer any. Eventually he would. Tonight though...tonight wasn't the time.

"To take young Laura somewhere safe. She may be...young, now. But she is still our guardian." Agni looked at Hania when he spoke, or at least two of his heads did. It seemed like he had more to say but decided against it.

"What's going to happen to her?" Thunderbird asked. Hania admittedly wanted to know but didn't care enough in his state of grief to ask.

"Well, the problem was that we introduced lord Phoenix into Laura's being after her body and mind matured. Her body couldn't take the power and stress, and her body essentially treated it like a disease. It wouldn't adapt, and with her being much more active with her powers, it made the corruption of her mind spread like...well, like wildfire. Lord Phoenix is still within her though, and the reincarnation has made both of them weak. Weak enough to grow together, so that Laura's body accepts the gift and the two can fully merge as she ages. Her body may fluctuate quite a bit, but I know of a place she can go and be free to grow and explore her powers." Agni answered.

"Do what you want with her. I'm going home." Hania waved Agni away. Normally, he switched to his Raiden garb whenever using his powers. Today though, he was physically, emotionally, and mentally drained. His eyes stung from crying and his body ached from how far he pushed his powers. In short; he didn't give a damn if anyone saw him. Hania took off into the sky, leaving a confused girl, a god who was slowly tearing away the fabric of reality, and his newly widowed father. He just needed some rest.

“You let me die!” Naira screamed at Hania, jolting him awake. He groaned and checked the clock and saw that it was only a quarter past seven a.m. Hania slept for a grand total of...about three hours. He managed to throw on a pair of shorts and a blue tank top on, but otherwise he looked disheveled. His body still ached a bit, but that wasn’t at the front of his mind. He needed a distraction. Fumbling around a bit, Hania managed to grab the remote off his night stand, and flick the TV on.

“Another devastating attack occurred last night by Phoenix, the arch nemesis with a weird obsession with local hero, Raiden.” The anchorwoman began, as images of the fire that Phoenix had unleashed upon the city flashed on screen. Hania watched on, as he hadn’t really gotten the full experience of what she had done. At the time of the pictures, Hania was blind and stumbling around. A young boy with sandpaper colored skin appeared on screen. He was rather scrawny, and fairly short as well. The baggy blue shirt that he was wearing practically hung off his body, although he appeared to have pulled it taut enough so that the storm cloud was centered on his chest. Hania didn’t even recognize the boy, until he started to speak.

“Jose?” Hania questioned, although his voice was hoarse from yelling.

“I thought I was going to die, but then Raiden came down and saved me! And he was super cool doing it. He told me he couldn’t see, but he was going to save everyone. So, he did! Some of the kids at school are acting all scared because their parents are nervous. They think he’s some kind of god or something because Raiden has a parent that's a god. But none of that matters. Raiden is a hero, and the coolest person ever!” Jose cheesed while he gushed about the hero. A tear fell from Hania’s eye as he spoke. If only Jose knew what he had done...then what would he think? Perhaps, there was no such thing as heroes.

"Thank you, Jose. Raiden's efforts certainly were appreciated. This tragic day could have been a lot worse, if it weren't for him." After the anchorwoman spoke, dozens of images of the aftermath displayed on screen. Two or three city blocks were completely damaged. Buildings and roadways could be repaired, but Hania couldn't help but think about Roy G Biv. Yet another villain that his actions created. "With great sadness though, not everyone was saved by Raiden during Phoenix's onslaught. Raiden was on the scene battling with Phoenix and rescuing people between the hours of eight and ten at night. During that time, or perhaps sometime after that, it appears that Naira Hawke, who lived in the outskirts of the city, fell victim to the villain. Her house was discovered to be completely ripped apart, and it is believed that Phoenix may have burnt her alive as evidence of the scorch marks that were present within the debris. Naira Hawke, forty-two, is survived by a single son, twenty-one-year-old Ha-"

"Damn it!" Hania threw his remote directly into the television screen with such ferocity, it became embedded in it. Cracks scattered across the glass like roaches when the lights flickered on. The images and sound quickly faded, before settling in on darkness. An empty and broken screen...like his heart. His fist were bawled so tightly, that his palms began to bleed. His anger and sorrow were so consuming, that he didn't hear someone knocking on his door until the sixth set of taps. In an almost zombie-like fashion, Hania rose from the bed and swayed over to the door. Normally he would be extra cautious and glance out the peephole about twelve times, but after last night, Hania was kind of over this whole living thing. He swung the door open, and once his eyes adjusted a bit to the morning light, Chief Valo's figure came into view. "Hi." Hania dryly greeted the police chief.

"Hello, Hania. My officers called your phone and left a message to tell you about your mother, but you didn't answer or return the call. I figure though...you were there. So, I came in person to check on you." Chief Valo explained. Hania had almost forgotten that the Chief had figured out his secret.

"Yeah." Hania wasn't quite in the mood for visitors. Even though Valo looked somber and seemed to struggle delivering the news, it wasn't like the police chief lost his mother or anything. Plus, he had to be careful not to say anything that might incriminate himself. He did technically murder someone after all. “Thanks for checking on me. I’m fine though.”

“Still playing the tough guy. It’s not weakness to admit you need someone, ya know?” Valo spoke to Hania. He was deeply concerned for the kid, even if it was currently falling on deaf ears. “Well, you have my number if you need to talk. Ever. There is another reason I’m here though.”

“Which is?” Normally Hania would have had some type of snarky comment to make. His mind was drawing a blank though. His voice was dry with little emotion behind it, like a male version of that actress from the show about the parks in Indiana.

“We’re covering your mother’s funeral cost. Also, I have a copy of your mother’s will. You were to inherit her home but...well, you’ll end up getting the insurance money for that once everything is processed. She also had you down as the sole benefactor for her life insurance. There are some other logistics, but I’m not too familiar with this stuff. I’ll arrange someone to be there after the funeral for a proper reading. I’d imagine the life insurance wouldn’t take too long for you to receive, but the insurance money from her home may need to probate.” Chief Valo explained. Hania had an idea that his mother had life insurance, but that was the last thing on his mind. Money wouldn’t ease the pain of loss.

“Why are you covering the funeral cost? Who is we?” Hania questioned. He cared a lot more than his voice let on.

“The city. Highly unusual, I know. But consider it the least we could do. The conclusion was made that paying for the funeral would benefit the city in the long run, as it would show unity against the villains that have been attacking our city.” Valo explained.

“That doesn’t even begin to make sense.” Hania pointed out. Not that he wanted to pay for his mother’s funeral or anything.

"Let's leave it at this. Someone higher up than me in the political food chain has a sneaking suspicion of what you do in your free time and wanted to ease your burden." Chief Valo shrugged. A few days ago, Hania might have went ballistic at the fact that yet another person figured out his secret. Who exactly was he trying to protect anymore though? If he even continued to be a hero, he had no real ties left. There was Kylie, but for her own safety, it probably would be best to cut ties with her.

"Fine. I'm not one to look a gift horse in the mouth. I'd like to get some rest now but thank you for coming. I'll see you at the funeral." Hania pushed Chief Valo out and closed the door before there was a chance to respond. Hania was crying off and on every few minutes, and he refused to let the police chief see. Hania didn't remember hearing his phone ring, but then again, his phone had been on vibrate since last night. After fumbling around for a bit, he found his phone on the floor. There were several voicemails left on it, that he thumbed through without much thought until he came across one that stopped him in his tracks. It was amazing how one simple name could make every nerve on his body light itself on fire. One word. One name. Mom. Hania hesitated for a bit, with tears falling from his eyes. The timing of the voicemail...she had to have called when he was coming towards her. His phone did ring when he was close, now that he could think back to it. He missed her last words...live, anyway. After several deep breaths, he finally worked up enough courage to hit the play button.

"Han. My wičháȟpi. I want you to listen to me, okay? I have a strong feeling...that I may not see the sun rise again. I know you, my son. Do not blame yourself. Please. I have never been prouder of you, Hania Hawke. The work that you've done as Raiden, the lives that you have saved, the people that you have inspired.... you are a hero. You are my hero. And no matter what happens tonight, or any other night, that will never change. I've always felt like I've been holding you back from your true destiny. Do not let my death be another reason to hold you back. New Mexico loves you, and you are good for New Mexico. But you are worth so much more. You can do so much better for the world. Stop limiting your talents. Start eating more balanced meals so that you don't grow older and have heart problems. That's really important. I don't want to see you follow me too early. Find someone to spend your life with. ALL aspects of your life. Someone who can support you and stand beside you, who isn't afraid to tell you when you're wrong if it means helping you become the best version of yourself. Who loves you unconditionally. That's all I have to say. I don't plan on going down without a fight. I mean, I conquered a deity's' heart, so you should know how strong your mom is. I just needed to tell you this...in case you don't hear from me again. I love you. I love you so much. Watching you grow has been my greatest honor, privilege, and achievement. I'll always be watching over you. Goodbye, my son." Naira's voice faded, as the sound of her dagger being drawn from its' sheath echoed in Hania's ear. The voicemail ended directly after that. She sounded so...calm. Strong, even when the end was nigh. He listened to his mother's voicemail three more times, each time sobbing harder than the last. He sobbed so hard that Hania hadn't notice that someone was knocking at his door, until it had flung open.

"Han…" Kylie called out to her friend from the doorway. She looked exhausted, as if she had ran up the stairs to his third story apartment without pause. Tears had filled her eyes due to both, her close nature with Hania's mom, and watching the normally strong Hania in such a state. She ran over and embraced him, allowing him to sob into her shoulders.

"She's gone…" Hania's voice trailed off.

Time seemed to pass slowly for Hania over the following week leading up to Naira's funeral. His mother's coworkers had reached out to offer their condolences, Chief Valo reached out twice to make sure he was okay, and Kylie checked on him twice a day, every day. Her family also checked on him twice that week. It was all appreciated, a fact that Hania made sure to tell each person, but all he wanted was to be left alone. The funeral though...he needed a little bit of emotional support to get through this. Kylie picked Hania up and agreed to sit in the front with him. It wasn't like he exactly had any family to lean on during times like this. His mother WAS his family. Without her, he felt empty. The compliments on his suit when he arrived barely reached his ears. "Hello, Han." Thunderbird had appeared in a black suit with a red tie. His son didn't know what was more surprising; the fact that he decided to wear funeral attire from this decade, or that he had shown up at all. Thunderbird had not reached out to Hania once during the long week of hell.

“Who is this?” Kylie, wearing a short-sleeved black dress questioned. Thunderbird had been waiting near the front, where the two friends had decided to sit.

“That would be my father. Father, this is Kylie. My best friend.” Hania looked Thunderbird in the eyes as he spoke, who had a certain look of guilt in them. Guilt, and pain.

“Do we like him now?” Kyrie’s combativeness was entirely warranted. After all, he often confided in her with his feelings about Thunderbird’s absence when the two were younger. Not the exact truth of his nature, but the feelings were genuine.

“Well, we’re trying to. That remains to be seen if it sticks.” Hania decided to leave it at that and sat down. Kyrie sat on his right side, while Thunderbird sat to his left. Surprisingly, Thor came bursting into the church. Like Thunderbird, he wore a black suit with red tie. However, it was clear that his suit was too small for Thor’s more muscular physique. Unless the goal that Thor had was to let onlookers trace the veins on Thor’s muscles without him having to pull off his clothing. In that case, the suit fit just right. Thor said little but pulled Hania into an incredibly tight embrace before setting into a seat beside his fellow deity.

“And that would be…?” Kyrie whispered.

“That would be my godfather. He goes by Tee.” Hania decided calling him Thor would just lead to questions that he wasn’t quite ready to answer.

“You have a godfather?” Kylie looked shocked. Hania just nodded however, while looking at his environment. Being in a church for his mother’s funeral felt a little strange, even if the stained glass and cherry wood were a beautiful blend to look at. His mother didn’t really have much of a belief system minus her husband and his best friend. Hania, despite knowing multiple gods, did believe in God. Or rather, his belief in God directly correlated with the fact that he was a demigod himself. Hania had personally met many gods, and they certainly were not omnipotent, omniscient, nor omnipresent. Something had to preside above them. Plus, having two gods in a church felt wrong in many ways. Hania snapped out of his thoughts and continued to focus on the pastor. A few of Naira's coworkers had gotten up to speak on occasion in between the pastor's words. The pastor had offered Hania a chance to speak earlier, but the young man declined. The pain was too raw...too fresh.

"I would like to speak." Thunderbird stood, garnering a few murmurs from the crowd. The fact that it was a very small crowd made the shock that much more audible. He rose to the podium, where the pastor eyed him. No one here had ever met Thunderbird, minus Hania of course. Naira did gush about her beloved though and showed off her single picture that she owned of him whenever she met someone new. "Naira Hawke was my beloved. She was the mother to my wonderful son, Hania. More importantly, she was the owner of the most beautiful soul I had ever seen. There is no one on earth nor the heavens themselves that could ever replace her in my heart. Or Hania's. My biggest regret for all of eternity is that I let my...work rob me of time I could have spent with my family. I urge everyone in this room to never make that same mistake."

"Indeed!" Thor shouted.

"I could stop time, with a single thought of you. But I could not stop the rain. I could smile and get rid of all my pain. But I could not stop the rain. I could face all my fears with you by my side. But I could not stop the rain. Now that you're gone, I've lost everything. Everything but the rain." Thunderbird quickly returned to his seat after his poem. The father pulled his son's head onto his shoulder, allowing Hania to continue crying. Hania could stop everything, but he could not stop the rain.

"Do you two need a ride back to your...hotel?" Kylie asked Thunderbird and Thor once the funeral was over, clearly confused over where the duo were staying. Everyone had left the graveyard, leaving only the four-standing next to her tombstone. The words that Hania had chosen were short and simple: Naira Hawke, a star too bright for this world.

“No, we’re okay red.” Thor cheesed as he spoke. He was whispering, but it still sounded like normal level speech. It was an improvement from yelling though. “We would like a moment with my godson though.”

“Don’t call me red.” Kylie mentioned, before walking towards her car. “Just jump in when you’re done with them.” The three watched as Kylie walked away from earshot.

“Tonight, we will come for you.” Thunderbird told a confused Hania.

“I don’t need a pep talk.” Hania retorted.

“You do. But, no. That isn’t why.” Thunderbird sighed deeply. “Zeus has called for a summons.” For a split second, all three of the lightning wielders had been on the same emotional wavelength. Anger.

“For what?” Hania was immediately annoyed all over again. He never wanted to see Zeus again.

“We aren’t at liberty to say. Just...be ready.” Thunderbird warned. The two deities walked away, before vanishing in a blur of blue. Hania was now alone, next to his mother’s grave. Alone….and confused. What would happen with Zeus in a few hours?

Crime & Punishment

"So why exactly am I here?" Hania had been wearing a simple pair of grey sweatpants and a black t-shirt. He felt underdressed in the god realm, in all honesty. Thor had picked him up a few minutes ago, but his father didn't show.

"I can't say. What I can tell you is that this is a very serious manner." Thor explained in his not so whispery tone. The two had been walking down the hall towards the guardian chamber, where the lords of lightning all gathered. Thor hadn't turned once to look at his godson, which was a drastic change from his usual cheery and overly affectionate self. Hania felt his stomach bubble from nerves.

"Should I change into my Raiden gear?" Hania questioned, while struggling to keep up with Thor's pace.

"No, my son. Let the see you as you are." Thunderbird had been leaning against the large red doors that lead to the gathering chamber. Most of Thunderbird was, at least. It seemed that he misplaced his left arm somewhere since the funeral.

"Where is your arm?" Hania questioned in a slight panic. His father definitely had all his limbs at the funeral.

"My penance from Zeus for raising a hand against him. I made a comment about him being too literal when he took my left hand, so he took the rest of my arm too. I guess I let my anger get the best of me." Thunderbird motioned towards the blank space that used to be his arm. To him, it seemed like a minor inconvenience.

"He took your arm? It wasn't even your mistake! Can you grow it back? Can you even turn into the bird anymore?" Hania was enraged.

"I'm afraid it doesn't work like that. Ichor can help heal nearly any wound, as long as the body is still whole. Once my arm was severed, ichor ceased to help it. I can still transform into my avian state and fly. I'll just have to shape my left wing out of lightning is all. I've already tested it." Thunderbird walked over to Hania and embraced him. "Whatever happens in there, know that I will give my life to defend you." Thunderbird's words set Hania into a full out panic. Neither his father nor his godfather were the type to get particularly worked up over anything.

"Are you ready?" Thor patted an unsure Hania on the back. Nevertheless, Hania nodded and pushed the large doors open. Once he stepped through, his paternal figures vanished from his side and appeared on top of their storm cloud.

"Welcome, Hania." Indra, the red-skinned god greeted the guardian of lightning in a pleasant, yet stern tone. In the eight years that he had known Indra, Hania still couldn't tell if Indra liked him or not.

"Do I get to find out why I'm here now?" Hania looked directly at Zeus when he spoke. All the anger and hatred immediately came back with a single glance.

"You broke the most important rule that we gave you. You killed the fire guardian." Zeus picked the wrong thing to say to Hania.

"She revived! How the hell does that count?" Hania let his emotions overcome him and his better judgement.

"It matters not!" Zeus bellowed so loudly that Hania's heart rattled in his chest. "She revived, so you killed her again. Repeatedly!"

"I only killed her because you stopped me! If you would have just let me go, my mother would still be alive! This is on you!" Hania was in full outrage at this point. It was taking everything in his power not to fly up and strike Zeus.

"Shall we break this down? You fought her multiple times, yet you failed to capture her. Like a hero is supposed to do. You were blinded by her and let her get away. You made the wrong decision on who she would attack. You let her figure out your identity and who mattered to you the most. I had nothing to do with your mother dying. She died because of your own incompetence as a hero. Shut up and wallow in your despair, you pathetic child." Zeus was clearly annoyed with the conversation. Hania let out a scream of absolute rage, before pointing an open palm at Zeus.

"TAKE THAT BACK!" Hania let out both the loudest scream and the largest ball of lightning that he had ever mustered thus far in his lifetime. Zeus was able to deflect the blow, albeit after sustaining severe damage to the arm that he had used to swat the attack away.

"This is not a personal attack on my son. Talk to him like that again, and no hierarchy will save you from my wrath." Thunderbird spoke once the smoke cleared.

"I WILL FOLLOW THOROUGH, TENFOLD!" Thor bellowed. Zeus barely acknowledged the threat but did decide to change subjects.

"Intentions matter not in this scenario. You broke the rules. Even as we speak, some of the other lords are preparing for war. We have decided to put this matter to a vote." Zeus explained.

"What matter to a vote?" Hania questioned.

"If we are going to keep you on as a guardian or release you from your services." Zeus's answer made Hania's heart drop. Being a guardian may have been a pain, but it had become who he was at the core of his being. The extra power was what helped him be a superhero. Hell, the pride that he felt knowing how many lives he helped being a guardian was what drove him to get up in the morning some days. "If we vote against you remaining in our servitude, we will remove your powers immediately in order to find a more suitable host, though you'll still have your basic powers as a demigod. The process may kill you, but luckily you don't have very many people to say goodbye to." Zeus spoke nonchalantly when it came to Hania's potential death. "I will start the voting off. I vote that we revoke his guardianship immediately. He has caused a potential war, directly defied my words, and killed another guardian."

“I will go next.” Thunderbird immediately chimed in. “I vote that he remains a guardian. Hania has protected more lives than any other active guardian. This circumstantial blemish does not define him.” Thunderbird seemed to be talking directly to Zeus with his vote.

“My vote is to revoke his guardianship as well.” Indra spoke with very little emotion. “Nothing personal against Hania but revoking his guardianship may be enough to convince the other sides to back down from this war.”

“Are you all mad?!” Thor spoke, in his typical shouting fashion. “We do not abandon our warriors in the middle of the fight! Not only do I vote that he keeps his guardianship, I vow to stand beside him should war come to pass!” Thor’s wink towards Hania did little to calm his nerves.

“A punishment must be dealt. If blood was spilled on one side, blood must be spilled on the other.” Set growled. “I vote that his guardianship is revoked. I also add on that if he does not die from the removal of guardian status, that we kill him ourselves.” Set bared his jackal like teeth at Hania.

“Having the boy here while we decide his fate is unnecessarily cruel.” Raijin pointed out. Raijin appeared like a traditional Japanese oni, with pale blue skin and twin horns. His pumpkin shaded hair spiked upwards, and his eyes had the same hue as his hair. Raijin was sitting on top of his drum, with a dog composed entirely of lightning sitting beside him. “The boy should keep his guardianship. Kagutsuchi started this war, not our guardian. How would we look if we bowed to his whims? Hania didn’t. He should continue bringing pride to the ‘Rai’ clan as he has thus far.” Raijin petted his beast, Raiju, as he spoke. Hania’s made a mental note to thank his thirteen-year-old self for picking a hero name without putting any research into it. It may have just gotten him a vote and saved his life.

“I suppose that makes me the tie-breaker.” Perun pointed out. Perun was a lord that never spoke much, and typically was content with observing the actions of others. He was shirtless, like many other gods, although he had metal shoulder pads on for some odd reason. His eyes, mustache, and long beard were pure gold in hue; contrasted by the matted hair on his head that was metallic silver in color. "Hania, you broke our most sacred rule. You killed another guardian and disobeyed the words of your ruler. However, your service to us over the last eight years deserves merit. Never once did you refuse a mission from us. Whenever you were involved in a mission, there were no casualties. You've given people hope and something to believe in. Weighing both sides, I vote that you keep your guardianship."

Hania, Thor, and Thunderbird all breathed a sigh of relief. Indra looked indifferent towards the situation, whereas Zeus and Set were clearly furious at the outcome. Raijin and Perun simply gave Hania a thumbs up. "That was only half the battle, however." Raijin broke the silence, despite it only lasting a few fleeting moments. "This will perhaps be more difficult than simply dying. I have no doubt in my mind that you will be hunted by the other guardians. Perhaps even the gods themselves. We won't be able to help or talk with you directly either, although we can help behind the scenes. There is no resolution to this war yet." Raijin didn't rattle Hania though. For the first time since his mother died, Hania smiled. A true, genuine smile.

"I bet it's eating you up inside, knowing your hatred of me couldn't be passed on." Hania gloated to Zeus.

"You are arrogant, defiant, and grossly overconfident in your own abilities. You are strong beyond human capabilities and that makes you a threat. You are more suited for our company than you may realize. I do not hate you. I hate your pointless obsession with the human world and your human side. You should be focusing on how to get closer to your godly side, than your human one." Zeus rubbed the dead flesh where Hania's lightning hit earlier in their visit. "You also took on the name of the wrong lord. Zeusling or Kid Zeus would have been much more suited for my representative." Hania said nothing but looked on at Zeus. Just who did he think he was? Besides an all-powerful god who ruled over other gods. Right, stupid question.

“Someone just take me home. I have something I need to do.” Hania explained. Now that he knew there was a war coming, it was time to start getting serious.

Saying goodbye

"Hania? What are you doing here?" Kylie had thrown on a black hoodie to answer the door. It was after ten, so the visit came as a shock. "Did you have a nightmare?"

"I have something to talk to you about. Can you come out?" Hania had only been back from the meeting with the lords of lightning for about two hours. He hadn't even had a chance to change his clothes. Kylie nodded, before throwing on a pair of kitten slippers and closing the door.

"What's up?" Kylie asked. She got no response. Instead, Hania grabbed her hand and led her to the side of the house. He held her hand tight...and started to lift himself off the ground.

"I'm Raiden." He pulled Kylie closer into his arms, before flying straight into the air. Once they had gotten a fair distance above the ground, out of the view of the average person, he stopped. Kylie looked down at how far the ground was, before looking back at Hania. His brown eyes had a few flakes of gold in them. The two then dropped from the sky; landing gracefully on Kylie's rooftop. "You don't look all that surprised." Hania pointed out, once Kylie had been released from his arms. He had sat down on the top of the roof, with Kylie sitting down to join him.

"I think in the back of my mind I've always known. I mean, I've always suspected. I just told myself I was crazy because there's no way that you could have possibly hidden superpowers from me for nearly fourteen years." Kylie ignored the look of guilt on Hania's face. "Plus, I recognized Phoenix's face as that bimbo who approached you that day." She added. How could Hania have missed that?

"If you suspected all this time, why did you keep quiet?" Hania knew that if the shoe was on the other foot, he would have asked Kylie immediately.

"Would you have told me if I had asked you?" Kylie questioned. Hania's hesitance spelled the answer out for her, without any words being spoken. "Exactly. I figured if it were true, you would tell me eventually. So that stuff about your father being the Thunderbird…"

"True. When you met my father, he was in his human form. And my godfather is Thor." Hania admitted.

"That kind of counts as cheating in those mythology classes then, doesn't it?" Kylie's joke forced Hania to crack a microscopic smile.

"I have to go away for a while." Hania blurted out, changing the atmosphere entirely. The two sat in silence for what felt like an eternity.

"Are you in trouble?" Kylie finally sorted out her thoughts and feelings. Hania considered lying to her, but he currently lacked the mental capacity to do so. He still felt empty inside.

"Yeah. If I don't leave, I could drag everyone and everything else into my mess. Plus, I have to figure out how to keep on living with this hole in my heart." Hania looked drained as he spoke. Everyone who had spoken to Hania since his mother died commented on how he wasn't his usual, vibrant self. Even though Kylie knew the truth, that deep down Hania was a victim of depression, she had never seen him this low.

"Then do what you've got to do. But don't you dare forget about me and the countless other people here who have crossed your path. We are all here for you. Especially me." Kyrie gently rubbed Hania's arm, before he pulled away.

"There's another thing I have to talk to you about. I need you to let me go, Kylie. I think of you as an amazing person and friend, but I don't want you to hold on to the hope that we will be together. I can't drag you down with me, and I need you by my side as my friend." Hania quickly spat.

"You're really self-centered." Kylie smiled as she spoke, but Hania could tell sense a level of annoyance behind it. "You seriously haven't realized that I'm dating Ben, have you?" Hania stared for a minute in disbelief, before putting the pieces together in his head. The two were spending a lot of time together. Whenever Hania wasn't with Kylie, it seemed that Ben was with Kylie.

"Why…" Hania was cut off.

"Didn't I tell you? Honestly, it's because I felt like you were hiding something from me. That you were making this...distance between us. So, I did the same, hoping you'd notice and correct yourself. Which obviously worked out in the exact opposite of how it was supposed to." Kylie walked closer to Hania so that she could peer directly into his eyes, although the slight height difference meant she had to look up. "Listen to me, Hania. I might have some slight lingering feelings for you, but I will not put my life on hold for you. Even if you felt the same way, which I could already tell from the way you treated me that you don't. You are a very good friend, and I hold you close to my heart. Don't misunderstand that as my life revolving around you like I'm some girl pining after you in your little fantasy world. Got it?" It was like a weight was lifted off Kylie's shoulders. Having to hold those feelings in all this time must have been draining. She hugged her friend tightly, as though she feared that she went too far in his fragile state.

"It's okay. No... it's better than okay. You're right. I've been selfish, and a jerk. I'm sorry." His apology probably contained the most emotion that Hania had felt since the death of his mother. This entire time Hania had been so focused on his life and his story, that he failed to pay attention to what had been going on in the background. "Now it makes sense why Ben always looked so nervous around me."

"You don't remember Ben very well, do you?" Kyrie retorted.

"Should I?" Hania was genuinely confused. He had met Ben in their junior year of high school, so it wasn't exactly like there was a bunch of history between them. Even then, Ben seemed skittish around Hania, which would make sense if

Ben had been crushing on Kylie for that long. Even though they had broken up the year before, Hania and Kylie were still very close around that time.

"Remember that kid in the third grade that kept teasing you about not having a dad? The one that you punched so hard that he had to go to the hospital. Which now that I know everything, I guess makes sense." Kylie's words seemed pointless to Hania. Who cared about some kid in the third grade? Certainly not Hania. He didn't even bother to remember the kid's name…

"That was Ben?!" Hania exclaimed; Kylie nodding in response. "I guess I should send him a fruit basket or something." Hania joked, before sighing. "I need to get going."

"Take your phone. I don't want any excuse why you can't contact me while you're away." Kylie hugged Hania tightly as she spoke. He returned the hug; albeit weakly. The young, weary hero looked both ways, before picking Kylie up and floating her back down in front of her door. Hania then flew off back towards his home. Even though he hadn't planned on taking much, he still had some packing to do.

"I didn't leave my door open…" Hania muttered once he landed. His door wasn't wide open, but he didn't leave his door slightly ajar either. Cautiously, he peered inside. Someone had turned the lamp off as well, leaving nothing but darkness in his room. "You picked the wrong apartment to break into, if you're still in there." Partially, Hania was referring to his superhuman abilities, but mostly about the fact that he was dead broke. The only thing of value in his apartment that could be stolen was his television, and Hania had already put a hole in that. He stepped into the apartment and closed the door, only to see a figure with two glowing red eyes atop his bed. Hania recognized those horrid, crossed shaped crimson eyes anywhere and immediately lunged.

"Wait..." Hunter tried to speak, but Hania had already pinned him against the wall with his arm digging into his throat. With his free hand, Hania began generating lightning. Hania was in no mood to play any of Hunter's creepy reindeer games. Still though, Hunter held his hands up in surrender. Hania lifted his hand off Hunter's neck and let him slide to the ground. "I heard about your mother." Hunter managed to spit out between coughs. The villain pointed at the bed. Something was sitting on top of it, but Hania couldn't make out its shape in the dark. He took a cautious stride over to close the door for his apartment, and flick on the light switch.

"Beer?" Hania was perplexed. Why did Hunter bring a six pack over?

"In times of hardship, men drink." Hunter removed the mask that covered the bottom half of his face for the first time since Hania had met him. His jawline was rather sturdy, with a budding beard the same shade of sand as the slightly spiked hair on the top of his head.

"What did you do? Drug the beer?" Hania was understandably skeptical. For some reason poisons, drugs, and admittedly alcohol were all several times more potent when introduced into his bloodstream. Hunter was, to Hania's knowledge, fully aware of this. The crimson eyed villain held up a receipt showing that he purchased the beer and sat down on the bed. "I have a couch ya know. This is weirdly intimate."

"That barely qualifies as a couch. But I will move over there, and we will share a drink. You can select any one of these beer bottles and I will drink out of whatever one that you wish. Losing your mother...it isn't good to have that pain in your heart." Hunter sounded surprisingly sincere; talking in his normal voice rather than one of the forty-five horrendous and mildly racist accents that he typically used. Hania decided that he had nothing to lose, and the two walked over to the couch and opened a beer.

"So, is this the pre hunting feast or something?" Hania was still wary.

"I do not hunt the wounded unless I am the one who did the wounding. There is no honor in that. And no matter how much you may try not to admit it, Hania Hawke, you are wounded. Your eyes are filled with pain. Take this time to recover and heal. Make no mistake, I will hunt you eventually, but you will know when that happens." Hunter chugged the rest of his beer and popped open a second one.

"How honorable." Hania was only being partially sarcastic. Hunter had proven to be an enigma to Hania. "Who are you? Really? What is your real name?"

"Hunter." Hania had opened his mouth to reply, but Hunter continued speaking. "As far as I know, anyway. I don't have any memories of my life prior to seventeen. From what I understand, this is the fate of all who have Judas' blood in their veins. The curse of the betrayer to humanity. We gain abilities that make us adept at killing and making money, at the cost of our humanity." Hunter looked down at his beer once he finished talking. Hania almost felt bad for him, in a way. Currently however, Hania was emotionally stunted. Until Hania could figure out how to truly feel again, there was no way Hania could offer up any real sympathy. Instead he raised his beer bottle up, clanked it against Hunter's, and the two downed their bottles together.

"What will you do while I'm gone? Terrorize this place?" Hania was wishing right about now that he didn't throw a remote into his tv. Beer and wall watching didn't exactly go hand in hand.

"I only came here to hunt you. With you wounded, I will just go find something else to hunt."

"You mean someone." Hania clarified.

"Something." Hunter repeated. "I hunt the supernatural and the mythical. I don't hunt you because you're a human. I started hunting you because your powers proved that you were an irregular. I kept hunting you once I found out that you were a demigod. I hunt other things too though. Werewolves, vampires, mermaids, things like that. Big game. Don't take it so personal." Hunter chuckled.

"It feels pretty personal. Especially since you just said I'm not human, even before the demigod stuff." Hania hated to admit it, even if it was just to himself, but he respected Hunter. More perturbing to admit, he could sense that Hunter respected Hania as well. Their relationship was different compared to Roy, who hated Hania's guts, or Phoenix, who Hania hated with all his being. Hunter was Hania's first supervillain, and Hania was the first creature to ever force Hunter to admit defeat.

"Just don't let anyone else kill you before I do." Hunter stood up and began to walk towards the door.

"Wouldn't dream of it." Hania called out as he watched Hunter walk out of his apartment, leaving behind four bottles of beer. "You can come in now." Hania called out after a few seconds. It was silent for a moment, but Thunderbird walked in through the door shortly after. Hania had now gotten used to the sensation of a lord arriving in the mortal plane by means of Hania's lifeforce. It was a faint, tugging sensation arrived in the pit of his stomach whenever they landed.

"Odd fellow." Thunderbird spoke as he walked in. Like the rest of the Lords and deities that Hania knew, Thunderbird didn't really believe in Hunter's claims when it came to his ancestor. The different pantheons didn't put much stock in the existence of the monotheistic beings. In their eyes, there was no evidence that proved anything regarding their existence, but Hania had figured that wasn't the reason. The thought of a singular God, being able to do what it took multiple gods to do frightened them. Truth be told, even though he was the son of one of these gods, Hania never truly believed that they were gods. Considering Hania's beliefs were closer to Christianity than anything else, he had written it off in his mind that deities were not the same as God, and that deities were simply creations of God.

"Well he does hunt other living beings for a living." Hania had pulled out a duffle bag from under his bed and began to throw clothes in it.

"You don't have to go, son. I will stand by your side as much as I am able to." Thunderbird pleaded.

"I know, dad." Hania caught his father by surprise. For the first time in twenty-one years, Hania called Thunderbird his dad. "This isn't about running, or about the war. Well, maybe a bit. I don't want to pull my city into whatever mess that I started. Really though, I have to go to find myself. I don't know what it means to be alive anymore and staying here isn't going to help me find my way. I don't want to feel so lost and empty…" Hania trailed off and continued to finish packing his bag.

"This is your journey. I will not stand in your way, if this is what you think you need." Thunderbird walked closer to Hania. Just as Hania zipped up his bag, Thunderbird pulled him into an embrace. "Things are not going to be easy from here on out. It will be harder for me to come and contact you like this. Just don't ever forget that I am doing everything I can for you." Hania returned the hug, albeit half-heartedly.

"Don't start getting mushy on me now, old man." Hania pushed Thunderbird away and slung his bag over his shoulder. "I'm leaving now, so you can head back to…" Hania was standing in a room by himself. "Well, you didn't have to be in such a rush." Hania turned off his light and walked out his apartment, eyeing the remaining beers that the two did not drink previously. At the last minute, he grabbed them and stuffed the bottles into his bag, before heading out the door. Out of habit, Hania locked his apartment door despite the lock having broken last year and took off into the air. He wasn't running...and he wasn't trying to forget what he had went through.

He was seeking redemption.

Tales of what's to come

"So, did you talk to your brother?" Susano'o, the Japanese god of the sea and storms sat on a beach overlooking an unnaturally blue ocean. His long, black hair was pulled into a tight ponytail. The lord of water took his sword from his waist and sat down in the sand beside the Emperor of water, Poseidon.

"Yes, I did." Poseidon had looked similar to his brother, Zeus. The few key differences were that Poseidon had more of a tan compared to his brother, deep blue eyes, and dark hair with light blue streaks within it. Like Susano'o, he also had matching stubble on his chin, which was not quite long enough to be considered a beard.

"What did he say?" Susano'o had picked up a stone and skipped it along the ocean. It never stopped however and continued skipping across the ocean and towards the horizon.

"άντε γαμήσου." Poseidon picked up a stone of his own and tossed it across the ocean. While Susano'o's stone skipped across the ocean infinitely, Poseidon's stone split the ocean in two, as if the water itself moved out of the way of the rock.

"Vulgar. So, what will we do about their guardian?" Susano'o pondered. When they had learned that the guardian of lightning had struck down the guardian of fire, Susano'o was the first to suggest that something needed to be done. Poseidon had wanted to talk to Zeus first to find out the full story, and Susano'o put his trust into Poseidon's plans. The two were longtime friends after all.

"The same thing that Repun suggested two weeks ago when we found out. We're sending in our guardian. An eye for an eye, a tooth for a tooth." Poseidon and Susano'o both walked into the water and vanished underneath the sea.

Made in the USA
Middletown, DE
17 August 2019